T0110215

"I was wrong, Leo."

"Wrong?" Cross turned to him, a frown marring his face. "How could you be wrong?"

"They aren't computer chips, or that sort of technology. My ignorance *was* showing, just not in the way everyone thought."

"How are you wrong?"

"Those look like some form of nanotechnology. I'm not up on all the current stuff, but I don't remember anything that has that configuration. And besides, it's not a natural human configuration."

"Natural human…" Cross turned back toward the screen. He didn't say anything as he studied it.

For the first time since they'd been working together, Bradshaw felt that he finally understood something Cross didn't.

"Even computer code is in binary, Leo," he said softly. "When humans make tools they usually have a dual function. A tomahawk has an edge and a handle."

"Advanced societies make tools whose usage isn't obvious," Cross said slowly. "These are clearly advanced."

"And their purpose isn't obvious," Bradshaw said. "But their configuration is just not something any human society has ever come up with …"

THE TENTH PLANET

Dean Wesley Smith
and
Kristine Kathryn Rusch

Story by Rand Marlis
and Christopher Weaver

A Del Rey® Book
THE BALLANTINE PUBLISHING GROUP • NEW YORK

A Del Rey® Book
Published by The Ballantine Publishing Group
Copyright © 1999 by Creative Licensing Corporation and Media Technologies Ltd.

All rights reserved under International and Pan-American Copyright Conventions. Published in the United States by The Ballantine Publishing Group, a division of Random House, Inc., New York, and simultaneously in Canada by Random House of Canada Limited, Toronto.

Del Rey is a registered trademark and the Del Rey colophon is a trademark of Random House, Inc.

www.randomhouse.com/delrey/

Library of Congress Catalog Card Number: 99-90139

ISBN 0-345-48515-7

Manufactured in the United States of America

In memory of Richard B. Weaver

Section One

DISCOVERY

1

240 Days Until Arrival

International Space Monitoring Buoy Number Six was alone. Since it had left Earth over three years ago, it had been alone, traveling through the depths of space to the seventh planet, Uranus, then settling into a wide elliptical orbit. For the past six months, ISMB 6 had faithfully done its job, taking readings of the surface of the planet, using its cameras and sensors and equipment to explore the outer reaches of the solar system.

ISMB 6 was a hardworking little craft, although from the outside it seemed like little more than a piece of space junk in an area devoid of anything else man-made. A silver craft, the diameter of a small bedroom, its surface was cluttered with a myriad of dishes, antennas, and measuring devices, making it look like a spider. On the side of the craft, in one of the only small, open areas of the main body, were the letters *ISMB* followed by the number *6*. Under the letters were a dozen tiny stencils of flags, indicating the countries that had helped in the joint project.

Out here, everything familiar seemed remote. Even the sun was nothing more than a distant hole of light in the massive field of stars, not even strong enough to cast real shadows, or supply any real warmth.

Not that ISMB 6 cared. It was one of seven buoys designed by American and Japanese engineers, and sent outward by a consortium of twelve countries, all believing that the heavens needed to be monitored as the seas were once monitored. The early scientists saw the ISMB system as a twofold project: the buoys would act as ways to gather information in deep space, and they would also serve as the markers of Earth's boundaries.

Surprisingly, the nations making up the consortium did not want to consider the boundary issue. To them, having boundaries meant defending them, sending weapons into space, perhaps even developing a fleet.

Such things are not necessary, the politicians said, *unless there is a perceived threat.* And of course, there was no threat and no hint of one ever appearing. The politicians believed we were alone. The scientists weren't sure.

So the consortium took its funding and built the seven buoys, launching them over a three-year period. Three buoys orbited the three largest planets in the solar system: Jupiter, Saturn, and Uranus. Two buoys were stationed over the sun's poles, holding positions above and below the plane of the solar system at a distance from the sun about the same as Mars. The seventh was completing the last year of its flight to catch and orbit Pluto.

All seven sent a constant stream of data Earthward, powered by batteries designed to last thirty years, even without solar reenergizing. The data was received at stations all over Earth and relayed to a classroom-sized area three floors under a complex outside of Sydney, Australia. The complex housed, at times, upwards of a hundred scientists from around the world, studying on-site the information being sent back from the buoys.

At the complex, ISMB 6 was the only buoy that hadn't been assigned a nickname. The nicknames suggested by the English-speaking scientists were too crude to use, even accidentally, at press conferences, and besides, the jokes did not translate well into the complex's other approved languages. As a result, the scientists who tried to create a shred of personality in their tools imagined ISMB 6 as a serious, unimaginative little worker, who could be relied upon at all times.

ISMB 6 wasn't aware of any of this. ISMB 6 really wasn't aware of anything. It simply went about its job, orbiting Uranus, sending telemetry back to Earth. It's entire mission was routine, as routine as a pioneering mission could be until ISMB 6's third orbit of the day, a day artificially measured in Earth time.

As ISMB 6 rose slightly above and beyond the dark, cold surface of Uranus, a blackness seemed to loom near the little craft, almost as if an invisible cloud of soot was filling space.

Then, with a weak, reflected flash of light from the darkness, all data stopped flowing toward Earth.

All instruments shut down.

ISMB 6, the faithful, hardworking little buoy, was dead.

August 16, 2017
4:56 A.M. Pacific Daylight Time

240 Days Until Arrival

Orange and yellow bands of light cut through the morning mist as the sun peeked above the Coast Mountain Range. The morning air had a thick dampness that felt more appropriate to winter than to August, yet by noon the chill would be gone and the temperature would hit eighty.

Dr. Edwin Bradshaw ducked out of his tent and pulled his jacket tight around his shoulders, shivering slightly in the cool morning air. A mile to the west the Pacific Ocean rumbled as the surf hit the beach. He couldn't see the water—the tall pine trees that surrounded him prevented that—but he could hear the ocean. Its sound was constant, sometimes a low murmur and sometimes an angry explosive pounding. And sometimes this rumble.

He found that the ocean's constant conversation soothed him. He knew he would miss it, as he always did, when he had to go back to the Valley. He would miss all of this. He was lucky to have ended up here, in Oregon, rather than some po-dunk university somewhere, a place with no credentials and no budget to send him anywhere. Oregon State University liked his background, despite the controversies, and for the most part, the administration left him alone. He was able to choose his dig sites, and his assistants, and use university funds to continue his research. Fortunately for him, his research centered on the Native American tribes of the Oregon Coast, and he got to spend his summers, and an occasional winter, in what he considered to be the most beautiful place on Earth.

But he was getting older. The morning chill got into his bones these days. In September, he would turn sixty, and lately, he had begun to feel it. Sleeping in a tent, even with a thick sleeping bag and an air mattress (something he wouldn't have considered in the old days), left him stiff and sore. It took a few minutes of movement every morning before his joints stopped creaking.

No one stirred in the dozen other tents around the small

clearing. Twenty-four Oregon State University students had signed up for this dig, more than any other summer. He was having trouble just keeping them all busy. The dig site wasn't big enough for all of them to work at once.

He grinned. He always woke before his students. On the second day of the dig, most of them had groaned their way through the work, and he hadn't felt old at all. These days students got no exercise, except for the federally mandated stuff in the public schools. Remotes, handheld computers, and the new personal assistants, which were little more than headless robots, ensured that anyone who wanted to spend his life in a chair could do so without any effort at all.

Bradshaw was an old-fashioned guy, old enough to remember when kids spent their summers outside playing baseball and kick the can until their parents forced them inside. Old enough to remember when color television was an unusual thing. Old enough to remember only three television channels—all free—and changing those channels by twisting a dial. When he was a little, little boy, it had taken him two hands to go from one channel to the other.

Now some of his students brought their own televisions with them, tiny things that attached to the wrist and changed channels with a soft verbal command. On the first day of the dig, he had Kelly Flynn, his graduate assistant, help him with what he called the Great Electronics Search. He confiscated most of his students' "necessities"—generally, watches that served as small computers, with television, radio, gaming, and Internet capability. He wanted them to focus on the lives of Native Americans before white settlers found this beautiful place. His theory was that if his students were able to think like the tribe that filled this area, they would do better when they searched through the earth for remnants of that life.

He hated the day of the Great Electronics Search. It made

7

him the most unpopular man in camp for the first week of the dig. But he had done it often enough to know that by the end of the summer, his students would thank him. They would say things like "I really got to enjoy the woods, Doc. I'd never done that before."

And never would again, he would wager.

Most of those students would be angry if they knew that Bradshaw always brought his own electronic equipment to the dig site. They would be even more upset if they knew that he spent part of his evenings on-line, keeping track of current research. His favorite on-line site was a place he lurked, a place where some of the best archaeological minds of this generation argued theory in terms that were as far beyond these students as computers were beyond the tribes that once lived in this very spot. Bradshaw's only contribution to the site—for that matter, to most archaeological publications, print or on-line—was to list the location of his dig and the reason he was excavating the site.

Imagine his surprise when he was awakened this morning by the vibration of his watch against his wrist. He had only set that private computer alarm for messages marked urgent, be they phone, fax, or e-mail.

This one was an e-mail message, sent only a few hours after he had updated the dig information for the archaeological site. It was from Dr. Leo Cross. Cross was not the world's most famous archaeologist. Bradshaw had no respect for the famous people, the brand names, to whom recognition was more important than research. They usually let their grad students handle the hard work, and then took credit for the findings. No. Cross was the best-known archaeological historian among his peers. They all envied his intuitive ability. It was almost as if the earth spoke to him, revealing to him secrets that none of the others could ever hope to hear.

8

The thing that made Cross so very very good was that he did the things that other archaeologists hoped to do, and probably would never achieve. Cross used the myths of history to find actual archaeological sites. And Cross hadn't just done that once or twice. He'd succeeded dozens of times, which to Bradshaw meant that Cross had more going for him than just luck.

Cross worked at Georgetown University and had, in the last fifteen years, developed its archaeology department from one whose reputation was in decline into one of the best in the world. Sometimes Bradshaw wished he were young again, or young enough to justify going to Georgetown for some post-doc work. He would have loved to spend a semester listening to Dr. Leo Cross.

Bradshaw stretched, wishing the tall pines let some of the sun's warmth through. Later in the day he knew he would be thankful for those trees, but now he wanted just a little of the morning sun to take the chill off.

But maybe the chill he was feeling had nothing to do with the lack of sunlight. Maybe it had more to do with the message he had received from Cross.

Already, Bradshaw could recite it from memory:

> *Dr. Bradshaw:*
> *Greetings. I see you are working a dig on the Oregon Coast this summer. Would you please inform me if you find a thin layer of black residue covering your site at any level?*
> *Thank you for your consideration.*
> *Leo Cross*

The message had Georgetown's stamp, and Bradshaw used his EncryptionChek program to confirm that the message also used Cross's personal code. This had been sent by the man himself, not some automatic program sending a standard e-mail message every time someone updated a dig site on the archaeological bulletin board.

Cross wanted information, and before Bradshaw replied, he wanted to make sure he had some to give.

He glanced once more at the tents. No one stirred. Thank heavens. He really didn't want to discuss this message with anyone, not even his indispensable graduate assistant.

Bradshaw walked quietly through the tents and down the worn trail toward the site. The dig area was staked and roped off, carefully detailed so that any discovery would be exactly placed in a numbered grid. Even the tiniest scrap of artifact could be traced back to an exact location, both in direction and depth, long after it was removed.

The site was under a rock bluff that had sheltered bands of Native Americans from the cold winds in the winter, yet allowed them to remain close to the ocean and the nearby river. This dig was focused on the Tillamook, who were native to the area. Bradshaw had chosen the area because he knew, from some of the aerial photographs and the migration patterns of the tribe, that his students would find something here. But he didn't expect it to be anything important.

Bradshaw already knew a great deal about the Tillamook, and had excavated several other sites relating to them, one that got mired in yet another controversy when his students discovered skeletal remains and the local Native American tribes, most of whom knew nothing about the Tillamook and their dead culture, had demanded that the dig end while they researched Tillamook cultural values to know if Bradshaw was violating an ancient burial site.

He had already known that he wasn't violating anything—the body had no evidence of traditional Tillamook death rituals. Instead, the skull was cracked and a large section in the back was depressed, indicating that either this guy had fallen and hit his head or that he had been murdered. Eventually Bradshaw won this argument and continued the dig, but not without some personal pain. The fight with the local tribes had inspired *The Oregonian* to investigate Bradshaw's past.

That was the thing that surprised him the most about the message from Cross. No archaeologist with a good reputation had spoken to Bradshaw in twenty years, let alone asked for his help. He supposed he was flattered by Cross's message. And intrigued. But he felt something else, something he didn't want to feel, especially at his age: just a little bit of hope.

Bradshaw passed the dig site and crossed behind it, toward a thin Douglas fir where he had had the students dig their first test hole. The test hole went very deep—this one went deeper than it should have, since the students were being overly cautious. This was called a depth-gauge dig, and it was done so that he could examine the layers and see how deep the dig site had to go to reach the ideal location for their search. Bradshaw's students were going back three to five hundred years, but they had dug the test hole so deep that he figured it went down five thousand years.

He smiled as he remembered double-checking their work. "No need to go any deeper," he had said. "Much of the Northwest Pacific Coast culture was just forming right about the point you're at."

The students had stopped as if they had been burned. Apparently they hadn't realized that you didn't have to dig five hundred feet down to get to five hundred years. "This was why," he had said to his students on their first day of class, "you actually dig instead of read about digging. Archaeology is a hands-on science, just like all the others. Knowing theory only takes you so far."

11

Now he was glad they had gone down so deep. Because he remembered other test holes from other digs in the area, and they all showed what he thought this one would show: the black layer Dr. Cross had been looking for. Only the layer was thousands of years old.

Bradshaw crouched, hearing his knees crack, and knowing it would take some work to get out of this position. He peered into the hole, and saw exactly what he remembered: a very thin black line several feet down. He knew without checking that the five other depth-gauge holes would also contain this black line. It was about an eighth of an inch thick and in the same level in each hole.

Considering the depth of the line, his guess was that at least four thousand years ago something had created this black layer. He knew from the look of the layer that it was caused by an exogenic process, but he hadn't cared what that process was. It was outside his area of concern. When a student had asked him, he had said that he thought, without testing, that a massive fire had gone through the region. And that was all the thought he had given it, until this morning's message.

Bradshaw stared at the thin, black line cutting across the thick dirt of the wall. Why would someone like Dr. Leo Cross want to know about such a line? Tracking volcanic eruptions? Large regional fires? Neither seemed likely, considering Dr. Cross's reputation.

But clearly something interesting to Cross had laid down that line of black soot four thousand years before.

Bradshaw shrugged and pulled his coat even tighter around his middle against the chill. Then he turned and headed back to his tent. He didn't trust voice commands for this message. He wanted to make sure each word was the one he intended, no misunderstandings, no misspellings. He would write to Leo Cross, and he would use his full-sized keyboard to do it.

This was the closest Bradshaw had been to cutting-edge science since his disgrace twenty years earlier. And he was still ambitious enough not to want to screw this up.

August 16, 2017
9:23 A.M. Eastern Daylight Time

240 Days Until Arrival

The black racquetball flashed past, just out of Leo Cross's reach. He twisted, his momentum slamming him into the hardwood wall, shoulder first. He rolled along the wall, ending up with his back against the wood, breathing heavily. Sweat dripped from his forehead and down his bare arms. His T-shirt was soaked and his heart was beating like it wanted to get out and run away from the torture of this racquetball court. Forty-six years old and he was more out of shape than he had ever been in his life. How had he let that happen?

"Leo?" Doug Mickelson said, leaning against the other wall, clearly breathing and sweating just as hard. "You all right?"

"Yeah," Leo said. "I just can't believe you beat me. Have you been practicing?"

"As if I have the time." Mickelson wiped his forehead with the back of his arm, and then shook his arm once. Leo was glad he was on the other side of the court. He knew that Mickelson maneuver—he'd seen it on their first day of college twenty-eight years ago in, of all things, a racquetball class they were taking for an easy PE credit. They had been friends ever since.

"They don't have racquetball courts in Southeast Asia?" Leo asked. He had his hands resting on his knees, and he was still breathing hard. Served him right, going after this game as energetically as he had, after not playing for three months.

"I think the Sultan of Brunei has a racquetball court," Mickelson said. "But then, he can afford anything."

"You should know," Leo said. "Check it out. Research. Tell them while you're handling the latest diplomatic crisis that you need a racquetball break."

Mickelson grinned. It was the same boyish grin he'd always had, one that hadn't been on his face much since he'd been appointed secretary of state. "Yeah, right," he said. "And have you fly in at someone else's expense so I have someone to play with." He glanced down at his running shorts and filthy tennis shoes. "Somehow I don't think this is proper attire in Brunei."

"Have you ever been to Brunei?"

Mickelson's grin faded. "I think it's the only place I haven't been. I thought I'd love this job, I really did."

"And you do." Leo had finally caught a breath. He stood, already feeling the workout in his muscles.

"Not like I thought I would, Leo. Not when we were in school. Remember those mock debates? Remember how hyped I would get?"

"I never understood why you liked it then," Leo said. "It seemed dry to me."

"It's not dry." Mickelson picked the ball up and held it in his right hand. "It's fascinating work. It always has been. It's just . . . so much is at stake. So much is always at stake."

They had had variations on this conversation before. It was one of the benefits of being old friends. Leo knew that Mickelson talked to him in ways he didn't talk to anyone else. He couldn't.

14

"You knew that going in. Hell, you've been flirting around this level of government for a long time."

"Flirting around the corners is not the same as being the one in charge." Mickelson glanced at the ball. He seemed about to say something, and then stopped himself.

Leo watched him, waiting. Leo was a bit out of his depth. He didn't entirely understand the differences Mickelson was talking about. The kind of power Mickelson had was something that Leo couldn't get close to, and didn't want to even if he had the opportunity.

Then he shivered. If his research turned out, he might need to make use of such power.

He shook off the thought. "Four months is a long time to go from crisis to crisis."

Mickelson smiled. This time it was the press briefing smile. "I was home for a few days."

"Not long enough to play racquetball."

"Long enough to call you and cancel." He shook his head. "Thank God for the plane. You know, if I didn't have time on that jet to meet my staff and concentrate on the next country, I wouldn't know what time zone I was in, let alone what U.S. interests were in the area."

"You've always known what our interests are. Everywhere," Leo said.

Mickelson nodded. "True enough. But going from a conversation on the International Cloning Treaty violations in China to brokering the latest economic crisis in Greece requires a different set of protocols, different knowledge, different skills. You know, I'm very good with the Chinese."

"I've heard."

"But the Greeks baffle me every time. You'd think I'd do better with them."

"Why?"

"Because of the influence of their culture on ours."

"Their ancient culture," Leo said. The conversation had now moved into his specialty. "A hundred years makes a huge difference in our own culture. Imagine talking to someone who survived the influenza pandemic of 1918 and trying to explain how conditions helped it spread. You can't expect the Greeks to be anything like their ancient ancestors."

"I suppose not." Mickelson sighed. "You caught me on a bad day, Leo. I guess we should have waited until I was back for a week before we had our racquetball date."

"Only to have you cancel again because of another terrorist incident in Milan? No thanks."

"I hope that never happens again." Mickelson started across the court. "I'm supposed to be back for at least a month. Maybe as out of shape as we are, we should schedule twice a week."

Leo smiled. "Whatever you want, Mr. Secretary."

"You're not going anywhere?"

"Research is keeping me home." Leo stood up completely, and walked to the glass door. On the bleachers sat Hank, the head of Mickelson's Secret Service detail. Two more Secret Service officers stood outside the private door leading into the racquetball courts. Since Mickelson had become secretary of state, privacy had become a thing of the past.

At first Leo felt uncomfortable even talking to his friends with the Secret Service around. But Mickelson pretended they weren't there, and Leo felt that if Mickelson was comfortable discussing personal matters around these men, then Leo could be to. Still, every time he came out of the racquetball court to see a burly man in a black suit, with the most sophisticated electronic equipment on his wrist, and a gun in a shoulder holster ruining the line of the man's jacket, he was astonished. Astonished because, in his mind, he and Mickelson were still students at Columbia, their theoretical discussions simply continuations of all-night pizza sessions at the dorm, the ups and downs in their personal lives just more grist for the conversation mill.

To think that, in twenty-eight years, Leo had risen to the top of his profession and Mickelson had risen to the top of his made Leo feel like a grown-up. He wondered if this was how his parents' generation felt when they woke up one day to discover their friends were successful bankers and doctors, and a man their age was president of the United States.

Perhaps that was what got Leo the most. The president was only five years older than he was, and Mickelson—the guy who had once called himself king of the mosh pits, who had gotten his nipples pierced on a dare—was now secretary of state for the United States. A man who wore Saville Row suits because they told leaders of foreign countries that he was conservative and cautious despite his relative youth (forty-six, apparently, was considered babyhood in international politics).

Leo himself had reached the age where anyone under thirty called him "sir"—and rightly so, since he could have fathered most of them. He hadn't fathered anyone, however, and he hadn't married. He had dedicated his entire adult life to his work, and he didn't see that changing. Archaeology combined the best of all the sciences. He had to know chemistry and biology and physics, as well as geology and paleontology. In the last year, he'd learned more about astronomy than he ever thought he would, and he'd been to a lot of classes and meetings in archaeoastronomy, a growing branch of his own field.

Yet the more he learned the more he realized he didn't know. And that worried him. He was beginning to think he was running out of time.

As Leo pushed the glass door open, he said, "Hey, Hank."

Hank nodded, just as Leo expected him to. In the years that Hank had been assigned to Mickelson, Leo hadn't managed to get more than a "Yes, sir," and "No, sir" out of the man. There was no way of telling if he had enjoyed watching two middle-aged men play racquetball for the past forty minutes. There was no way of telling anything about Hank at all.

"Dr. Leo," Hank said, and Leo started. Hank had never addressed him directly before. "Your computer alarm has been buzzing off and on for the last ten minutes."

Mickelson frowned. "You should have interrupted us. It might have been something important."

"No," Leo said. "Being my secretary is not part of his job description."

Leo grabbed his towel off a lower bleacher and wiped off his face and chest. Then he wrapped the towel around his neck and picked up the watch.

Watches weren't really watches anymore, but all the trendy names like Infometer by Swatch failed to catch on. Even though watches could do everything but drive your car (and Leo sometimes wondered why someone hadn't developed a program to do that), they were still called watches. They were thick little creatures though, and the older models, like his, were bulky. He just didn't believe in upgrading every time someone improved the sound speakers. He simply waited until the upgrades were something he could use. And in the last three years, no one had thought to upgrade the business programming.

He didn't buckle the watch onto his sweaty wrist. Instead, he sat on the bleacher and called up his e-mail.

Mickelson stood beside him, toweling off. "It's kind of nice to see someone else get the urgent message these days," he said to Hank.

Hank, characteristically, didn't reply.

Leo stared at the e-mail response from Professor Edwin Bradshaw in Oregon. Part of him had hoped that he wouldn't get another e-mail like this, but the scientist in him, the part that loved discovery, was thrilled.

"Problems?" Mickelson asked.

"A pet project," Leo said. "A worrisome one."

"Something you need to talk about?" Mickelson was a good friend; he always asked that. And once or twice Leo had taken him up on it. But archaeology was not Mickelson's strong suit. He didn't understand how ancient civilizations had a relevance in modern society.

This time, though. This time, he might need to know. But Leo would pick his moment, and this certainly wasn't it.

"Actually, I might need to talk to you," Leo said, "in an official capacity."

"You're not a head of state, Leo," Mickelson said, only partially joking.

"I know," Leo said. "But sometimes you open the doors you can, not the doors you should."

"And I suppose on that cryptic statement, you're going to let this go."

Leo grinned. "Yeah." He flicked the watch to voice-activation. "Phone."

"You don't need to lean in like that," Mickelson said.

"You always tell me that," Leo said as the phone icon appeared on the tiny screen. He leaned in again. "Office."

The watch dialed his office, and he turned the switch on the side back to normal function. The phone rang, and then his secretary Bonnie picked it up. Bonnie was an elderly woman who refused to give him her age. She had raised her own children, and then her grandchildren, and then, two years before, had decided to rejoin the workforce. She'd had a lot of trouble finding a job; secretaries were a dying breed, replaced by automation and computers. Leo hated doing a lot of the work himself, even though it took nanoseconds instead of days, and he had convinced the university to find room in the department's budget for a secretary.

Leo wouldn't have gotten that luxury if he hadn't been the centerpiece of the department.

He had interviewed nearly forty highly qualified women, most of them elderly, and had finally settled on Bonnie, not because she was more qualified—there were others who were just as qualified as she was—but because she made him laugh.

"Dr. Cross's office," she said in her best schoolmarm voice.

"Dr. Cross," he said, and she burst out laughing. He had done that to her on her first day, and inadvertently launched her into a surreal conversation where she was trying to explain that Dr. Cross wasn't available, and he was trying to explain that he was Dr. Cross. Later she had called it an Abbott and Costello moment, and when he hadn't understood the reference, she introduced him to the joys of their "Who's on First" routine.

When she stopped giggling, she said, "I thought you were coming back here after your racquetball game."

"Change of plans," he said. "I need you to book me a flight to Portland, Oregon. I need to leave as soon as possible."

"Want me to bring your overnight bag to the airport?" she asked. Her question wasn't an idle one. She was booking his flight as she spoke to him, and she was efficient enough to use the conversation to gather information. Someone had once pointed out to him that in the time he spoke to her, he could have booked his own flight. But he really hated that sort of work, more than he admitted to anyone, except Bonnie.

"Depends on the flight time," he said. "I might have a chance to stop at the office and pick it up."

"Good," she said, "because you were supposed to have student conferences this afternoon. It would be nice if you were to leave the vid message canceling instead of me."

He sighed. "If I have time."

"You'll have time," she said. Then he heard a slight ping on the watch. "There. You've got a flight leaving from Dulles in three hours. You'll have time to stop."

"Nothing earlier? It'll be late afternoon by the time I reach Oregon."

"I can work miracles," she said primly, "but only on every other Thursday."

He laughed. "Thanks, Bonnie," he said. "See you in a few." Then he hung up.

Mickelson was still watching him. "I thought you said your research was keeping you here."

"It was," Leo said. "But things change at a moment's notice."

"In archaeology?" Mickelson said. "If it's been sitting there for a thousand years, what difference does another day make?"

Leo stared at him for a moment, wondering if this was the time to broach the subject. Then he shook his head slightly.

"You'd be surprised how much difference a day makes, Doug," he said. "You'd be really surprised."

2

August 17, 2017
7:06 A.M. Pacific Daylight Time

239 Days Until Arrival

The Oregon dig site, like most student-run sites, was remote. Leo Cross had the choice of flying into Newport, the
largest town on the Oregon Coast, and renting a car at a local
car dealership; commandeering a helicopter; or flying into
Portland and taking the scenic route. He had tried to rent a car
in Newport fifteen years before, and vowed never again. The
helicopter ran the risk of disturbing the site. So he went directly to Portland, and he was glad he did. The flight had been
delayed due to bad weather in the Midwest, and he hadn't arrived late in the afternoon after all, but closer to one in the
morning. It was all he could do to stumble out of the Portland
airport and find a hotel room. There he caught a few hours of
sleep before starting his drive across the Coast Mountain
Range.

Leo had traveled all over the world, and had always enjoyed the unspoiled beauty of Oregon's Coast Mountains. He
timed his drive through the Van Duzer Corridor so that he
would go through it at sunup. He wanted to see the reddish

bands of daylight touch trees so tall that he felt dwarfed. Except for an occasional RV, he was alone on the road.

On mornings like this, as the sunlight turned the dew into a silver mist that floated along the road, he wondered what his life would have been like if he had chosen a true specialty, settled in an area, and continued to study the lives of, say, the Chinook, or the Tillamook, as Dr. Bradshaw had been doing. Would he be married by now? Have children? Maybe even grandchildren? Or would he still be as obsessed, as driven?

The dig site was on the coast itself, near the town of Cloverdale. Oregonians called Cloverdale a town, but it was really a village, with fewer than three hundred residents. The town's businesses huddled in a lump on the North Coast Highway, also known as 101. He passed a school, a veterinarian's office, three restaurants, a church, and a general store. There were two T-shirt shops, which appealed to tourists driving through, even though, from Cloverdale, the ocean was invisible.

Leo hadn't been in a town like this since he was a child. No supermarket, no video rental. Just a few shops and some familiar places to eat. If he had time, he would have slowed down and tried to see if one of the buildings still had a revolving red and white barber pole outside. He would have laid good money on the fact that one of them did.

He followed Bradshaw's directions, taking the old highway that went up what he would call a mountain, but what the locals would call a hill. Halfway up, he saw a faded sign that had the name of a town scratched off of it; a few miles later, the highway became a narrow dirt road. Communities on the Oregon Coast, particularly older ones built in the middle of the previous century, sometimes disappeared without warning, swallowed up by the ocean. He knew of at least two that had disappeared like that, and if his memory served, he had just passed a road sign still giving directions to one of them.

A shiver ran through him. Even after all these decades of study, it still made him nervous to think that a town, a city, a country, could disappear without warning. Human life was a very fragile thing.

He took the turn marked by a red bandanna tied to a tree, a bandanna probably left by Bradshaw or one of his students. Here the road became little more than a memory; weeds had covered most of the dirt. Only the deep ruts on either side showed that there was once a lot of traffic along this route.

As Cross followed the bumpy course, the car's computer came on, warning him about the damage the road was doing to the shocks and telling him, in a rather rude tone, that if he had wanted an off-road vehicle he should have rented one.

"Voice activation off," he snapped. He hated this part of the twenty-first century. Computers seemed to think it was their job to monitor adult behavior. It was like traveling everywhere with his elderly parents.

He rounded another corner and saw five cars parked near some trees. Four of the cars were battered and old. Two were rust-covered. Only one, an off-road vehicle liberally coated in mud, was new enough to be the professor's. Leo had found the site.

He got out of his car and stretched. From here he could hear the shush-shush of the ocean and smell the salt on the gentle breeze. Several tents were pitched to his right, and he thought he saw a trail that probably led down to the dig proper. A shout echoed from below—someone had seen him. Moments later, a solid, gray-haired man came up the rise, two students, both female, trailing behind him.

Dr. Edwin Bradshaw looked nothing like the man in the

grainy newspaper photographs and the yellowish video clips that Leo had looked at on his flight out here. Then, Bradshaw had a square-jawed, reedy look; the look of a man who spent too much time thinking and not enough time eating. Now he had a slight paunch around his belly, and his hair needed a good trim. He wore a dirt-covered flannel shirt over a faded T-shirt with the words *Grateful Dead* still visible. His jeans were tucked into heavy workboots, and he carried thick gloves in his right hand.

The students behind him were dressed similarly, although their T-shirts weren't faded and bore names of musicians or vids that Leo knew of only vaguely, because his own graduate students had the same shirts and the same tastes.

He wiped his hands on his clean blue jeans, feeling slightly self-conscious. He had left in such a hurry that he had forgotten his own workboots, and it had been long enough since he had supervised a dig that his own clothing made him look like a tourist among experienced locals. He reached into the open car door, and removed his pack, slinging it over one shoulder before he slammed the door closed.

"Dr. Cross," Bradshaw said as he stepped into the parking area. "Edwin Bradshaw."

They shook hands. Leo studied the man before him. He was shorter than Leo had expected, and there were sorrow lines around his eyes. He had been through a lot over the years, and it showed in his face.

Leo remembered studying Bradshaw's work as an undergraduate. He also remembered the gleeful debunking his professors had engaged in during graduate school, after Bradshaw announced his findings of a technologically advanced civilization operating in the South American rain forests. His findings had been based on several sites in one small area, and the tiny fossils he found embedded into rock from twelve thousand years ago. Bradshaw thought he had proven, beyond a shadow of a doubt, that those tiny pieces he had found were similar to the microchips that ran computers at the time, only on a nanotechnology level. His story became an overnight media event, and Bradshaw had become famous.

It took a year, but his rival archaeologists examined the same evidence and found it lacking. Bradshaw's credibility was destroyed and he became the laughingstock of the field. Leo had always thought that a shame. Even if Bradshaw's South American hypothesis was wrong, his other work had been stellar, so much so that Leo had based some of his own early work on Bradshaw's research.

It had been a pleasant surprise to discover that Bradshaw was still in the field, even in a limited capacity.

"These are two of my students," Bradshaw said. "My graduate assistant Kelly Flynn—"

The short, brown-haired woman nodded. She had freckles across her nose and a look of competence to her.

"—and an admirer of yours, Bet Cambridge."

Bet Cambridge was traditionally pretty, with high cheekbones and blond hair that Leo would have bet was dyed. Her blue eyes were a tad too bright as she looked at him, and he wondered if she'd seen those archaeology documentaries he had narrated, thinking they would be aired in schools only and that, to his surprise, became a popular Sunday night program on many PBS stations.

"Would you like some coffee, Dr. Cross?" she asked.

He made himself smile. He hated groupies, of any sort. "I've been up since four," he said. "And I'm already floating. Thanks though."

He turned to Bradshaw. "I'd like to see the site if I could."

"Certainly." Bradshaw led them down a well-worn path,

packed sand covered with pine needles and leaves. There was no grass poking through.

Leo could hear the dig site before he could see it. The rustle of human beings in a natural environment mixed with the exchange of soft conversation between a couple of the students. He thought he heard his own name come up once before Bet announced loudly that they were there. A flicker of annoyance crossed Bradshaw's face and disappeared.

Leo expected it. He hadn't come to watch students work. He had come to see the black layer.

They went over a small rise, and suddenly they were upon the dig. Leo could see why Bradshaw was working this site. It was a logical campsite for the Tillamook, or anyone else who was living in this area. It was far enough to be off the ocean, close to fresh water from the stream below, and sheltered from the wind by the rock bluff. He was surprised that this site hadn't been worked before now.

The area under the rock face of a shallow bluff had been completely roped off and crosshatched in squares with ropes for reference points. Three fifty-year-old pine trees were scattered over the site and were being used as anchors for the ropes. Ten students were carefully working different areas, some using only toothbrushes to help clean and loosen finds.

Leo smiled. The site looked no different from a dig that he would have worked on twenty-five years before. Very few of archaeology's data collection tools had changed—at least, not when it came to this kind of work.

Some of the dig areas were only about two feet deep, suggesting a shorter time span than the ones Leo had been working with. His breath caught between his teeth. Maybe his hypothesis had been wrong.

He hoped so.

"How far back are you working?" he asked.

"Mostly just two to five hundred years," Bradshaw said. "Although we think this site might have been a regular camp of a number of tribes farther back than that."

A few of the students looked over their shoulders at Leo, but none of them stopped working. Usually when he visited a site, they all acted like Bet—not just because of the documentaries, but because so many of them had studied his book on methodology. It was the definitive work these days (and he knew how long that would last) on how to take information from various disciplines and form a hypothesis, not just during the interpretation stage of a dig but throughout.

Bradshaw glared at one of the students who had stopped working, and he bent over his little area of dirt again. Even Bet had climbed into the dig site, her left hand braced against the smooth wall of dirt, her right hidden in a corner. Kelly still stood beside Bradshaw. Apparently she was his right-hand man, ready for any special orders he might give.

When the students all looked away, Bradshaw grinned at Leo, and Leo saw that what he had mistaken for sorrow lines were really laugh lines. When he smiled, Bradshaw had a puckish face. Leo smiled back, almost because he couldn't help himself.

Bradshaw led Leo over to the extreme edge of the roped-off area. Kelly followed half a step behind. When Bradshaw got to a section, he crouched. Leo knew exactly where they were and what Bradshaw was looking at. Bradshaw had used the spot to sink an exploration hole, working back into the past through the dirt, like a time machine.

This exploration hole was about three feet across and about six feet deep into the brown soil. The black soot line was clear about four and a half feet down, ringing the hole like something had put a blanket flat in the ground and Dr. Bradshaw's hole had cut right through it.

Being that deep in the test hole was a clear sign the black ring wasn't close to the present, as Leo had hoped it would be. He forced himself to take a deep breath and not show his disappointment. If only he could find a soot layer closer to the surface, he'd start sleeping at nights again. But this wasn't to be the place.

"How far back is that?" Leo asked, knowing almost certainly what the answer would be.

"I'd say around four thousand years," Bradshaw said, "considering the buildup of soil in this area. I'd have to run tests to be sure. You never know with some of these coastal areas."

Four thousand and twelve years, Leo wanted to say, but instead only nodded. It was as he had feared. He didn't want to tell Bradshaw that if he went down even farther with his hole, he most likely would find another band at eight thousand and twenty-four years. The same soot bands, at those same depths, had been found as far south as Bakersfield, California. This was the farthest north. So far.

"We dug other depth holes outside the site," Bradshaw said. "After I saw the ring."

"Do they all show the same thing?" Leo asked, knowing they would.

Bradshaw nodded.

"Was it a fire, sir?" Kelly asked. Her voice was husky and deep, confident, and not at all what Leo had expected. "Or did one of the volcanoes drop a ton of ash here in one of those strange wind swirls that sometimes bring debris from the east?"

Without answering, Leo dropped to his knee and put his pack on the dirt and pulled out his mineral test kit. It was the size of a shoe box, large for most computerized devices, but samples of varying sizes had to fit inside.

29

"Wow," Kelly said. "I've never seen one of those."

Leo glanced at her with some amusement. "You still do the initial analysis the old-fashioned way and then confirm it when you get back to the lab?"

"Our archaeology budget is fairly small," Bradshaw said before Kelly could answer. "I've been saving to get one of those for myself."

It was a shame that one of the field's most eminent researchers, however badly he had once been disgraced, couldn't even afford what most archaeologists considered to be an essential upgrade in their data collection tools.

But Leo didn't say that. Instead, he said, "They are expensive."

He took a small spoon and dish from the case and eased himself down into the hole, using the steps cut into the side. He was glad that the upgraded tool kit had drawn attention away from Kelly's question about fire. He didn't want to answer it if he didn't have to.

The sandy, damp smell of earth was comforting, even if the depth of the black band was not. Carefully, he scraped a sample of the ring right out of the center of the one-eighth-inch-wide black streak, making sure to get none of the surrounding dirt.

Then he placed his sample in the top of his case and grabbed two more containers, filling them with the black samples and sealing each. Then he climbed out of the hole and knelt in the dirt beside the test kit. As he poured the first sample into the examination dish, he moved slower than he normally would, so that both Kelly and Bradshaw could see how the new equipment worked.

The computerized test kit analyzed the soil sample without destroying it. For that reason alone, he preferred doing it this way. It allowed him to work on the smallest bit of data without losing it. The computer only took a moment to analyze the sample. He ran the second, to check his result, and then did the third. The results were what he had expected.

"The streak is exogenic, as I expected, and partially organic," he said to Bradshaw.

Bradshaw nodded, but before he could say anything, Kelly frowned.

"So doesn't that confirm it was a massive fire?" she asked.

In her position, without any background, Leo would have thought the same thing. The mostly organic composition would have been a preliminary confirmation that a fire had leveled everything in this area. Cultural research and more data collection added to or changed the result.

But it hadn't been a fire, Leo knew that much. And to form a one-eighth-inch-wide ring at that depth level, a fire would have had to create almost two inches of ash. No fire dropped two inches of ash uniformly over the ground. Bradshaw hadn't said a word, but Leo suspected the man had thought of fire and instantly ruled it out for that very reason. Plus there was another very basic reason.

Neither Kelly, nor Bradshaw, had the benefits Leo had. He had samples from fifty sites all over the world, and he had conducted extensive tests on those samples. Not one site had shown any signs that heat had caused those black lines. Plus there were large quantities of magnetite in every soot line, no matter what the area around it contained.

But what bothered him the most was the consistency of every site. He had visited digs where there was a soot line at 16,048 years and found the exact same elements in the sample as one found half a continent away and several thousand years younger. Remains from natural events, such as fire, didn't respond that way. It should have been different in different time periods, different in different parts of the world, different, for god's sake, in different types of soil.

But it wasn't.

"Dr. Cross?" she asked. She wasn't going to let her idea go.

He suppressed a sigh. He didn't know what had caused the soot layers, so it was just easier to let everyone listening believe it had been a fire. His answer wouldn't satisfy Bradshaw, but he hoped the older man had enough sense not to say anything until the student was gone.

"It's a good theory," Leo said to Kelly. "But never jump to conclusions until all the tests are in."

She smiled. "That's what Professor Bradshaw always says."

"Now do you believe me?" Bradshaw asked her.

She shrugged. "That's not the issue," she said. "Something else is happening here, and you don't want me to know."

Leo glanced at Bradshaw who had a slightly paternal smile on his face. He was clearly proud of this student, and thought she had potential.

She caught the glance, and smiled. "It's all right, you know," she said. "I understand how these things work. Someday I'll be the professor, and I'll be able to torture lowly graduate students."

"I already allow you to torture lowly undergraduates," Bradshaw said.

"And for that I'm eternally grateful," she said. "I'll leave you two to your mysterious black dirt." And with that, she walked away.

Leo watched her go. She spoke to one of the students in the dig site, and then crawled in herself. "That's a smart one," he said.

Bradshaw nodded. "I rely on her a little too much. Good students like that don't show up every day."

Leo brushed off his hands and folded up his kit. "I appre-

32

ciate your help," he said to Bradshaw, hoping to forestall the inevitable questions.

Bradshaw smiled. "You don't get off the hook that easily. We both know that ring wasn't caused by a fire."

Leo placed the mineral kit into his pack. "That's right."

"And frankly, I'm surprised you knew it would be here, especially since you didn't know much about the dig, the site, or how deep we would be going." Bradshaw sat on the scrubby grass beside the test hole before going on. "Which means you've found this in other places. You've seen it in other time periods. I ran your site visits last night, Dr. Cross. You haven't been to a dig in Oregon since you were a student yourself. You couldn't have remembered something like that black line from a two-day dig twenty-seven years ago."

Damn, he was good. Leo should have known that Edwin Bradshaw would put his finger on part of the problem immediately. None of the other site managers had. A few had tested the sample themselves and asked questions later, but none of them had figured out the most confusing part of all of this: that the black soot had turned up in a number of digs and a number of time periods. Bradshaw had got it in one.

It made Leo wonder if Bradshaw had stumbled on this before.

"I ran some tests after I got your e-mail," Bradshaw said. He nodded toward the pack. "Nothing as fancy as yours, but I learned a few things. There's no carbon or any other signs of fire in that layer. Trace elements of a number of local area minerals, plus magnetite. There's no magnetite anywhere near here. And we won't even discuss the thickness of the layer."

Leo glanced back at the students down the hill and the clean, carefully worked site. Clearly Bradshaw was a man who just might be trusted, and who could think on his own.

Leo would have to do more investigating on Bradshaw's errors, to see if they were reasonable assumptions based on the evidence and that the discrediting had come from jealous colleagues, or to see if Bradshaw had truly lost his ability to make reasonable deductions from the data at hand.

Leo had always assumed that Bradshaw's work had only been preliminary and the findings had gotten blown out of proportion. If he was right, and Bradshaw's methodology was okay, then he might hire Bradshaw to help him. One thing the man's work had shown was that he had a quick, nimble, and open mind.

"Well, Dr. Bradshaw," Leo said.

Bradshaw held up his hand. "Edwin."

Leo nodded. "Edwin. As you have guessed, there's a lot more to these black layers. I'm calling them soot levels, even though 'soot' isn't really an accurate term. I'll wait for an official name until I know what I'm dealing with."

"That's sensible," Bradshaw said. He looked expectant.

Leo would have to crush those expectations, for the moment anyway. "Right now, though, I can't tell you much beyond what you already know. But give me a few days and I'll fill you in with more. I promise."

The light in Bradshaw's eyes dimmed. How many archaeologists had made the same promise to him since he lost his reputation? Probably countless ones. Leo felt sympathy for the man and more than a touch of worry. He might be facing the same sort of reaction himself.

Still, Bradshaw put a good face on it. He smiled, even though the smile wasn't as bright as it was before. "Since I ran those tests I've been laying awake wondering what caused that layer. So please don't keep me waiting too long. At my age I need my sleep."

"I won't," Leo said. "I'll make sure you hear something quickly."

That much he could promise, because that promise was one he could keep. Then he glanced back at the site. The students were still hunched over, gathering evidence. The fact that Bradshaw was here meant that Leo wasn't the only one who remembered Bradshaw's past. Oregon State University had enough courage to hire him, even though they took advantage of his misfortune and hired him at one-fourth his old salary. Still, by giving him a haven, they were giving him an opportunity to rebuild, and it seemed as if Bradshaw was taking it.

"Do me one more favor, would you?" Leo asked.

"If I can," Bradshaw said.

"It's going to mess up your sleep even more."

Bradshaw smiled, and this time the look reached his eyes. "It's always nice to have something to ponder."

"Well, trust me, you'll ponder this a great deal," Leo said. "Take one of those outer exploration holes, and when you can, dig down a few more feet, past the ten-thousand-year level. Do this without student help or student observation. I don't want anyone else to know about this. Let me know what you find, if anything."

Bradshaw stared into Leo's eyes. Leo could see the concern in the older man's eyes. Bradshaw had clearly put key elements together quickly. He wasn't surprised by the mention of another layer at a deeper depth. Leo felt a shiver run down his back. Bradshaw might just be the assistant he so very much needed.

"I'll do it," Bradshaw said. "And I won't let anyone know."

"Thanks," Leo said.

He shook Bradshaw's hand, then started up the trail alone. Leo wanted to get away from the site. He was starting to feel twitchy, just as he had at the previous sites. His imagination was very vivid. Without any effort at all, he could see this whole area without a tree, without a plant, covered in black soot so thick that his feet would disappear in it if he walked through it. He could see it as clearly as if he had lived through it.

And he hadn't.

But he was afraid he might.

August 23, 2017
12:19 A.M. Australian Eastern Standard Time

233 Days Until Arrival

"You're workin' too hard, mate," said Thomas Kingsford. "You should do what all good Yanks do when they're in over their heads. You should take a break."

Craig Stanton pushed his chair away from his monitor and glared at Kingsford, only because it was expected. "No matter how hard you try," Craig said, "you should never use a phrase like 'take a break.' It sounds funny coming from those Aussie lips."

Kingsford laughed, a sound so rich and full it should have come from a man three times his size. "I'm not tryin' to be a Yank, mate. I'm just tryin' to use language you'll understand."

"Try harder," Craig said with a bit of an edge as he got out of the chair. Kingsford was right. He did need a break. He walked through the large white room filled with monitors and desks and an overhead screen that, at the moment, was show-ing real-time pictures being beamed back from Mars. The pictures seemed familiar even though he was sure they were new. The Martian landscape had become as familiar as his own, maybe even more familiar than the view outside his window in that tiny apartment he had found near the Hawkes-bury River.

No one had bothered to tell him he would have to drive across half of Sydney to get home every day. Nor had anyone told him that there was nearby housing available at a reduced rate to people hired by the International Space Monitoring Agency. He had discovered all of that after he had signed his lease.

Craig only minded when people like Kingsford brought the feeling back, the feeling he had had his first weeks in Australia. It was as if he were truly on his own for the first time in his life, even though he had been living on his own for seven years. Australians, at least those connected with the project, had a kind of survival of the fittest attitude. If a man made a mistake, so be it, and if it cost him a lot of money or a lot of time or if it hurt a little, well, then, maybe he would learn from it. Craig had always thought the American West—particularly Wyoming, where he had grown up—was tough, but Americans were soft compared with their Australian counterparts.

No one person looked up as Craig threaded his way to the break room to get some of that swill they called coffee. In his old office in San Francisco, where he had worked for a multi-national conglomerate, not an international agency crammed into a university, the lunchroom had actually had a *barista* who had been employed there for more than thirty years. Here, half the guys still made instant in the microwave.

He shuddered involuntarily, and when he want into the break room, he opened the refrigerator and removed a Coke instead. He glanced at the ancient sandwiches tucked among the fake lettuce in the glass case, then looked at the dough-nuts, which had just arrived, and then glanced at the lunch he had brought. None of them appealed. He didn't want food. He was just concerned about what he had found. He went to the door of the kitchen and stared at the room.

Dozens of people worked third shift here. The buoys didn't stop transmitting data just because humans wanted to rest. And the buoys were transmitting so much information it was keeping a hundred scientists busy around the clock.

There had been an uproar when ISMB 6 had stopped transmitting almost a week before, mostly from the international scientists who had been counting on ISMB 6 teaching them all they wanted to know about Uranus. But the agency director had calmed them by reminding them that in its short six-month orbit around Uranus, ISMB 6 had already sent back more information than they could process in three years. And that didn't count the information it had sent on its journey to the planet. And, the director had reminded them, equipment failed. No matter what they planned for, equipment failed. A piece of space debris might have taken the buoy out, or something might be interfering with transmission. The current team was hoping that the problem was something they could fix from the agency here in Australia.

Craig wasn't so sure, and that was what had been bothering him. He wasn't part of the ISMB 6 team, at least not the original assembly team, although he had felt a small fondness for the buoy. It had been his job to monitor that buoy in real time, and he had felt that they were companions, two creatures alone in strange and sometimes hostile worlds.

And then ISMB 6 had died on him.

Since ISMB 6 had died, the assembly team and several other scientists had been called in to try to reestablish contact with the buoy. They assumed it was still there, and that the problem was nothing more than a glitch.

He took his Coke back to his console. Kingsford was gone from his desk, which was a good thing. Craig wasn't in the mood to talk anymore. He pushed his chair in and punched up the data he had been struggling with for the past four days.

The experts were wrong—that was the conclusion he was coming to. They saw the problems with ISMB 6 as internal or as something that could be fixed. He didn't. No matter which way he looked at the information, he came to the same conclusion: Something external had happened to ISMB 6 right before it stopped sending—and it wasn't something expected, like collision with space debris. He had been watching the event happen in real time and he had seen a series of patterns in the data stream that he had never seen before. They had blipped past him too quickly to analyze, of course, and at first, he wasn't even sure he had seen them. So, after hesitating for two days, he finally decided to analyze the twenty channels of data that had come through the buoy in the last eight hours of its life to see if he could come up with what had stopped the transmissions.

He hadn't asked permission and, in fact, no one seemed to care that he was not following the usual protocol. It made him wonder if anyone watched over his work, like the project manager had said they would do when he was hired. He suspected no one did.

Even with that suspicion, though, he felt odd following this data trail. He just couldn't stop. He and ISMB 6 had been buddies for a long time, and even though he was supposed to work backup on ISMB 5 until ISMB 6 came back on line, he couldn't bring himself to do it. He had a hunch that ISMB 6 wasn't coming back, and he had to know why.

After four days of research, he knew a number of things. First, there had not been a freak collision with space debris. Even if a rock had come in fast, ISMB 6's sensors would have spotted it. There had been nothing. Two days ago he had shared that information with the restoration team and they had applauded, since they thought it meant they had a good chance of restoring contact with the buoy. But they hadn't taken the thought any farther. They had gone back to work reestablishing contact with ISMB 6.

No one had even yelled at him for turning his attention away from his new job.

Craig hadn't told them the rest of his findings. He wasn't ready to. He had discovered a lot of things. He had eliminated the possibility of an electrical spike through the system causing everything to shut down. Nor had the buoy received a signal to shut down. Both of those events would have left clear fingerprints in the last seconds of the data streams. Neither was present.

On his monitor, Craig punched up his chart showing the twenty data streams in the last second of transmission. He had plotted each stream on a graph showing intensity and clarity. All twenty streams, at the same moment, had downward slants. They went from normal power to no power in one second's time.

Impossible, but true. The data streams went from a measurable quantity to zero faster than he could blink. He had double-checked his information. All of it was exact. And that wasn't the creepiest part. The creepiest part was that they all hit zero at the exact same instant. Different CPUs, different backplanes, three separate battery backups—everything had cut out at the exact same time.

His training told him such a thing wasn't really possible. It was as if something had covered ISMB 6 like a blanket covered a bed, almost instantly draining the power. Yet within that instant, the signal had stopped in a familiar way: The chart looked the same as one he would do of a car battery being drained by a stuck horn. The battery got weaker and weaker. Yet on the buoy, the drain of a very powerful set of primary, secondary, and backup batteries had happened within a second. It was only the high speed of the data sent that allowed him to even see the diminishing power.

But what would have that effect? And did the buoy just get swallowed by something, as the last second of data transmitted Earthward seemed to suggest? He had mentioned to the team the possibility that the batteries were drained. They had laughed at him.

"Craigie, lad," said one of the scientists, "the batteries were to last thirty years. They've barely gone through three, and there were two backups."

He had had that thought as well. But his evidence showed that the power cells were dead. And if the batteries were dead, the buoy was dead.

He knew he was right. He just had to prove it beyond a doubt. Craig had no idea what would cause the drain. But he was sure any conclusion he came to was going to be laughed at by the others if he didn't present it carefully. And maybe even then.

He sat back down in front of his monitor and went back to work. If he had to be laughed at, he was going to make damn certain his information was exact and correct. And if that took him a few more days, then fine.

Nothing would bring the buoy back. Of that he was certain. A few days didn't matter either way.

August 24, 2017
8:03 P.M. Eastern Daylight Time

232 Days Until Arrival

Edwin Bradshaw leaned back in the cracked plastic seat of the cab, and stared at the dirty buildings of Washington, D.C.

It had been a long time since he had been to this place, a long time since he had been welcome. Even now he felt nervous. He really wasn't sure he should have come.

But Dr. Leo Cross had sent for him. Cross had paid for his plane ticket and had said he would take care of Bradshaw's lodgings and meals. They had made the arrangements by e-mail, but Bradshaw had been unable to let things rest. Just before he had called an assistant professor to take his place on the dig, he had called Cross. To his surprise, the man had answered the phone himself.

"Dr. Cross," Bradshaw had said without much preamble, "I am quite flattered by your offer to help you on this project—God knows, I'm intrigued—but I'm not sure you know who I am."

"Of course I do, Dr. Bradshaw," Cross said. "I've studied your work."

"But do you know about—"

"The advanced civilization scandal? Of course I do."

"Forgive me," Bradshaw had said, "but I've lived with that disgrace for a very long time. My presence on your project might take it from a respectable realm into the realm of tabloids and kooks."

"Your research has always been impeccable, Edwin," Cross said.

Bradshaw had been glad he was not using the video option on his phone. He had to sit down when Cross said that. It was the reassurance he had been looking for from a colleague, a confirmation that Bradshaw had always done good work, not that he had made a mistake and would get over it.

"I'm glad you think so," Bradshaw had said a beat too late. "But others might not. I would compromise your work."

"I'd be a fool if I said I hadn't thought about that," Cross said. "But frankly, I need you more because of that 'disgrace' as you call it than if you hadn't had it."

"I'm not following," Bradshaw said.

"I work on hunches, and the gathering of information from a variety of sources, just like you do. My tendency is to bulldoze ahead, even if doing so might compromise the work. The problem is that we may not have much time on this project. I suspect you'll make sure I'm fully prepared before any of this leaves my office."

"I'll do that," Bradshaw said. "But that still doesn't prevent the reaction after it has left your office. I'll taint your work."

"That's one way of looking at it," Cross said. "Or I might be able to rehabilitate yours. You still stand behind your research, don't you?"

"I don't discuss the case," Bradshaw said primly.

"Discuss it with me," Cross said. "Do you stand behind your work?"

"It was preliminary data," Bradshaw said. "I put the information out there, not so that it would be criticized but so that others would evaluate it. So far no one has."

"And the press circus?"

"Was my naïveté. I didn't realize how many people would latch on to my findings as confirmation of their own crazy theories."

"If you had, you never would have published that paper," Cross said. "I read it again last night, by the way. You were quite clear about the preliminary nature of your research and, contrary to media reports, you never drew a single conclusion. You only marked possibilities based on cultural contexts, and you outlined the need for further research. I think you've been in exile long enough, Edwin."

Bradshaw hadn't been able to agree more. "I'd feel better about this if we kept my involvement quiet."

"Let's make that decision after you've seen what I'm working on. You might want to go back to your beautiful dig site on the Oregon Coast." And with that, Cross had hung up.

The conversation had reassured Bradshaw enough to get him on the plane, but it wasn't carrying him through the streets to the address Cross had given him. What was getting him through this was his own curiosity. He hadn't been able to get those black lines out of his head.

The afternoon after Cross left, Bradshaw had gone to an outer test hole and dug while some of the students were working and others were running errands into Cloverdale. Just as Cross had suggested, Bradshaw dug down and, at what would have been right about twelve thousand years in normal depth, he had found another black soot ring, same thickness. He quickly took samples, then filled the hole back up to its previous level so no student would ask questions he couldn't answer. He wasn't sure that even Cross could answer the question of what had caused two soot rings in the ground, eight thousand years apart in time.

Bradshaw did some tests, coming up with the same results as the first soot ring. Exactly the same results—something he knew wasn't possible. He had e-mailed Cross with his findings, more than likely before Cross had even arrived back in the nation's capital. That night Bradshaw had received a simple message in reply.

Thanks. I'll be in touch shortly. Cross.

Two days later the offer to come to Washington, D.C., had arrived.

The cab pulled up in front of a stately brick home that was probably two hundred years old. In its day, it had been a man-

44

sion, but by modern standards it was a good-sized home, well-maintained. It was certainly not what he had expected, even though Cross had told Bradshaw that he would be coming to Cross's home.

It was drizzling as Bradshaw got out of the cab, but the air still felt sticky with heat and humidity. The cabdriver helped him get his bags out of the back—Cross had told him to pack heavily in case they decided to work together. He carried his bags up the wet brick steps and rang the bell.

A woman at least twenty years older than Bradshaw answered the door. She wore a two-piece blue suit and a strand of pearls around her neck. She was considerably shorter than Bradshaw, but she had a lot of presence. She smiled when she saw him.

"Dr. Bradshaw," she said. "Dr. Cross has been expecting you. Come on in."

He stepped into a hallway with a polished wood floor, paintings hanging from the white walls, a chandelier that formed the centerpiece of the room, and a wide wooden staircase leading to a balcony on the second floor. Whatever he had expected of Leo Cross's home, this wasn't it.

He continued to hold his bags, afraid to set them down on the expensive wood.

"I'm Bonnie Oldham," the woman said. "I'm Dr. Cross's secretary. He's waiting for you downstairs, but before you go, I think you should at least have time to freshen up. Constance—!" That last was a bellow, so harsh that Bradshaw was relieved it wasn't aimed at him. Bonnie Oldham grinned at him as if she expected his reaction. "Raising children gives you a good set of lungs."

A woman came out of the kitchen, wiping her work-roughened hands on a white towel.

"Where does Dr. Cross want Dr. Bradshaw?"

"The blue bedroom," Constance said. "I just finished getting it ready."

"You're about to go, aren't you, dear?" Mrs. Oldham asked. "Finish your dinner preparations. I'll take Dr. Bradshaw upstairs."

"Thank you, Mrs. Oldham." And Constance went back into the kitchen.

Seeing Bradshaw's startled look, Mrs. Oldham said, "She's his housekeeper. Dr. Cross comes from an old, distinguished, and very wealthy Virginia family. He's always been a bit sensitive about it, but that doesn't stop him from living comfortably. This part of the house, as well as the guest rooms and the formal living and dining rooms, still reflect his mother's tastes. The rest of the house is all his. I think he keeps Constance on because he wouldn't eat properly if he didn't. Not to mention the fact that the place would be a sty."

She led him up the stairs and across the balcony into a wing. The blue bedroom was done in royal blues, with a queen-sized mahogany bed as its centerpiece. The bed was an antique. It even had mosquito netting folded back as if the guests were expected to make use of it during the night. Bradshaw found himself wondering how many generations of Cross guests had actually slept in here.

She opened a door. "You have a wardrobe through here," she said, "and a bathroom on the other side of that. The next room over is the sitting room, also for guests. There's an entertainment center as well as enough reading material to take you through the next century, if you're so inclined. I've never figured out why Dr. Cross's guests leave. This setup is so much better than anything I have at home. I keep waiting for him to invite me to sleep over."

46

Bradshaw gave her a startled look and she laughed. The sound was deep and full, so filled with life that he had to laugh too.

"You'll just have to get used to me, Doctor," she said. "I say what I think—and don't blame it on my age, because I have always done so. Get freshened up, and then go down to the basement. The stairs are in a door off the hallway you were first in. It's the only closed door. You can't miss it."

Then she left. He stood in the center of this stately room for a moment, noting the solidness of the antiques—no spindly French furniture here, just well-built American pieces, some more than three hundred years old. The paintings on the wall were originals too, American primitives all of them. He was educated enough to recognize the style but not the painters. If someone had told him the week before that he would be standing here, and not be in the middle of some Oregon forest, he would have laughed.

He picked up his suitcases and carried them into the wardrobe. There he was surprised to see clothing in various sizes. He had never before been in a home that provided outfits for the guests, should they find they needed something. Formal gowns hung on one wall, and formal men's attire right behind them. Shoes were on the floor, and there were brand-new shirts on shelves, as well as a variety of ties. He shook his head slightly. No. He hadn't expected to be here.

He unpacked quickly, then took a fresh shirt out of his bag and went into the bathroom. It was the only bow to the twenty-first century in the place. The shower was computerized and even had a dual head in case couples were staying here. The toilet was an automatic flusher, and the sink had a motion sensor instead of faucet handles. There he used the unscented

47

soap from the basket that gave him more choices than he dreamed possible. He smoothed back his hair, peered into the mirror, and thought that he didn't look as tired as he felt.

Then he took a deep breath and gripped the sides of the sink, moving back in surprise as it turned on. "Damn," he muttered. There were benefits in the old ways of doing things.

He wiped his hands on the towel and shook his head. This was his last chance to back out. He might be doing both Cross and himself a favor.

But he knew as clearly as he knew his own name that he couldn't back out. He was committed from the moment he read that first e-mail. This was an intriguing mystery, and more than that, it was probably his last chance to work on something larger than a student dig.

He left the room, and went down the stairs, not seeing anyone. He heard pots bang in the kitchen, which meant that Constance the housekeeper hadn't left yet. Then he walked through the hallway, past more antiques, all American colonials, from the pie shelf that was being used as pottery storage to the wig rack near the door. He found the closed door to the basement beneath the staircase. He pulled the door open and was surprised to see stairs carpeted in green shag.

Lights were on below, and he could hear voices. Mrs. Oldham—laughing—and Cross sounding, well, slightly cross. "I thought you said he was here."

"He just got off a long flight, Leo. He needed a moment to himself."

"I wanted him here first. If he doesn't like what we're doing, he has a whole day to himself before he can fly out again."

Bradshaw made sure he made a lot of noise as he came

down the stairs, which ended in a long but wide room that had a fireplace and a pool table in the very center. The cues were in a rack on the wall, which someone had painted a forest green to match the shag carpet. From the wear patterns, Bradshaw figured this carpet had been in place since he was a boy—more than fifty years ago.

He crossed it and entered the open door. This room looked more comfortable. It was well-lit and warm, with oak paneling on the walls and thick carpet. There were a few chairs and a couch facing a wide-screen television that looked like it wasn't HDTV. Clearly it was some sort of family room or game room.

Cross was pacing in front of it. "Edwin, at last," he said.

"Let's try again," Mrs. Oldham said. "How about 'Hello, Edwin. Welcome to my home. I hope you had a safe flight.' "

Cross grinned. "Can you believe I pay her?"

"The university pays me," she said. "You take advantage of that."

Cross walked to Bradshaw, and shook his hand. "Sorry about my rudeness," he said. "Constance got you settled?"

"I got him settled," Mrs. Oldham said.

"Good," Cross said. "Now that we're through the pleasantries, let's get down to business."

Bradshaw felt as if he had been run over by a steam roller. He hadn't said a word, yet he felt as if he had been the center of the conversation. His hand ached from the intensity of Cross's grip.

Cross moved to a closed door in the far wall and inserted a computerized key.

"We put the map room back here," Cross said. "It's safer than at the university. We don't get questions we don't have answers for."

Bradshaw followed Cross inside. This was a working office, complete with computer plasma screens and digital fax machines. Printers lined one wall along with a large document printer for maps and architectural drawings. In the very center of the room was a cluttered table surrounded by several chairs. Some desks were pushed against the printer wall, and that was the only furniture. There were no windows. A second wall was covered with several two-drawer filing cabinets that looked as if they belonged to another era. But the wall directly in front of them was blank.

Cross pressed a button on one of the computers and several large flat screens, like most modern television sets, unfolded. He hit two more buttons on his keyboard and the screens sprang to life.

A three-dimensional map of the world appeared on the biggest screen. Tiny dots glimmered as the world spun on its axis. Another screen contained a detailed map of North America. A third held a map of South America. Europe and Asia each had their own screens as did Indochina and Australia.

Colored dots covered each map in various locations. Other areas were entirely covered in a light color, as if the entire space had been highlighted.

"Black dots represent soot rings found at levels indicating it was laid down two thousand and six years ago," Cross said.

"Six?" Bradshaw said, glancing at Cross. No archaeological site could ever be that accurate about dates without outside information.

"I'll get to that." Cross pointed to the South American map. "Red dots show layers of soot at four thousand and twelve years. Green are six thousand and eighteen years. Your dig site, of course, shows red."

Bradshaw walked up to the North American map. His site,

in Oregon, looked lonely. A red dot and orange dot side by side. There were no other sites with markings in Oregon at all. The nearest was in California. And its dot was blue.

"Blue is eight thousand and twenty-four years," said Cross, noting where Bradshaw was looking, "and orange is twelve thousand and thirty-six."

Bradshaw noted several orange dots in South America.

"White dots mark fourteen thousand years and over," Cross said. "They're harder to track exact dates."

Bradshaw stared at the maps, letting the information Cross had just given him sink in. The soot levels like the two he had found were a worldwide phenomenon. He felt a slight chill.

This was some sort of recurring event.

Something external, something that could be predicted— at least in its regularity. Bradshaw stared at the markings. But clearly it didn't happen in each place at the same time. It didn't spread all over the Earth when it hit; just certain parts of it.

"Is the chemical analysis the same at all the sites?" he asked.

Cross nodded. "There's a slight variance for local minerals, but otherwise it's exactly the same. And each site is laced with magnetite."

"Magnetite," Bradshaw said, shaking his head at the strangeness of it all. Magnetite was a fairly common mineral found around the world, with the largest deposit being in northern Sweden. But it was never found in thin layers like this.

Cross only shrugged. "I've been putting this information together for the past two years and I still don't have even a guess as to what is causing this."

"What do the highlighted areas mean?" Bradshaw asked,

51

walking up to the North American map and studying it. There was a red-tint covering an area stretching from near Los Angeles to Southern Oregon. A green one over most of the central part of the country and a red oval in Texas and New Mexico.

"Since we have the most data on the events two, four, and six thousand years ago, we tried to figure the extent of the soot cover. Last year we did almost a hundred test holes in the central United States, locating the parameters of the three soot levels."

Bradshaw couldn't believe what he was hearing. The green highlight covered most of seven states, right out of the very center of the country. And the red highlight covered most of the West Coast.

"Your dig extended the northern boundary on the four-thousand-year West Coast area," Mrs. Oldham said. "We thought it stopped at the Siskious Mountains before."

Cross nodded. "Seems mountains mean nothing to whatever is causing these soot layers."

Bradshaw walked slowly around the room, noting all the work that had gone into tracing all the soot levels around the world. Only someone with Cross's reputation and influence could gather this much data. It was impressive all by itself, outside of the amazing facts it was showing.

"So," Bradshaw said after his mind finally balked at looking at any more. "How did you pinpoint the time so accurately?"

Cross sat down in one chair and slid a notebook toward Bradshaw. "We started with carbon dating and worked backwards," Cross said. "The two-thousand-year-old events were the easiest to pinpoint." He pointed to the black highlight covering part of central and northern South America. "The South and Central American cultures left us records that were helpful. I found references from the Izapas of the Guatemalan region as well as the Nazca People who had heard of the phenomenon all the way down in the area we now call Peru."

Bradshaw felt a slight irritation at Cross's tone. Obviously Cross had explained this to people who weren't familiar with these cultures, but Bradshaw was. He peered at the South American map. "What of the Mayas? They should have had information you could have used."

"Their records call this the great blackness," said Cross. "It was ignored by Mayan scholars because no one knew what it meant. We still don't, but the timing can be worked almost exactly."

Bradshaw looked around at the maps. Large black areas covered parts of China, central Asia, South Africa, and North America. He could see how, using data from historical records, those times could be pinpointed. There were a lot of witnesses around.

"In all areas, the event is called the Time of Blackness, or Giant Black Cloud. From what we've been able to tell, something black comes out of the sky and covers a large area, destroying everything it touches. And all occurred the same year: nine A.D."

Suddenly the room seemed to spin. He was holding his breath. What Cross had been telling him finally struck home. Before he spoke, he made himself breathe. "You're saying the last event had been two thousand and six years ago?"

"Yes," Cross said.

"And that means we're due this year for another?" Bradshaw stared at all the black highlighting that covered huge areas of the maps. All taken together, he figured it covered a size far larger than the entire North American continent.

If everything was killed inside that much area, billions would die.

"That's right," Cross said. "Whatever caused this is due back anytime now."

3

September 1, 2017
10 A.M. Australian Eastern Standard Time

225 Days Until Arrival

The conference room was gray and dark. It hadn't been upgraded since the building had been built in the late 1990s. One overhead fluorescent was sputtering; the other one was burned out. The only concession to the modern era were the small lights built into the table by each chair. Craig turned his on.

His stomach was all acid, and it didn't matter how strong the stomach pills he took were, the acid wasn't going away. He rubbed his damp hands on his chinos, and then double-checked the equipment.

His bosses were outside, getting coffee he had bought especially for this meeting, and the special cream cakes the bakery near his apartment made. Craig knew scientists; they always appreciated a meeting that had food.

He couldn't eat, and more coffee would burn a hole through his tortured intestinal lining. He was normally in bed at this hour, but he couldn't very well tell his bosses to meet him at the beginning of his shift. Instead, he had asked for, and been granted, this meeting.

He kept trying to tell himself that he had been through the worst. He had told his project manager that he hadn't been doing his assigned duties, that he had been investigating ISMB 6 instead. His manager, Tracie Smithers, had looked a bit stern until Craig told her that he had found something, and then she had asked what that something was.

It was she who called the three who were going to meet with him today.

One by one they came into the room. Vijay Du Bois, a slender man who always wore white to set off his dark skin and even darker eyes, carried his demitasse cup on his palm. In his other hand, he held a half-eaten cream cake. Du Bois had been in charge of the original team that planned the buoy's missions. Since ISMB 6 had disappeared, he had headed the effort to get the buoy back on-line.

"Where did you find these cakes?" he asked in English so melodic that it was clear it was not his native language. "I have never had anything like them."

"A bakery near the Hawksbury River."

"You'll have to give me the name," he said. "I will send a treat to the engineers."

Craig nodded.

The second boss came in. Athena Terizopolis held a full-sized glass of the instant coffee they served in the break room. Craig could still see the crystals undissolved through the side of the glass.

"Cream cakes," she said, patting her round thighs. "You could have thought of something less fattening."

"But then you wouldn't have eaten any, my dear," Du Bois said.

Terizopolis laughed. She was short and round, with dra-

56

matic features that overpowered her face—except when she laughed. Then those features worked together to form a great beauty. Craig always felt as if he had to look away at those moments. She was the on-site head of the International Space Monitoring Agency, the one who made sure relations with the scientists and the university and the international agency sponsoring everything went smoothly. She intimidated him, and discovering that he found her beautiful when she laughed made him uncomfortable.

She sat beside him and called, "Martin, we're waiting for you."

A muffled response came from outside the door, and then Martin Kellog entered, wiping some crumbs off his face with a napkin. Kellog was head of data retrieval and one of the few other Americans on this project. His bolero ties and cowboy boots clashed mightily with his afro, and sometimes Craig wondered if Kellog wasn't trying to be everything American to the Australians.

"Sorry," he said. "Didn't have breakfast. Those cakes are sinful."

Craig smiled, and as Kellog slipped into a chair, he turned on the light above. All three faces turned toward him expectantly.

He sighed. "I spoke to Tracie and she said it was imperative that I talk to you." His voice sounded raspy and uncertain. He cleared his throat. In his six months at ISMA, he had never made a presentation before people as important as these.

"She said you were to talk about ISMB Six?" Terizopolis asked, almost like a prompt.

"Yes," Craig said. He was the only one standing. He clasped his hands behind his back. "We're never going to make contact with ISMB Six again. It's dead. And instead of trying to contact the dead like we have been doing"—he blushed, hoping Du Bois wouldn't take that as an insult—"we need to treat this like a murder mystery and figure out what killed the buoy."

"I do not believe the buoy is dead," Du Bois said.

"Obviously, or you wouldn't be trying to revive it," Kellog said. He leaned forward. "Tracie said this wasn't idle speculation. She said you had data to back up your theories. Is that true?"

Craig nodded and hit the button that released the thin television screen. It scrolled downward. He then punched up one of the large charts he had made for this meeting. The computer displayed it on the screen. The chart showed all twenty data streams transmitted by ISMB 6.

"On August 16, at 16:04:08 Greenwich Mean Time, ISMB Six was functioning perfectly." Craig pointed to the beginning of the chart. "I have separated each data stream into its primary and secondary bands, just as we received it here almost two days later. I recombined the data to form just one line for each data stream and the power level of each received."

All three scientists nodded. They looked interested. He felt the muscles in his shoulders relax slightly. He was used to doing this sort of presentation. He had done it all the time in San Francisco. Just not here, and not with such strange data.

"If the buoy had remained functioning normally over the thirty years of its projected life," he said, "the drain on the battery would have been evidenced by slow deterioration in power output, frequency sensibility, and amplitude imperceptibility, according to a standard log curve, for the first ten years. Then the deterioration in power would have accelerated over the last twenty years until we finally experienced transmission loss."

Craig traced the transmission lines on his chart as they remained basically flat for a time then curved down rapidly to the bottom of the graph.

Again everyone nodded. Du Bois looked slightly impatient. It had been his team, after all, that had designed those batteries, and Terizopolis who had approved them. Even the chart should have looked familiar. Craig had pulled this chart out of preliminary data done years before the first buoy launching.

Craig took a deep breath and punched up his other chart. It was bigger and more elaborate. He had overcompensated for his nervousness by making the chart pretty. Next to the first one, it looked almost fussy and he cursed silently, wishing he had seen that before.

"At 16:04:09 Greenwich Mean Time, something happened to the buoy that caused it to start discharging its batteries."

"Drain its batteries?" Terizopolis repeated. "Why wasn't I told of this?"

"No one else found it, ma'am," Craig said. "I wouldn't have either if I hadn't been watching the data streams when they came in. Even then it registered as something unusual, nothing more. I had to dig for this."

"You're sure about the discharge?" Du Bois asked.

Craig nodded.

"It's not possible. Do you know how many fail-safes we set up within the system?"

"It's space, Vijay. We don't know everything about it," Kellog said.

Du Bois looked as if he were about to answer, but Terizopolis interrupted him. "What drained those batteries?" she asked.

"I don't know," Craig said.

"Are you sure they were fully discharged?" Du Bois asked.

"Yes," Craig said. "This is what I found."

He pointed at the chart that had the exact same downward curve to all twenty data channels, only elapsed time was two seconds instead of thirty years.

It had been striking to Craig when he'd first discovered that both charts were exactly the same. He could only imagine how his audience was feeling.

No one spoke. So Craig said, "I've documented all my research in an encrypted file that I can download to you if you'd like. I'm sure you're going to want to check it. But I think you'll find you're wasting your time trying to contact that buoy again. Something inside, or outside, that buoy sucked out the remaining twenty-seven years of its life in less than two seconds. ISMB Six is dead. It told us so itself."

"This changes everything," Kellog said, moving up and examining the chart carefully.

"Yes, it does," Terizopolis said. "Before we send another buoy out there, we need to know what happened to this one."

"If your data is accurate," Du Bois said, with a hint of challenge in his voice, "then can you tell us what drained the buoy's batteries?"

"I don't know," Craig said, sinking into his chair. "That, I'm afraid, it didn't tell us."

September 3, 2017
5:09 P.M. Eastern Daylight Time

222 Days Until Arrival

Cross took the butter dish off the counter and placed it between the basket of warm cornbread muffins and the plates Constance had left out. The coffeemaker dripped behind him.

He grabbed the morning paper, still unread despite the lateness of the afternoon, and set it on the table.

Bradshaw sat down in the padded chair across from Cross and grabbed one of the muffins. "This is the life," he said, putting the muffin on a plate and pulling it toward him. "You have no idea how lucky you are."

"Hmm," Cross said, scanning the front page of the paper. The usual political news. He really didn't read much of it, only enough to keep up with Mickelson. Actually, he had an on-line clipping service that sent him all the *Washington Post* and *New York Times* articles that mentioned Mickelson (and there were too damn many!) as well as articles that dealt with his own discipline. But he didn't log onto the service every day. He did scan his paper every day—in fact, he felt as if he hadn't had a good day if he didn't. Old habit. They said that the number of actual newsprint copies of the *Post* had been declining in the past decade even though readership had been going up. The reason was that people who wanted to read an actual hard copy, one that smelled of ink and smeared on the fingers, were dying off, to be replaced by people who self-selected their news like he did on-line.

Sometimes, he felt, it paid to read everything.

"It's the two thousand and six years that's bothering me," Bradshaw said.

Cross glanced up from his paper. The older scientist had buttered his muffin heavily and the butter had melted, dripping onto his plate as he took a bite and then went on. "And the great blackness. I suppose you've looked at eclipses and how they manifested across the globe."

Cross suppressed a sigh. He wouldn't get to the rest of his paper. Constance came in the back door, her arms filled with groceries. She smiled at Cross when she saw them snacking on the muffins.

"Not too much now," she said. "I'm making a roast for your dinner. It's fun to cook for someone who appreciates it."

That last was directed at Cross and he knew it. He often ate the dinner she left for him and then couldn't remember, the next day, what it was he had eaten. She had long ago stopped asking whether he had liked or disliked something. She simply fixed his meals. In the week that Bradshaw had been staying here, though, the older scientist had complimented her on her cooking every time he saw her.

"Muffins are wonderful," Bradshaw said, right on cue.

Cross watched as her smile grew.

"The blackness was not referring to a celestial event," Cross said, ignoring the interchange as best he could. The warm sweet smell of the muffins was getting to be too much for him. His stomach growled. He grabbed a muffin off the pile and didn't bother with a plate. "It was referring to the way the Earth looked after this event happened. As if it were covered with darkness, at least that was what an assistant to King Mentuhotep of Thebes told the court when he returned from a long journey. I suspect the journey took him to Italy, if you look at the map, but I'm not sure, and the documents don't say. Octavian received a similar report two thousand and six years later, this time about the British Isles."

"I thought it came from the sky," Bradshaw said.

"A number of reports said that." Cross popped half the muffin in his mouth. Constance gave him a disapproving stare.

"How good is your archaeoastronomy?" he asked

"Lousy," Bradshaw said. "It wasn't even a discipline when I was coming in. I know enough about it to mention it in my 101 classes, and then I don't touch it after that."

"I spent the last few years boning up on it precisely because of this. The heavens were very important to ancient

62

peoples. They didn't have electric lights, or cities that blotted out the skies. They saw things we don't."

"And what did you find?"

Cross sighed. "I was looking for similarities of descriptions. And that's tough between cultures, let alone cultures that were thousands of miles and thousands of years apart. I found a few. The blackness of the Earth being one, and the mention of something in the sky. But that's it."

"What were you hoping for?" Bradshaw asked.

"Something you could pinpoint." Cross put the rest of the muffin in his mouth. "You know, something so unusual even the ancients would be able to extrapolate from it."

"Like Haley's Comet."

Cross stopped chewing. A shiver ran up his spine. "Huh?" he asked.

"Haley's Comet. You know—"

"Shit," Cross said, and pushed his chair back. He went to the sink and looked out of the kitchen window. The sky was gray and hazy, covered with late afternoon clouds.

An orbit.

Of course. He was so damn dense sometimes.

"What did I say?" Bradshaw asked.

"An orbit," Cross said, turning back to face Bradshaw. "I was so busy looking at the ground, even though I knew the sky factored into it. I was looking for an earthly event, something predictable. And even though I was boning up on astronomy, I never really thought about it. Damn stupid."

"Well, I haven't boned up on astronomy. Tell me what you're thinking. Are we dealing with a comet?"

"Maybe," Cross said.

"But how would that affect the ground? I've seen what meteor and comet strikes look like and this black ring isn't it."

"I know," Cross said. "Maybe something comes through

63

the atmosphere somehow, or we enter into some kind of dust cloud—I don't know. But now I'm sure we are dealing with an orbit here. A damned long one. Two thousand and six years."

"Which means we're dealing with something big," Bradshaw said.

"No," Cross said, shaking his head. "Just something regular. We can't hypothesize on what it is yet. We just know that it happens."

Bradshaw had taken a second muffin and he was picking it apart.

"Here's what we know," Cross said, ticking off on his fingers as he went along, "we know that it appears every two thousand and six years. We know that whatever it is, it comes from the sky. And we know that it leaves areas of the Earth blackened. You double-checked me. There was nothing endogenic about this, right?"

"Right," Bradshaw said.

"So the celestial event didn't cause earthquakes or volcanic eruptions. Whatever caused this layer came from outside, like a fire. But it wasn't a fire."

Bradshaw frowned. "So if it has an orbit, shouldn't we be able to track it? We're not the ancients. We have stuff up there."

"Buoys!" Cross said. He grabbed the paper he had been scanning. There it was, bottom of page two, only a few columns long: SPACE BUOY LOST.

He had only seen the headline, hadn't read the article because he thought it hadn't concerned him. But now he did.

The article said that the International Space Monitoring Buoy Number Six that had been orbiting Uranus since early last year had suddenly quit transmitting. Scientists in the Sydney headquarters of the internationally funded research organization were still working to make contact with the deep-space buoy.

The article went on to quote the costs to the United States and give a quick background of the other buoys still functioning normally. It was the next to the last line of the article that really caught Cross's attention.

"U.S. scientist Craig Stanton, who has been with the ISMA for less than a year, believes that something caused the buoy's sudden malfunction. 'We have evidence of a sudden, massive power drain,' Stanton said. 'I'm not sure we'll ever get that buoy to function again.' "

"What time is it in Australia?" Cross asked.

"It's tomorrow," Constance said. "That's all I know."

"Bradshaw, you worked over there. What time is it?"

"Eighteen hours difference from the West Coast," Bradshaw said. "Which would make it—"

"Fifteen from here, or about eight A.M." Cross picked up the house phone and asked for the international operator. Within minutes, he had the number for the International Space Monitoring Agency in Sydney, Australia. He had the operator ring him through, and when someone answered, he asked for Craig Stanton.

He was put on hold briefly, and then a young voice said, "Yeah."

"Mr. Stanton, my name is Leo Cross. I'm an archaeologist working on a project that, believe it or not, your buoy might have relevance to. I really can't go into the research I'm doing now, but answer me one question."

"If I can," Stanton said, his voice sounding tired and very distant to Cross.

"The buoy, before its power drain, did it record anything unusual?"

"You mean besides the rapid power drain itself?"

65

"Yes."

"Like what?"

"I don't know. A comet, maybe, or an asteroid."

"Nothing that gave us any clear picture," Stanton said. "Look, Dr. Cross. I've been working all night, and I'm late getting off my shift. We're buried in data here, and since the Sydney news nets reported the story, we've also been buried in phone calls from reporters who want to know why we're spending so much money sending malfunctioning equipment into space. So unless there's anything else I can do—"

"What did it report before it went dead?"

"Nothing," Stanton said, with a sigh. "The power just drained."

"Nothing?" Cross repeated.

"Yeah," Stanton said. "All the sensors went black at the same time."

"They went black, or they ceased functioning."

"You're splitting hairs, Doctor." And in that one faintly annoyed sentence from Stanton, Cross realized he was on to something.

"So split them for me," Cross said.

"In the second plus that it took for the power to drain," Stanton said, "the sensors continued to send telemetry as if they were working properly. But all we received, at least from the visual data streams, was a slight flash in inky blackness. I don't know if you know, but—"

"Space isn't an all-consuming blackness. I do know that, Dr. Stanton." Cross's heart was pounding hard. He had finally found it. He didn't know what it was, and he didn't know how he knew he had found it. All he knew was that he had. "Tell me, Dr. Stanton, is such a blackness unusual?"

"Yes."

"And that's all you know."

"Yes," Stanton said.

"What would you say the blackness was?"

"If I could tell you that, Dr. Cross," Stanton said, "I'd get a raise and better hours. Now I'm heading home to bed."

"Thanks for your time," Cross said, but Stanton had already hung up.

"What was that all about?" Bradshaw asked.

Cross caressed the top of the phone, then clenched his hand in a fist. "I think we found it, Edwin."

"Found what?"

"The cause of those soot rings. I think it's near Uranus and heading toward us."

"From an article in a newspaper, a talk with a scientist halfway around the world, and the mention of orbits?"

"Yeah," Cross said, knowing how ridiculous hunches sounded to people who hadn't followed the thought process to get there.

"So what is it?" Bradshaw asked.

"I don't know," Cross said. "But I finally think we have a chance to find out."

September 3, 2017
23:19 Universal Time

222 Days Until Arrival

Just inside the orbit of Uranus, the cold and emptiness of space seemed almost untouched by the distant point of brightness that was the sun. Yet the warmth and life-giving rays of that distant star were having an effect on the tenth planet of the solar system, like an alarm going off after a long night's sleep.

The tenth planet was small, more than twice the size of Earth's moon, only larger than Pluto and Mercury in the brotherhood of planets. Now it hurtled sunward, passing Uranus, sensing the weak light, like a flower turned toward the morning sun. The tenth planet spun slowly, moving to get all sides facing the sun. And as it spun, sensors buried in the thick, hard shell of the planet's surface felt the slight increase in temperature, the barely perceptible increase in energy.

The surface of the planet started to wake up.

As the sun's energy washed faintly over an area, parts of the hard, thick shell moved slowly aside and black, solar panels deployed, covering every meter of the surface. Before the planet reached Saturn's orbit, it would change from a survivor of deep-space cold and blackness to a highly efficient collector of the sun's energy.

Then, inside the tenth planet, the awakening would continue. Again.

September 3, 2017
7:44 P.M. Eastern Daylight Time

222 Days Until Arrival

Doug Mickelson cut himself a slice of roast beef, piled mashed potatoes on his plate, and heaped steamed broccoli in the remaining spot. Then he poured gravy all over it and tried to ignore his inner voice that lectured him about calories and cholesterol and fat.

"Mashed potatoes," he said to Cross as he sat down, "that's a twist. I thought Constance usually roasts them."

"I mashed them," Edwin Bradshaw said. He was a man who seemed to be nearing sixty, with unusually bright eyes and the demeanor of a child who had just been told he had a thousand Christmas presents and didn't want anyone to take them away. "I think gravy is best with mashed potatoes."

"Can't disagree there," Mickelson said, as he shoved a forkful in his mouth. The other two men had finished eating, but he hadn't had a home cooked meal in, what?, four months? He was taking seconds no matter how impatient Cross was getting.

And Cross was impatient. Mickelson had known his old friend long enough to see all the subtle signs. Cross wanted to talk to him when he had come in the door, but Mickelson had reminded him that he had been promised dinner. So they ate, and Bradshaw had taken plates out to the Secret Service guarding the doors, but of course, they weren't allowed to eat on duty.

Cross had remained relatively patient through all of that, but since Mickelson announced his intention to have seconds, Cross had been exhibiting all of his old bad behaviors. He had taken a piece of the blueberry pie that Constance had left for them, put ice cream on it, and then proceeded to stir the entire mess on his plate. The fingers on his right hand tapped against the arm of his chair, and his gaze kept going to the morning's *Post*.

The newspaper, to Mickelson, was the most curious part. There hadn't been much in the *Post*. The paper had covered the official events surrounding the Japanese prime minister's visit, and then there had been that wretched write-up of last night's state dinner. Ralph Ewers, the society columnist, had written a nasty piece on the White House chef and his out-of-date cooking techniques. It was all an attack on the First Lady, who was the first presidential spouse to keep her day job while her husband was in office. The crusty old guard of Washington hated it, and attacked the smallest thing.

"You know, you could tell me up here," Mickelson said after he watched Cross mash the blueberry/ice cream/pie crust mess into a pancake with his fork.

"No, I have to take you downstairs."

Mickelson found himself looking at Bradshaw for confirmation. Bradshaw had an apologetic smile on his face. "It is better that way."

"Well," Mickelson said, deciding his diplomatic skills were in order here, "will Constance kill me if I eat downstairs?"

"Naw," Cross said as he stood up. "She'll just kill me."

He headed toward the basement without waiting for either of them. Bradshaw took Cross's pie plate and put it in the sink. Mickelson took that moment to grab a roll from the plate in front of him, and to put more gravy over his potatoes. Then he took a napkin and followed Bradshaw downstairs.

Carrying a full plate to the Cross basement, after walking through Mrs. Cross's bevy of antiques, made Mickelson feel like a college student again. For one semester, Cross had lived at home—his mother was ill and wanted him nearby— and so Mickelson often studied in the secret room that Cross had discovered behind the pool table.

He chuckled as he walked down the familiar shag-carpeted stairs. The basement smelled faintly of mildew, as it always had, and the pool table looked even more inviting than it used to on study evenings. He glanced longingly at the cues, but no one else noticed.

The door to the hidden room was already open, and for the first time, Mickelson felt a pang. Part of his past was gone. Instead of being full of Game Boys and clothing covering all the unwanted furniture Mrs. Cross had originally hidden in the garage, it had a real table in the center, desks on the side, and several screens already scrolling their way down the walls.

70

"Can you think and eat at the same time?" Cross asked as he kicked a chair toward Mickelson.

Bradshaw looked alarmed at what must have sounded like a rude question, but Mickelson laughed. Bradshaw didn't understand that parts of Mickelson's relationship with Cross were stuck in their nineteen-year-old selves.

"If I couldn't think and eat," Mickelson said, "I would have lost my job in two days."

He took the chair, propped his Gucci loafers on the table-top, and rested the full plate on his stomach. He had come to Cross's house straight from the State Department, after Cross had told him that he had an urgent matter to discuss. At first, Mickelson had thought the matter personal, but then Cross had reminded him of his cryptic comments the last time they had played racquetball.

"I had been planning my first evening at home in several months," Mickelson said.

"What were you going to do?" Cross asked. "Eat something unhealthy, have a glass of wine, and watch the pundits on TV until you fell asleep on the couch?"

Mickelson laughed. Cross knew him too well.

"Here you can have Constance's roast beef, a glass of wine, and listen to me for two hours."

"Can I fall asleep on the couch?"

"Only if you agree to help me with my proposition," Cross said. He sounded partially serious.

Cross had never imposed on their friendship before, had never once asked Mickelson to do anything for him, from helping him obtain funding to getting visas to some of the exotic dig sites Cross had gone to the last few years. Others, who had less of a claim to Mickelson's friendship than Cross, had imposed for years.

Mickelson didn't mind this request, although he had minded

71

the ones from other people. He had been waiting nearly two decades to repay Cross. Cross had gotten him through the required science courses at George Washington, not by helping him cheat but by finding ways to explain the concepts so they made sense.

"Well," Mickelson said, seeing that a holographic image of a rotating Earth had appeared on the center screen. "Is this my television viewing for the evening or will this get a little more risqué?"

"Not risqué," Bradshaw said.

"More like gloom and doom," Cross said. "I really need your help on this one, Doug."

"I have to warn you," Mickelson said. "My scientific knowledge hasn't advanced much since Doc Flo's Physics for Poets class."

"Not that that class helped you much anyway," Cross muttered. "Okay, bear with me, because this will take some explaining."

"I'll listen," Mickelson said. "It'll give me a chance to consume another fifteen hundred calories."

Finally he got Cross to grin. But the grin faded as Cross turned toward the screens, and then punched a few keys on his computer. The other screens sprang to life, showing maps of various regions all over the world. Mickelson felt the first twinge of indigestion. He had a hunch Cross didn't know how close this setup was to some of the meetings Mickelson had had with the president's security advisers.

"Five years ago," Cross said, "while I was visiting an archaeological dig in South America, I noticed a thin, one-eighth-inch-wide layer of a black sootlike sediment that had been dug through. I figured, as the site leader had figured, that it showed a large burn sometime in the past. Normally, that type of layer would indicate a burn, but usually wouldn't leave a layer so thick and uniform."

Mickelson nodded, waiting. Cross was too serious for him to even crack a joke.

Cross went on.

"Two weeks later I was in Germany at another site, and saw a similar layer of soot. A week later, while in California, another layer. All black, all approximately one-eighth-inch thick. To be honest with you, if I hadn't been to three sites in such rapid order, I never would have noticed this. But three layers, on three continents, got my curiosity up."

Mickelson set his empty plate on the table, and then sat up. Something in Cross's tone told him he needed to pay attention.

"I took a sample of the layer in California, then asked for samples of the black layers to be sent from the other two sites. They were all identical."

"That's weird, isn't it?" Mickelson asked, looking at Bradshaw for confirmation. Bradshaw nodded.

"Yes," Cross said, "that's weird. Obviously you remember a few things from those late-night cramming sessions."

"Not much," Mickelson said. "The state of the world was always more interesting." But he had a hunch this covered the state of the world. Those diverse regions, and the various maps before him, had attracted his attention.

"Over the last five years," Cross said, "I've spent more and more of my time and money chasing these 'soot' layers. 'Soot' really isn't an accurate term, but I don't know what else to call them. And I don't have the time to think up a proper name."

"That's the second allusion you've made to a ticking clock," Mickelson said. "I still don't know how anything in archaeology can have urgency today."

"I'm going to get to that," Cross said, "but as I said, bear with me. The more soot layers I found, another pattern started emerging. They were all laid down at the same times."

"I don't follow," Mickelson said, afraid that he actually might be understanding.

Cross moved over to the charts. "These black tinted areas indicate the regions where I think a soot layer was laid down two thousand and six years ago."

Mickelson stared at all the massive area covered by black tinted color. If he had to guess, it was a land area the size of the whole North American continent. "How do you know the exact date?"

"Carbon dating," Cross said, "and collaborating evidence found in many civilizations around the world. A number of cultures were completely wiped off the planet by this event. Their demise was recorded by the civilizations that survived, or by the things that they left—to go into more detail is to explain archaeology to you, Doug, and we don't have all night. What we do have are enough references on all the continents to pin the date within the year."

Mickelson didn't like the look of those maps. "So what caused these soot layers? Fire? Volcanoes?"

"That's what I thought at first," Cross said. "But the historical record never mentioned a fire like that, and the volcanic activity that I knew of never coincided with the timing." He pulled up a chair, turned it around, and as he sat down, rested his arms on its back. "What had me intrigued was one other thing. Most plant, and probably animal, life was destroyed in these areas. Sometimes it took hundreds of years for the area to return to normal. Sometimes the area never returned to normal."

"Fires do that," Mickelson said, having just dealt with a large one that devastated an entire city in Jamaica.

"Fires leave a certain kind of soot layer," Bradshaw said, obviously seeing the frustration that Cross was beginning to show. "Usually that layer is very thin, almost immeasurable. But this one is thick by comparison. In all the sites around the world it's the same thickness. No fire drops two inches of soot uniformly, which is what it would take to compact down into an eighth of an inch."

"All right," Mickelson said. "It's not a fire. Then what the hell is it?"

"I don't know," Cross said. "I honestly don't. But I believe it's something that comes from space. There are a number of references to 'blackness from the sky' in ancient records from the time. I think it's more than likely something in a two-thousand-and-six-year orbit around the sun that causes this damage."

"You mean like a meteor?"

"Orbit," Cross said. "More like a comet. But I doubt this has anything to do with comet or meteor impact. It's far too uniform in its destruction."

Cross moved to the other maps, the ones of specific regions. "Red indicates areas covered in soot four thousand and twelve years ago. Blue are six thousand and eighteen. And so on."

Mickelson felt that very good dinner slowly turn in his stomach. "You're kidding, right?"

Both Cross and Bradshaw shook their heads.

"I'm afraid, Doug," Cross said, "this thing returns every two thousand and six years."

Mickelson felt the muscles in his back tighten. "And the last one was two thousand and six years ago," he said softly, as the realization hit him. "That's the urgency you're talking about."

Cross nodded. "We're due right now, this winter or spring, for a return of whatever is causing this."

"And you have no idea what that something might be?" Mickelson asked again.

"None," Cross said. "Not even a wild guess."

Mickelson bowed his head, then ran his hands through his hair. This was beyond him. Not for the first time in Cross's presence, Mickelson wished science came easier to him, like languages or diplomacy. He also wished that Cross had one other friend in government, someone else to worry about this. Mickelson had enough trouble keeping peace in the Middle East.

He forced himself to look at the maps. Colored areas marked all of them, and the areas were large. He couldn't even comprehend that sort of destruction on such a huge scale. Inches of black soot over the Midwest, the South, Alaska. All plant and animal life killed. His mind wouldn't accept it.

"Now I want you to look at this, Doug," Cross said, as he laid the morning's paper next to Mickelson's plate.

Mickelson looked down, hoping, for the first time since he took his cabinet post, that the *Washington Post* would save him from his thoughts. He knew it was a vain hope.

Cross pointed to an article on a space buoy, one that Mickelson hadn't even noticed in his disgust over the treatment of the state dinner. He scanned the article, not sure why Cross wanted him to see it.

"I'm guessing that whatever is coming might have something to do with the loss of this buoy," Cross said.

"Why?" Mickelson asked.

Cross shrugged and only smiled. "Call it a gut feeling."

"Shit," Mickelson said. He knew about Cross's gut feelings. Cross only admitted to them under extreme duress. The horrible thing was that his gut feelings were never wrong.

Mickelson stared again at the maps. The rotating Earth was starting to irritate him. On it were all the colors moving and flashing in accordance with a little time grid that kept crunching numbers on the side of the screen. Damn Cross. He had built a model of his research, showing how the Earth changed over thousands of years as this phenomenon, whatever it was, laid soot across the land.

Cross was bringing this to him. Cross expected some sort of help. But Mickelson was baffled. What the hell was he supposed to do now?

"Who else knows about this?" Mickelson asked, conscious of the serious consequences a possible leak on destruction of this magnitude could have in the general populace.

"Not many," Cross said. "Edwin and Bonnie, of course. A few others around the world know there is something weird about these soot layers because I asked them to do samples, but as far as I know, I'm the first one to put it all together. It's taken me years."

"Do you have any suggestions as to what we do next?"

"Until I saw that article this morning, I didn't," Cross said. "I just wanted the government starting to get involved in this. But now I think we need to get some deep-space telescopes pointed toward that buoy's last location and see what we can see."

"Telescopes?" Mickelson said.

"Yes," Cross said. "The Hubble and her sisters, if possible."

Mickelson knew enough about the large space telescopes to know that they were international affairs. One didn't just tamper with them on a whim.

But if Cross was right, this whim might save the Earth from a horrible event.

Mickelson could imagine himself trying to talk the rest of the government into this. It wouldn't be pretty.

"I'm going to have to go through channels on this," Mickelson said. "Are you willing to talk to the president's science adviser?"

"I'll talk to anyone if it gets us moving on this."

"Great," Mickelson said. "I'll arrange it in the morning. Be prepared to make this presentation to him. He'll know where to take it from there."

Or so Mickelson hoped. Because if the president's science adviser didn't, Mickelson didn't know who did.

4

September 4, 2017
6:50 P.M. Eastern Daylight Time

221 Days Until Arrival

The president of the United States had several science advisers. They had different labels and concentrated on different projects, all coordinated by the only person with the actual title of science adviser: Yolanda Hayes. Leo Cross learned this in his mid-afternoon phone conversation with Mickelson. And he was glad Mickelson had warned him, or he would have been shocked to see four people sitting in Mickelson's formal office.

Cross had only been in Mickelson's office once, just after Mickelson had been sworn in. Unlike the White House, the State Department was not an open building. In fact, Cross's visit had to be approved through security channels, and Cross had been assigned a handler, who met him at the security checkpoint outside the doors.

The State Department was a long office building built in the middle of the last century. It had no striking characteristics. In fact, the current president had proposed demolishing it and replacing it with a more modern building, but architectural purists, who believed, apparently, that all historic buildings should be saved, even the ugly ones, campaigned to keep the State Department building.

Mickelson had complained about that often, and Cross could see why as he was led down the wide corridors with bland doors off to each side. The air smelled of mildew and outdated recycling. Most of the windows did not open due to security measures instituted before Mickelson got his job, and that caused great aggravation in the handful of beautiful days that the capital had during the spring and fall. Right now, though, Cross was relieved that the air-conditioning, however faulty, was on. He had worked up quite a nervous sweat in his summer suit.

He wished Bradshaw were here. He was getting used to the older man's wry humor and his ability to put anyone at ease. Cross was too prickly and intense for that; he was more concerned with the work. But Bradshaw was on a short trip to check out a newly discovered soot layer in Canada, and then to return home to Oregon to retrieve some things. He would be back in a few days. Cross missed him, and Bradshaw hadn't been too happy about it either. He had said that he wanted to hear all the details when he got back.

Not that there were a lot of details, at least about the location. Mickelson's official office was done in what Mickelson called "U.S. government drab." The carpet was a rich blue, the furniture expensive dark wood. A photograph of the president filled the center of one wall, and the seal of the State Department was displayed on another. Leather-bound books that probably hadn't been opened in fifteen years covered one wall; one of those permanently closed windows, reinforced with steel cross-hatching and an invisible security system, dominated the other.

The computer setup in the middle of the room had clearly been brought in especially for this meeting. Mickelson's computers were in his working office, where he did not hold meetings—except with his senior staff. Several large screens had been set up against the book wall. Cross placed his high density video disk in the drive, and let it run.

The science advisers had already taken their seats in the center of the room, and Mickelson had been talking to them softly when Cross's handler brought him in. Cross had thought the meeting would start at seven; he started to say so when Mickelson gave him a private grin.

"I asked the advisers here early to explain who you were," he said. "Turns out most of them already know."

Unfortunately, Cross had no idea who the advisers were. The introductions didn't really help. Mickelson had told him he would introduce the advisers in order of importance. Yolanda Hayes was a tall lanky woman with dark hair and even darker eyes. Her bright red suit showed off her chocolate-colored skin to advantage, and Cross was surprised to see, when she shook his hand, that her nails were painted red to match. Most government officials he had met through Mickelson didn't take the time on the details of their appearance.

He was then introduced to a slender colonel, obviously air force, whose close-cropped blond hair and perfect posture belied the humor in his pale blue eyes. This was Robert Shane, the head of the President's Special Committee on Space Sciences.

Next to Shane was an officious redheaded man whose name Cross did not catch, who was on the President's Special Committee on Biological Sciences. And next to him was another woman, this one so young that she could have been one of Cross's students. Her name was Amanda something and

81

she was a geologist who headed the President's Special General Sciences Commission.

By the end of the introductions, Cross's head was spinning. He didn't know what each of these committees and commissions did; he wasn't sure he wanted to know. He had asked Mickelson earlier in the day if these science advisers were working scientists instead of politicians, and he was assured that they were. Looking at them, Cross wasn't so sure. Except for the officious redhead, they all seemed more put together than the working scientists he knew.

After the introductions were over, Mickelson turned to Leo's handler, and asked him to wait outside. Then Mickelson closed the door.

"I want to thank you all again for coming," he said. "Let me explain why I brought you here. Leo Cross and I went to school together; we've been friends ever since. When his research turned up something he believed the U.S. government needed to know immediately, he called me because he didn't know whom else to turn to. He has convinced me that we are facing an urgent problem, and now I'd like him to talk with you. When we are through, I will need your help and suggestions as to how to proceed with Leo's rather unusual request." He turned to Cross. "All yours, Leo."

Cross felt like a Ph.D. candidate about to start his orals. He had made presentations before—countless times—but none with stakes like this.

The science advisers were watching him closely, all except for Officious Redhead, who seemed to have dismissed him from the start. Cross knew the type, and knew better than to tailor his presentation to him. Instead, he would talk to the other three, particularly Shane and Hayes, and let them work on Officious Redhead.

Cross punched a few keys and pulled up the maps that had convinced Mickelson. Then he turned to his audience.

It took him almost a full ten minutes to describe his discovery of the soot layers. The scientists listened, but squirmed imperceptibly—the movements of people who had already had a long day and wanted to go home. At one point, Officious Redhead glanced pointedly at his watch. Cross had given enough lectures over the years to know when he was about to lose his audience, and at the moment, he was about to lose this one.

So Cross jumped to the first startling piece of information. "For all practical purposes, the soot layers I found in those first five locations around the world were identical in size and content."

"That's not possible," Officious Redhead said, putting his hands on his thighs as if he were about to stand up.

"Content is possible depending on the event," the geologist, Amanda whatshername, said. "But in size as well, and in those regions—this is highly unusual, Dr. Cross."

"Yes, it is." Cross walked toward the screens. "The black areas indicated on these maps show the area we now believe the soot layers cover. All the areas here test virtually identical and were laid down at the same time two thousand and six years ago."

Now Cross had his audience exactly where he wanted them. All four of the advisers were watching him. Mickelson was too, as if he were reviewing the information for a test.

"You said each layer was an eighth of an inch thick?" Hayes asked.

Cross nodded. "All composed of the same organic remains, varied slightly by region, plus magnetite in all samples."

"At two thousand years," the geologist said, "that would mean an ash level of around two inches when it occurred."

"That's right," Cross said.

"Your tests have to be faulty," Officious Readhead said.

"It's his area of expertise, Andrew," Shane said. He had been following everything closely, but Cross could see the curiosity on his face as to why he was in this group. "It's not yours."

"But it is, Shane," the Officious Redhead, who was apparently named Andrew, snapped. "If we had an ash layer like that in our past, then all the biological material in the area would be dead. And I know of nothing like that."

"Actually," Mickelson said, "there are records of this in some ancient cultures."

Word from the secretary of state apparently silenced them. The difference, Cross assumed, between a high-level cabinet post and powerless advisers.

Thank you, Doug, Cross thought. He decided to move on. He pointed to the other six maps showing soot layers. He quickly explained that the different colors meant different years. When he finished, the science advisers sat silently, staring at the charts.

"You're sure of the two-thousand-and-six-year period?" Hayes asked, staring at the charts.

"Yes," Cross said.

"Was this soot, as you're calling it," Andrew the Officious Redhead asked, sounding somewhat subdued, "laid down over the existing plants?"

"All the evidence I have," Leo said, "is that the soot was caused, in part, by the destruction of the plant and animal life in each area."

The scientists said nothing. They stared at the screens.

"The reason that I called you here," Mickelson said, "is that this matter has some urgency."

84

"It's been two thousand and six years," Shane said. He had gone pale.

"My god," Hayes whispered.

"And I assume I'm here because this is not a terrestrial event," Shane said.

"That's right," Cross said.

"What?" Andrew asked.

"Regularity of that type, plus my presence at this meeting," Shane said, "means that this was caused by something with an orbit. But what you're showing us is not classic meteor debris."

"No, it's not," Cross said. "It's something else entirely, and I'm not sure what that is. But I believe I know where it is at the moment. I need your help to confirm it."

"How would you know that?" Shane asked.

Cross explained the difficulties the buoy had by Uranus, and the image it had projected in the nanoseconds before its power drained. Then he told them about how he wanted to turn the telescopes.

"That's not scientific evidence," Shane said. "Do you realize the enormous political and scientific implications of messing with those telescopes?"

Hayes held out her hand. "We can't authorize this," she said.

"I'm not asking you to authorize," Mickelson said. "I'm asking you to confirm. I need your scientific expertise so that when I ask, I won't be going out on a limb."

Andrew did stand this time. "I'm sorry, sir," he said. "But you're asking me to put my butt in a political sling. I work for the president, not you, and if I might say so, you're overstepping your bounds. You should be working with the head of NASA in the least, and the president at best. Not alone here."

"I want the president out of this loop at the moment," Mickelson said.

"Deniability," Shane muttered.

Hayes nodded.

"If this makes you uncomfortable, Andrew," Hayes said, "you don't need to stay. I, though, would like to examine Dr. Cross's information myself before making a decision."

"So would I," said Shane.

"And me," said the geologist.

Cross stood completely still, watching them all. Andrew looked at them, then at the maps. He shook his head.

"This is going to backfire on all of you," he said. "You're listening to an archaeologist, for god sake. He's not even a real scientist, just one of those pseudos. You can't make a decision like he's asking you to through back doors like this. It's not right. Mr. Secretary, I want nothing to do with this."

"All right," Mickelson said, sounding completely unruffled. Cross stifled a grin. When Mickelson sounded like that, he usually was pissed. "Thank you for your time, Doctor."

Andrew left, closing the door none too gently behind him. Cross was about to say something, anything to get the meeting back on track, when Hayes said, "Sorry about that. Every once in a while, we get someone like him in the science team. Officious little prigs who meet the president a few times, get their official photograph, and let working in the White House go to their heads. They forget all about science, which is the thing that gets them here in the first place."

"It's all right," Mickelson said. Then he grinned. "I'm used to it at State."

"I'd like to see this evidence," Shane said. "Particularly the information from the buoy."

"I don't have that," Cross said. "I got it in a phone conversation. But I can give you the name of my contact."

"Please," Shane said.

"These soot layers have me intrigued," the geologist said. "Can I see one of your samples?"

"Sure," Cross said, and then he spent the next two hours going over his work in minute detail, answering questions, and thinking through the theory. Midway through, Mickelson ordered pizza and beer, all three scientists called home to say they would miss dinner, and Cross felt the beginnings of a headache mixed with a growing exaltation. At the end, he had convinced them that he was right. Then they spent another hour planning how to get the telescopes turned.

Cross was making progress. Why then, he wondered, was he feeling even more nervous than he had before?

September 5, 2017
9:45 A.M. Eastern Daylight Time

220 Days Until Arrival

Brittany Archer set her briefcase down beside her desk, then carefully put her tall double cappuccino on the only empty space among a pile of papers. Her office was cluttered with paper and books. A computer stood on her credenza, its fan humming, its monitor showing the current Hubble downloads as its screen saver. The blinds on her solitary window were open. Johns Hopkins campus was full of new students this time of year. The rhythm of campus life always made her a little uneasy, made her feel something like an interloper on campus. She should have been preparing lesson plans instead of managing an organization.

She peered out the window. Two students were standing in front of a newly planted tree near the corner of the Steven

Muller Building that housed her office, and they were comparing notes. Britt couldn't hear them, but she knew that the discussion between them had to be serious because they were ignoring the way the mid-morning sun fell across the sidewalks and well-maintained grass.

Already she was longing to be outside, but she probably wouldn't be able to spend more than fifteen minutes in the sun. The day promised to be a long one.

The night certainly had been. The proposal review commission, which was supposed to break up at ten, had only reviewed one application by then. So the other commission members voted against her and opted to stay until they had reviewed at least three applications. At 2:30 in the morning, she had driven to her Greenbelt apartment and left an e-mail for her assistant saying she wouldn't be in until ten.

She was a little early, only because the line at JavaJivin wasn't as long at 9:30 as it was at 7:30. She was thankful too, because today she needed the caffeine. The commission would meet again this evening, and probably the next, considering how many proposals they had to go through.

The monthly proposal review was the worst part of her job, a job she generally loved. So many scientists from all over the world wrote to the Space Telescope Science Institute requesting anywhere from ten minutes to three days on any one of three giant telescopes orbiting the Earth. The oldest of the telescopes was Hubble, launched on April 24, 1990. It was supposed to have been decommissioned about a decade ago, but the advisory panel, composed of scientists from all over the world, opted to keep Hubble active until it could be replaced with a better telescope. That new scope had a scheduled launch date of June 15, 2020, and Britt was glad she was not involved in that project. Managing the day-to-day operations at STScI, working with the university and NASA and the international consortium, plus reviewing the proposals kept her busy enough.

She pulled the top off her plastic cappuccino mug and sipped the still hot liquid. Then she sat at her desk and pawed through the messages her assistant had placed on her keyboard. Britt stopped mid-paw. A message from the president's science adviser? A message from the head of NASA?

"Patti?" she called through the open door. "What's with the messages?"

Her assistant looked inside, her close-cropped hair spiked and held in place with green wire. Fashions of the young, Britt had mentally called the style, knowing one day her twenty-one-year-old assistant would look at photos and regret ever wearing her hair that way—just like Britt regretted the fifteen piercings and five tattoos she had gotten at the same age.

"Yeah," Patti said. "It's like Honcho Day or something. Just before you came in you got a call from"—she glanced at the paper in her hand—"a Robert Shane."

From the President's Space Commission. Something was up. "Thanks," Britt said. "What're you working on?"

"Got the download from Goddard and I'm making sure their info connects with ours."

Every morning, Goddard Space Flight Center, which shared some of the responsibilities for the telescopes, e-mailed the next day's operations schedule to see if it coordinated with the master observing plan issued by STScI. GSFC also sent over all data transmissions from the telescopes every twenty-four hours, but they went to the various project managers spread throughout the five-hundred-person team.

"Go ahead with that, then," Britt said. "I'll call you when I need you. And I'll get the phones or let voice mail take it."

"Thanks." Patti disappeared into her office. It wasn't part

of her job to answer phones, although she often did out of courtesy. Britt didn't have the heart to tell her that voice mail and e-mail were a hell of a lot more efficient. She wished she had gotten voice mail from the "honchos" as Patti called them. Then Britt would know what state of mind they were in.

She logged on, and was downloading her e-mail when the phone rang. She answered, only to hear a digitized male voice say, "Please hold for the secretary of state."

Startled, she said, "All right," and waited, her heart pounding harder. First the two science advisers, then the head of NASA, and now the secretary of state. What was going on here?

"Ms. Archer?"

She recognized the voice. She had heard it on CNN enough.

"My name is Doug Mickelson. I am the U.S. secretary of state. How are you today?"

"A bit startled," she said. "How are you?"

He laughed, and she felt a small measure of relief. "I can understand why," he said. "I'm a bit startled myself. I'm spearheading a project that is slightly out of my league. But it came to me courtesy of an old college friend, the archaeologist Leo Cross. Do you know who he is?"

"Vaguely," she said.

"Well, he's discovered something, and presented it to the president's science advisers last night. Later today, you should hear from them, as well as from Jesse Killius at NASA."

"They've already left messages," she said. "I haven't had a chance to return them." Her hands were cold despite their grip on her cappuccino. "Mr. Secretary, what is this project?"

"It's not really a project, Ms. Archer. It's a matter of some urgency. I assume you're familiar with the lost buoy out by Uranus?"

"Yes," she said.

"We would like to convince you to turn a few of your scopes that way, if not all of them."

"All of them?" Britt said. She wondered if she were still in her comfortable queen-sized bed with both cats pressed against her back, having a stress nightmare. "Forgive me, Mr. Secretary, but that's simply not possible. I was up until three A.M. last night reviewing proposals for projects that are two years out, all of them requesting time on the scopes. Maybe one in ten will get that time, even though ninety percent of the requests are deserving. I can't turn the scopes on a whim. Nor can I turn them on the request of the United States government. While we are a NASA agency, we are coordinating the telescopes for an international authority. We are simply one of many here, Mr. Secretary."

"I'm aware of the political problems of this request," the secretary said. "That's why I need you, and the others in charge of your project around the world, to give Dr. Cross ten minutes of your time. There's something you all need to see so you can decide for yourselves the correct course."

"Dr. Cross is an archaeologist," she said. "What would he want with space?"

"Let him make the presentation," the secretary said. "He made a similar one last night to the science advisers, and convinced them of the need to take this path. They'll talk to you a bit about it today, but they'll only confirm what I've told you. It's imperative—not just for the United States, but for the entire world—that we turn those scopes."

She shifted in her chair. "You have me intrigued, Mr. Secretary. But I must warn you, this has to be something extremely important for us to tamper with the schedule of one of the scopes, let alone all of them."

"I realize that," he said, "otherwise I wouldn't be making this call. Can we do this meeting?"

"I will not promise that the result will be what you want."

"I understand," he said. "Just let Dr. Cross make his presentation."

She sighed. The last thing she wanted was to talk to the coordinating committee. But this was a high-level request.

"All right," she said.

"Excellent. Dr. Cross will be driving up there this afternoon to show you his data personally. Then he will return tomorrow for the conference. You *will* be able to organize it by then?"

"Yes," she said, not certain if she could. But if she couldn't, she would tell Cross that afternoon. That, at least, would give her an out.

"Thank you for your time," the secretary of state said. "We'll be in touch."

Britt hung up the phone and sat for a moment staring at it, not really believing it had happened. Then she stood, nearly knocking over her cappuccino. She caught it before it sloshed on the nearest pile of proposals, and went to her door. Patti was sitting at her desk, a split screen displayed before her. The computer was double-checking the next day's schedule.

"Patti," she said, "I need your help."

Patti hit the pause command on her touchscreen, and turned. When she saw Britt's face, she frowned. "What is it?"

"I need you to get in touch with the people at the International Space Monitoring Agency in Sydney. Get me the exact last location of their lost buoy."

"It's the middle of the night there," Patti said.

"I don't care," Britt said. "I need that information, and anything else you can get me about that buoy. Why they think it disappeared. Everything. Now go."

"What about the schedule?"

"I think the schedule will have to wait a few hours," Britt said. "This is more important."

She wasn't going into any meeting blind. And she certainly wasn't going to take the word of an archaeologist if she was going to put her career at risk.

Patti picked up her phone, and Britt went back to her office. She had a lot of people to contact to see if a vid conference the following day was even possible. As she returned to her desk she had, for some reason, a sinking feeling that nothing was ever going to be the same.

September 6, 2017
12:15 P.M. Eastern Time

219 Days Until Arrival

Cross sat in the student union at Johns Hopkins, wondering why the last few days had sent him back emotionally to his Ph.D. orals. Was this the last time he had felt such strain? Or was it the pressure of giving information to people who could ignore it, and the severe consequences that would cause?

He hated this building. Student unions were supposed to be old funky places, filled with wooden tables covered with graffiti carved by bored students using ballpoint pens. Instead, this place was only a year old, and it still smelled new. The tables were a reinforced glass–clear plastic amalgam that didn't allow any defacing. There were skylights all over the place, and warm decorative lamps attached to the walls above the booths. The booths were also clear; the cushions were the only thing solid about them.

There was no privacy in this place, no place to go to just hide and recover, like he used to do as an undergraduate after his poli-sci and history exams.

Somehow, though, Mickelson always found him. Mickelson, who would tease him about his ignorance of current events, and who would then buy him a beer to settle him down.

That was the other problem. They did not serve beer in here. No wine, either. Not that he would have had any, mind you. It was the middle of the day, and he might still be called back for more of his presentation, but he wanted the familiar odor of beer and popcorn to permeate this place. Instead, the ventilation system made even the smell of the long coffee bar behind him disappear.

He had taken one look at that coffee bar, and bought himself a Diet Coke. It was his generation that introduced the coffee culture to the rest of America, but he had never really been a part of it. A rebel his entire life, Mickelson would say, and Mickelson would be right.

Cross bowed his head. For the fifth time he touched his pager, and felt its warmth. It was still on. No one had bothered to page him. What were they talking about? And why were they talking without him?

The afternoon before he had made his presentation to Brittany Archer in her cramped office. She was a tall, dark-haired woman, with intelligent eyes and a no-bullshit manner that he appreciated. She answered her own office door, listened to his presentation, asked several intelligent questions, and then told him to return at 10:00 A.M. the next day to present his findings to the heads of the entire consortium running the three scopes.

Later, Shane had called to see how the meeting went and Cross told him. Shane had whistled. "Sounds like you impressed her," he said. "And our lady Britt Archer doesn't impress easily."

Cross would hate to see how she acted when she was unimpressed.

This morning, she had taken him to a conference room, and he had made the same presentation to half a dozen scientists all over the world. Again she had been cool and reserved, not endorsing him but not criticizing him either.

He was beginning to hate politics even more than he had before—and he thought he had worked in the most political of all places, the sciences. He had never realized that, when you combined science with *real* politics, you got stress like this, not to mention cool players like Britt Archer who didn't let a single emotion show. He wondered if Mickelson was like that in his international dealings, and then doubted it. The few times Cross had seen Mickelson on television, he had seen all of Mickelson's passion laid bare on the screen.

When Cross was done with his presentation, he had left the room with Britt Archer. She had told him to go relax in the union—"We don't have a real waiting area here"; she would page him when the meeting was done. But that was half an hour ago, and Cross had no idea what was taking so long. Either his presentation was convincing or it wasn't. Isolating him from the scientists while they were trying to make a decision was isolating them from the information.

A group of students came in, laughing loudly as one of them did an impression of their new English professor. They took the table next to Cross and he eavesdropped because he had nothing better to do. He wondered what his students said about him. He hadn't taught a class in so long, because of this project, that he doubted students even remembered him.

Then his pager vibrated against his hip. "Thank god," he murmured.

He picked up his pack and tossed out the remains of his Diet Coke, then headed out of the wretched union building at full lope. Archer's office wasn't too far away, but he found himself dodging students on the curving sidewalks and cursing under his breath at how long it was taking him to get there.

Then he opened the door to Muller Building and followed the corridor to Archer's office. Her door was open, and her assistant was gone. Archer was sitting at her desk, her feet on top of it. She was holding a large cup from JavaJivin in one hand—apparently she didn't get her coffee fix at the union—and she was grinning at him.

Grinning.

The expression made her into a completely different woman. Not the cool professional who had been distressing him so much over the last two days, but a gamin-faced charmer whose grin made him want to grin also.

"Did you have lunch at the union, Dr. Cross?" Even her voice had a different texture. It was warmer, more mellifluous than it had been in their first two meetings.

Her question had surprised him. "No, I didn't eat there."

"Wise choice," she said. "There are several excellent restaurants just down the road from us. Would you like to go to one? My treat."

He sat down in one of her chairs, uninvited, he knew, but his legs didn't support him any longer. "They turned me down," he said.

"And lunch is the consolation prize?" She laughed, the sound running up and down the scale like a flute. "Much as I think you'll enjoy my company, I don't think it would make up for the fact that the commission turned you down. Which it didn't. But it was going to."

It took him a moment to parse out that last. "It was going to?"

"Yes," she said. "You don't know how much money your little request was going to cost us, how many projects it was going to interfere with, how much controversy it was going to cause."

"I had a hunch," he said defensively,

"I doubt that," she said, taking a sip from what had to be cold coffee. "But lucky for you I listened to your friend the secretary of state—how does one become old friends with the secretary of state, by the way?"

"He was just a skinny teenager when I met him." Cross couldn't believe this conversation. He couldn't believe this was the same woman he had met the day before. Where was that grim line she had in place of a mouth? Where had this sense of humor come from? And why in god's name did she gush? "So you listened to Doug?"

"And he said that I should meet with you. Which I did. And after hearing your presentation—which is quite good, by the way—and checking your credentials in archaeoastronomy—which aren't even in the same league as your archaeology credentials—I realized we had a twofold problem."

"Yes?" he asked, afraid of the answer.

"One," she said, "you may have found a very real threat to our planet, but you have no idea what caused it, and only, let's face it, a hunch backed up by the flimsiest of evidence that it comes from outer space."

He didn't answer that. He was afraid he might screw something up.

"Two," she said, "we had the more immediate problem of kicking astronomers and physicists with better astronomy credentials than you, and people who had gone through our rigorous proposal procedures, people who have been waiting for *years* to get on these scopes, off the scopes and potentially causing an international—or several international—incidences. I know my colleagues. They really aren't *hunch* sort of people."

Cross was getting confused. Hadn't she said they approved the project? "They aren't?" he asked.

"And neither are you, frankly," she said. "I sifted through your evidence last night and listened to your presentation again this morning. You've done a lot of research to get to this hunch stage."

"Thanks," he said. "I think."

Her eyes twinkled. "So, last night, I developed a backup plan."

"A backup plan?" he repeated.

"Yes," she said. "I knew the consortium would turn you down—and they did. They didn't want a single scientist to lose his scope time."

"I thought you said they agreed."

"To my backup plan," she said and took another sip of her coffee. She watched him over the rim of her cup. She reminded him of a cat playing with a mouse. She was enjoying this.

And if he had to be honest, if he weren't so damn nervous, he would be enjoying it too. Was she flirting with him? God, he was in college student mode wasn't he?

"What is your backup plan?" he asked.

"I thought you'd never ask." She took her feet off the desk and sat up, turning, before his eyes, back into the formal woman he had met the day before. "Did you know that even though the telescopes operate around the clock, not all of their time is spent observing?"

"No," he said.

"Some of the time is reserved for housekeeping functions such as receiving command loads or calibrating the equipment. I proposed that we take housekeeping time to honor your request."

"If I had known about it, I would have suggested that," he said. "It's brilliant."

Her smile was small, the patronizing one she had used the day before. He preferred the grin. "Actually, you probably wouldn't have, because this didn't resolve one of our major problems: turning the scope to find new targets. That's one of the housekeeping tasks. It's not easy moving these large scopes."

"All right," he said. "What did you do?"

"I checked what was going on with the scopes and gave you a scope order. You'll get all three scopes, just not at once. Lucky for you, Hubble is pointed close enough to your spot that, with some minor calibrations, we'll be able to get what you want. That will start later tonight. Tomorrow, after the current project finishes on Clarke, we'll turn it for a series of scans in the area of the lost buoy. Then, tomorrow night, we'll turn Brahe that way."

"You proposed this to them, and they accepted it?"

"Not at first," she said. "I let them argue the merits of your case. I figured it would be best to let them make their own decisions. They were unnerved by your presentation, but all agreed you would have to go through the proposal stage, just like everyone else. They vowed, though, that if you got your proposal done, say, within the week, it would be reviewed promptly and your time would be scheduled priority, before the end of the year."

He felt a flush rise in his cheeks. "Didn't they understand the urgency of this? I explained that this could be back at any point, that it's probably on its way—"

"But you don't even know what it is, Dr. Cross, and you don't know how something from outer space can cause those soot layers on Earth. These are people who like certainty." Then she leaned back and grinned. "So I took their fannies off the line, told them we could use housekeeping time, and showed them how, and they approved it in an instant."

"Couldn't you simply have approved the housekeeping time on your own?"

She shook her head. "Those housekeeping tasks are important. Hubble has broken down twice since her launch, and you remember the controversy when Brahe went up, don't you?"

He didn't, but he wasn't about to admit it.

"A year or so ago, someone suggested cutting back on housekeeping time, but no one else would hear of it. That's very important equipment out there, Dr. Cross. You're lucky that we found a solution for you at all."

He took a deep breath. He was lucky. He knew it. That was why he had that Ph.D. feeling all along. He was afraid he'd flunk these orals, and the entire world would suffer. At least now they had a chance.

"I should be the one buying you lunch," he said.

Her grin widened. "Yes, you should," she said. "But be warned. I'll take you to the most expensive place I can think of."

"For lunch, how expensive can it be?"

"I don't know," she said. "Now you've presented me with a challenge." She got up from her desk, left her coffee behind, and walked toward him. He stood. She extended her arm, and he took it, as if they were going to dance a cotillion. They walked toward the door, but they didn't fit through it, and they burst into laughter.

It was the first lighthearted moment he'd had in days, and

100

he enjoyed it, because he was afraid he wouldn't have many other lighthearted moments until he resolved this ancient, urgent puzzle.

5

September 8, 2017
3:12 A.M. Eastern Daylight Time

217 Days Until Arrival

Bradshaw was dreaming.

Soot was falling from the sky in big lazy flakes, like the snowfalls of his childhood. Only this was landing on everyone he knew—his students, his ex-wife, his accountant—and they were trying to catch the sootflakes on their tongues. The moment they did, they would start choking.

He tried to explain to them, he really did, that this wouldn't do, that they had to stop. He tried to get help. He even tried to get the president to make an address about the problem, but it wasn't stopping. And the sootflakes kept falling, faster now, and then even faster, and even faster than that. Finally they were going so fast that they were buzzing and calling his name.

In Cross's voice.

Bradshaw sputtered awake. He had been drooling on his pillow—a sign that he had been so sound asleep that almost nothing could have awakened him. Only the buzzer sounded again, and it came from the intercom beside the bed.

"Edwin!" Cross said, and he sounded irritated. "Wake up!"

Bradshaw fumbled with the buttons and finally found the correct one in the darkness. "What?" he asked, or thought he asked. The word actually came out as "Whaa?"

"I need you in the map room."

Bradshaw squinted at the digital clock on the nightstand. "Now?"

"In five minutes. I'll have coffee."

"And bagels?" Bradshaw asked.

"I'm not a miracle worker," Cross said, and the light on the intercom blinked out.

Bradshaw rubbed his eyes. That dream wasn't letting him go. It had been terrifying. This whole thing was terrifying, and it had gotten worse since his trip. The soot layer in Canada was exactly what they were looking for, and it was in the six-thousand-year level. Then he had flown home and gone into his garage. There, underneath the boxes of old clothes and his mother's things taken from her house when she died, were his research notes from his disgrace all those years ago. He hadn't had the heart to toss any of it, although the disks were corrupted. He had only hardcopy now.

He packed that into an old carry-on and brought it back to D.C. with him, just as Cross had asked. Bradshaw had tried not to look at the information, but even seeing the yellowed paper was hard. He remembered when it meant so much.

He wiped his hand over his face. No sense in being maudlin. Since he'd been back, Cross hadn't even asked for the documents. Bradshaw had placed them in his closet and had gone on, listening to the report of Cross's adventures while he was gone.

And now this.

He staggered into the bathroom, washed up, and then got

dressed. He still wasn't too wide awake, but he was awake enough to make it down the stairs, through the minefield of antiques, and into the kitchen to grab one of yesterday's blueberry muffins before going downstairs.

All of the lights in the basement were on. Bradshaw hurried down the green shag stairs, and as he walked beside the pool table, he said, "Don't you know an old man needs his rest?"

"Rest later, Edwin," Cross said from inside the map room. He sounded just like Bradshaw speaking to his students at a dig site.

Bradshaw stepped inside the room and stopped. A woman's image was on the main display screen. She wore a pair of jeans and a crumpled top that looked as if it had been slept in. Her dark hair was pulled back in a makeshift ponytail. Behind her were small maps and star fields. In her left hand, she clutched a cup of coffee like a lifeline. She was clearly in real time because when Bradshaw entered the room, she smiled at him. He was immediately charmed. Whoever she was, she got his vote.

"Edwin," Cross said, "this is Dr. Britt Archer. I told you about her."

"You didn't tell me about that smile," he said under his breath as he passed Cross and headed for a chair. Louder, he said, "It's a pleasure, Dr. Archer."

"All mine, Dr. Bradshaw," she said.

"Okay, Britt," Cross said. "We're ready." Even though he didn't look ready. She had clearly awakened him too. The hair on the back of Cross's head stood up like the beginnings of a mohawk. He hadn't shaved and he wore a pair of sweats with a flannel shirt that had seen better days. His feet were bare, and probably cold, given the temperature of the room.

Archer frowned. "Is Dr. Bradshaw familiar with—"

"Dr. Bradshaw has been brought up to date," Cross said. "Tell us what you found."

Archer nodded. "Over the past three days first Hubble then Clarke, in maintenance time, have been taking pictures of images in the area of the sky where Uranus is, using the Planetary Camera field."

A clear picture of a star field replaced her face on the screen. Her voice went on over the picture. "Here is one of the first day's pictures of one small area. The scope took hundreds of shots just like this one of different areas of the system around Uranus."

Bradshaw was amazed. There must have been ten thousand stars on that picture, so much so that parts of it looked almost hazy. And there were hundreds of other pictures, and this was only a small section of the sky. Archaeology suddenly looked simple compared to astronomy.

The screen flickered for a moment, then she said, "Now let me show you the second day's picture of the same exact area."

Bradshaw clearly couldn't tell if there was a difference, if there actually was a difference. He assumed he was looking for something to compare.

The picture flickered again, then Archer said, "And here's tonight's picture. I'm going to overlap the picture from two nights ago with tonight's."

Again the screen flickered. The two overlapping pictures looking like the same picture to him. Thousands of dots of light against a dark background.

"How big is this?" he asked.

"The photo?" she asked, "or the section of space?"

"Anything," he said.

"We took the photo at pinhead size if looked at from the ground."

Bradshaw sat down. Maybe he was dreaming. Space was so vast that it was almost incomprehensible to him.

"You're going to have to point out to me whatever you want me to see," Cross said.

Bradshaw agreed, glad that Cross had spoken first.

On the picture a white mark appeared as Archer drew a tiny circle, smaller than a dime, in one corner of the picture. Bradshaw's traitorous brain thought of the play-by-play lines that football commentators used to make on television screens.

"See the small star inside the right side of the circle I just marked?" she asked.

"Yes," Cross said.

"I'm pulling out the photo from two days ago. Watch what happens."

A flicker on the screen and the star vanished right out of the circle.

"Got it," Cross said.

"What?" Bradshaw asked. "What caused that?"

No one answered him. The screen flickered and the star returned as she put the original picture back into place. Archer erased the circle she had drawn and drew another one around another star close by the first. "Now watch the small star inside this circle as I remove tonight's photo."

"Okay," Cross said.

The screen flickered and the star vanished. But the first star remained. "Clearly I'm an archaeologist," Bradshaw said. "I don't get this."

"It's not as complicated as you're making it, Dr. Bradshaw," Archer said. "If you saw this in your line of vision on Earth, you would know exactly what happened."

"Something blocked the star?" He blinked at Cross who was nodding.

"But this thing is moving. It eclipsed a second star too."

106

"That's right," Archer said.

"Have you checked all known asteroids and satellites?" Cross asked.

"We did that first," Archer said. "This is something near Uranus's orbit, never tracked before."

"What about the size?" Cross asked. "It must be huge."

"Yeah," Archer said.

Her word hung for a moment.

Bradshaw looked at Cross. The man seemed even more intense than usual, if that were possible. This was what they were looking for. They all knew it, but instead of being excited about it, Bradshaw felt a shiver run through him.

"What is it?" he asked again.

"I can't answer that exactly," Archer said. "But here's what I can tell you. Our first guess is that we are dealing with something about twice the size of our own moon."

"That's huge," Cross said, whistling.

"There's more," Archer said.

Bradshaw wasn't sure if he wanted more at the moment. He was having a hard time grasping that something twice the size of Earth's moon was suddenly discovered out there, right where Cross thought something might be.

"I can tell you it's moving inward, toward the inner planets and the sun," Archer said.

"How fast is it coming?" Cross asked.

Archer's face replaced the picture of the stars on the screen. She looked tired and not at all overjoyed by this news. Bradshaw wondered if she would have rather had Cross's hunch be nothing at all.

"We don't know exactly how fast it's coming," she said. "We should have the rough calculations tomorrow."

"Guess," Cross said.

She shrugged. "Guessing, it should be inside Mars by next spring some time."

Now Bradshaw's mind was really swimming. But Archer went on.

"We ran some preliminary spectrograph shots on it. We can't seem to get much of a fix on rotation or chemical makeup. It's as if all light is just getting sucked down into this thing."

"Is it a black hole?" Cross asked.

"No," Archer said. "That much we're sure of. It seems to have normal mass, at least not enough to affect anything else out there. It just has no real light reflection that we can find yet. But realize, this is still early. We just spotted this thing two hours ago. We'll turn Hubble's NICMOS on it tomorrow and that might get us more data from the infrared."

"NICMOS?" Bradshaw asked, feeling so far out of his league that they could be talking ancient Arabic. Actually, if they were talking ancient Arabic, he would have a better chance at understanding them.

Although he was really afraid he understood enough already.

"It's the acronym for the Near Infrared Camera and Multi-Object Spectrometer," she said. "Among other things, it can detect light with wavelengths longer than the human eye limit."

"And that will tell us what?"

"If we knew that, Doctor," she said, "we wouldn't need it. There is just so much out there that we don't understand yet. And, thanks to Dr. Cross, we found one more thing. Only I think this one is very important."

"You think this one is our baby?" Cross asked.

"Don't you?" she asked.

"Yeah," he said.

There was a pause, and then she said, "But it could be something else. We just don't know at the moment."

108

Only her qualification came several beats too late to give any of them comfort.

Bradshaw stared at the screen. Somehow he hadn't thought Cross's hunch would come to anything. Up until this point, the entire thing had been an archaeological mystery that could come into the present, not something that actually tied to the cosmos, like Cross had thought it would.

"Can you keep a lid on this?" Cross asked Archer.

She nodded. "For now only four of us here and two monitors at Goddard know, and until we gather a bunch more data, nothing is coming out of either place."

"Good," Cross said.

"How long until we know exactly what this thing is?" Bradshaw asked.

"We hope to know size, makeup, and path of the orbit in a week," Archer said. "It might take longer, though, given those seeming light-absorbing properties of this body."

"A week," Cross said. "That seems like such a long period of time now that we know this thing is real."

"We don't know that this body is what's causing your soot layers, Leo," Archer said gently, and her tone made Bradshaw wonder if they had more fun at that lunch than Cross wanted to admit. "We just have confirmation that something is out there, like you suspected."

"I know," he said.

"Don't get ahead of yourself. Get some sleep, keep researching those soot layers. We'll do what we can here."

Cross nodded.

"Sorry to wake you in the middle of the night."

"No problem," Cross said. "I would have rather known."

"Good," she said, and signed off. The screen before them went blank.

"I would have rather waited until morning," Bradshaw said, picking up his uneaten blueberry muffin.

"It's not my imagination, Edwin," Cross said, and he sounded a little relieved. "There's something out there, just like I knew there would be."

"If that's supposed to reassure me, Leo," Bradshaw said, "it's not working."

"It's reassuring me," Cross said. "Knowledge is always the first step toward a solution."

"Let's just hope it's one we can live with," Bradshaw said.

September 12, 2017
10:40 A.M. Eastern Time

213 Days Until Arrival

Cross staggered to the corner of the racquetball court and grabbed his towel. He wiped the sweat off his face and neck, then picked up the bottle of water he had left there and drank until the bottle was nearly empty.

It had been years since he played racquetball this badly. Every time that little black ball zoomed toward him, he thought about its trajectory and rotation, and the fact that it looked like a sphere from outer space, a sphere that did not reflect light.

"Okay," Mickelson said as he leaned his racket against the wall. "I can't think that you had a sudden change of heart and decided to help my ego by losing this badly, and we're not playing for money, so I know that you didn't suddenly want to make me rich. All I can assume is that you're so preoccupied that your brain is on Mars instead of in this court with me."

"Closer to Uranus," Cross said.

Mickelson raised his eyebrows. "If I didn't know you better, pal, I'd take that as an affront."

Cross laughed. He hadn't realized how that sounded. "I meant my brain. It's closer to . . . oh, never mind."

"I thought something was happening," Mickelson said. "You haven't kept me informed, Leo."

"You had to make a sudden trip to Beijing."

"I got back yesterday," Mickelson said.

"I figured it could wait until today." Cross braced himself against the wall and finished the bottle.

"You gonna tell me, or do I have to pry it out of you?"

Cross smiled and hung the towel over his shoulder. He was short of breath and his heart was pounding hard. These irregular racquetball matches were the only exercise he got. He would have to change that, and soon. As soon as his time became his own again. If it ever would.

"Those scopes found something, didn't they?" Mickelson asked.

Cross nodded. "It's preliminary, but something about twice the size of Earth's moon just passed inside the orbit of Uranus and is heading inward."

"Something?" Mickelson asked. "What is 'something'?"

Cross held up his hand to silence Mickelson. He was going to tell this his way or not at all. "It's going to come in, swing around the sun just outside of Mercury's orbit and head back out. It will miss us and all the other planets, both coming in and going out, by a wide margin."

"Like a comet?" Mickelson asked.

Cross looked at Mickelson with surprise. The man was smarter about science than he let on. "This is similar," Cross said. "But you have to realize that what we're looking at is bigger than most moons and two of our planets. It has a

111

regular orbit, so it wouldn't surprise me if it will be called the tenth planet."

"A tenth . . . planet?" Mickelson struggled with the word. "As in another Earth?"

"I doubt it," Cross said. "It's too far out to support life."

"But another planet?"

"Finding a planet isn't as unusual as it sounds," Cross said. "Pluto was confirmed in the 1930s. No one knew much about Neptune until the 1980s. That's not what's unique about this thing."

Cross closed his eyes for a moment. He had promised not to say anything. But the conversation with Archer that morning had rocked him even more than finding the planet had. He had to tell Mickelson. Mickelson understood. And besides, Cross would just feel better if his friend understood.

"All right," Mickelson said. "Enlighten me."

"It's the orbit." Cross watched Mickelson out of the corner of his eye.

Mickelson's expression froze.

"Remember the soot layers?"

"Of course," he said, looking annoyed at the question.

Cross raised his eyebrows, as if that explained all. It had to him. But Mickelson didn't have a scientific brain.

"All right," Mickelson said. "I'm missing the point. How could a planet have anything to do with soot layers here, especially if it's not coming close to us?"

"I don't know," Cross said. "I wish I did."

"But . . ." Mickelson said, waiting.

Cross looked up at his good friend. "They worked out a preliminary estimate of the new planet's orbit length." Cross took a deep breath, letting the sweat drip off his forehead.

"No," Mickelson said, his eyes wide in disbelief.

"Yes," Cross said sadly. "This thing comes in close to the

112

Earth every two thousand and six years. Just like it is this year. There's no doubt in my mind that whatever caused those areas of destruction in our planet's past came from, or with, this tenth planet."

September 13, 2017
13:17 Universal Time

212 Days Until Arrival

In the absolute blackness and cold of the chamber of The First, a change started, slowly. No light penetrated the thick walls, but with a faint click the temperature started to rise. It was only a fraction of a degree, but it was the first move in two thousand years. Using the faint energy gathered from the distant sun, funneling the energy into this one small space no larger than the size of a human coffin, the temperature again moved upward another fraction of a degree.

A dark figure, shrouded in black, dull material, lay frozen inside the chamber. For two thousand years the one known as The First waited, not realizing the time had passed. For twenty-six passes of the sun he had had the honor of being The First, the one to be awoken from the sleep of the cold before even The Leaders of the Segments.

His job was to awaken before all others, and then watch over the awakening of the rest of his people. It was a great honor, and a great task, one that he had fulfilled without flaw for twenty-five passes.

The temperature clicked upward slightly in the small space above The First's body. The awakening would be slow, only accelerating during the last few hours of the sleep of the cold, as the precious stored energy flooded into his body, filling him again with life. The process would take twenty-four Earth days. When compared to the sleep of two thousand years, a twenty-four-day awakening seemed quicker than a single inhaled breath. Quicker, but just as important to survival.

Section Two

FIRST CONTACT

6

March 8, 2018
4:10 P.M. Eastern Standard Time

36 Days Until Arrival

Dr. Leo Cross set a Starbucks cup filled with mocha for him and a larger cup filled with cappuccino for Britt Archer on the fake wood conference table. He didn't even bother with coasters. Nothing would destroy that surface. If it had survived from the eighties unmarred, it would survive another thirty years in the same way.

He was the first to arrive. Britt was outside, conferring with Hayes, the president's science adviser, and Jesse Killius, the head of NASA. Robert Shane, from the president's space sciences committee, had left the conversation when Cross had, although for a different reason.

Shane believed the planned mission to the tenth planet was ill-advised. He believed that human lives should not be put at risk this early in the proceedings, and he was quite passionate in that belief. The mission project was an international one, and Killius had gone with the consensus opinion: that robotic probes would make the first pass, and humans would proceed from there. The discussion had continued this morning, even though the decision was made, and as Shane left it, ostensibly to go to the men's room, he had muttered as he passed Cross: "Human missions in space have always been p.r. tools, and in this case, there's no p.r. to be had."

The comment was still going around in Cross's brain as he entered the conference room. Screens were down on all sides, covering the windows, waiting for the video uplinks all over the world. The entire international consortium was meeting this morning to discuss that very issue: whether or not the tenth planet's presence should be made known to the general public.

Cross sank into his chair. It too was from the eighties, made of solid metal and upholstery that needed to be replaced. The government had modern equipment in these secret conference rooms—of which he had been in several in the last six months—but they never seemed to see the need to update the furniture.

This conference was being held in one of the several unmarked government buildings near the Capitol. Cross had a hell of a time finding it the first time—the building had a designation known to government employees, and that was it. Fortunately, his instructions had been good, and the building he had wandered into (a bit confused) was the one he wanted. He knew that when a handler met him at the security checkpoint and called him by name.

He was getting used to these strange meetings. They had to be held in buildings like this because it was important that the video calls were scrambled, and since they were bouncing off satellites, that required some special equipment. Even now he felt odd about discussing such sensitive matters on airwaves, but none of the news had broken in the six months these meetings had been held, so he was reassured that the links were somewhat private.

Voices rose and fell as the discussion continued in the hallway. Cross took the lid off his mocha and took a sip. Britt had gotten him started on this habit about the time he had stopped thinking of her as Dr. Archer. She was a lot of fun to be with, and if they weren't working together, he would consider asking her out. Then he smiled. As if they had time for that. During the last six months, they'd barely had time to catch a meal, let alone spend some time alone.

On a day-to-day level, it felt as if things were changing rapidly on the Tenth Planet Project, which was what the group was unofficially calling itself. When Cross actually examined their accomplishments, it felt as if they hadn't made any forward movement at all.

What they had learned in all this time was that they didn't know much. Only now they had confirmation of the things they didn't know.

The research into what the tenth planet was had turned out to be the most frustrating. It seemed the thing just didn't reflect light, at any point of the spectrum. Nothing seemed to come off of it. No heat, no light, no energy. And since it was still just outside the orbit of Mars, there was no way to tell what the planet was even made of. The only way to get more information, it seemed, was to go there. And doing that wasn't going to be as easy as it sounded, considering the speed of the planet as it was coming in toward the sun.

That was the center of the discussion outside the room, even though what they would do for a first attempt was already settled, and not to everyone's satisfaction.

Robert Shane came into the room and sat in his usual chair. He templed his fingers and sighed. "I hate being in the minority," he said. "Especially when I'm right."

Cross made a sympathetic noise but didn't say anything. He didn't dare. This part of the work was outside of his expertise.

119

"We need to send out probes, do equipment work. This argument that we don't have enough time is bullshit."

Cross started. That was the first time he'd heard Shane swear.

Then Shane smiled sheepishly and rubbed the bridge of his nose with his thumb and forefinger like a man who was used to wearing glasses. "Sorry," he said. "I shouldn't bitch to you. Your group is the only one making any progress on this thing."

"If you can call that progress," Cross said.

"I do," Shane said. He got up and went to the back table where someone had put out beverages. "Want anything?"

Cross held up his mocha and shook his head. Shane turned his back and went through what looked like an elaborate tea ritual. Cross suppressed a sigh of his own.

After they had discovered the tenth planet—six months ago to this very day—they had formed this advisory group. It had a large contingent of Americans, who represented various groups and interests, including Clarissa Maddox, a member of the Joint Chiefs of Staff who everyone knew spoke for the president. There were also several international members, representing various governments, the head of the Japanese Space Agency, the European Space Agency, and several smaller space powers. The work was top secret, and Cross had had a bad moment when it looked as if his upper-level security clearance wouldn't go through. But it had, and he was here. Not that he always wanted to be.

But without the panel, he wouldn't have had as much success as he had in the archaeological part of this work. Through Hayes and Shane, he was able to get more than enough government funding to try to figure out what had happened during the last pass of the tenth planet.

They'd found out parts of it. Over these six months, they

120

had managed to map even more exactly the destruction areas coinciding with the tenth planet's last three passes near Earth. A large part of Eastern Asia had been destroyed, along with an eight-hundred-mile-wide circle in South America, a six-state area of the central United States, two large areas in Africa, and a small area in Australia. There were no patterns to the destruction areas, and the only records of the events from nearby civilizations were a variation on that phrase he was beginning to hate: "A black death from the sky."

If that black death from the sky came back to those exact areas now, hundreds of millions of humans would die. Cross didn't want to even think about that possibility.

What he hadn't been able to learn, and what frustrated him more than he could say, even to Bradshaw, was what had caused the destruction. In that area, even with twenty people doing research into a dozen ancient civilizations' records, Cross hadn't learned much more than he had before. He just had more confirmation. He had only become more certain that some form of destruction came with the tenth planet. He, and all the others, just didn't have a clue as to how the tenth planet could have caused that destruction.

Cross took another sip of his mocha. He was about to get up and bring Britt hers when she came into the room and flounced into her chair.

"Now they're arguing about whether or not to name the planet before we make the announcement," she said. "I suggested Proserpine, in keeping with mythological names . . ."

"Nice," Cross said. Proserpine was the name of the minor goddess who ruled the underworld as the wife of Pluto. She spent half her time in Hades or darkness, and the other half in the real world or light. It sort of fit the tenth planet. "But I think her Greek name, Persephone, would be better."

"Most of the planets use the Roman names—"

"Except Pluto."

"*Dis* is a dumb name for a planet," she said, referring to the Roman word. He had to agree.

"Is that what they're arguing about? The name?"

"No, whether or not the name is the right thing to do at this point. Hayes is worried about causing an international incident. You know, the Japanese may want to name her. I said, let them. The language is different enough anyway, at which point they all jumped on me—"

"Saying you'd better not say that in the meeting." Shane sat down with a small grin on his face. "I heard that chorus. Pity they don't think you politic enough to understand that."

She smiled at him, the wide grin Cross so enjoyed. "I'm just trying to make this meeting interesting. We're going to rubber-stamp the announcement. We basically agreed to it before we got here."

"But we need the approval so that someone doesn't complain," Hayes said as she came in the door. Maddox of the Joint Chiefs was right behind her. Maddox was a solidly built, athletic woman who had posture so straight that Cross believed he could put a level on her back and it would read perfect.

"At this stage," Maddox said as she took her seat at the head of the table, "a rubber stamp is fine with me. I'm more concerned with the upcoming mission."

"Aren't we all?" Shane muttered.

"Well, I have a concern," Cross said, partly because he wanted to forestall a repetition of this conversation, and partly because he'd been meaning to bring this up for some time.

"Does it need to be aired to the whole team or can you tell us now, Dr. Cross?" Maddox asked.

Killius came in, started for the beverage table, and then, realizing that something was happening without her, wandered to the table.

"I'd rather tell you now. Then we can present a united front," Cross said.

Britt looked at her watch. "We have three minutes."

"Is that enough time, Dr. Cross?" Maddox asked. She usually ran these meetings. She had a crisp no-nonsense attitude that worked well with the structure.

"Yes," he said. "All I was going to ask was that if—when—the announcement is made, we keep my name out of it."

"And why is that, Dr. Cross? We wouldn't have found the planet without you."

"In the beginning, I asked a lot of archaeologists to report those soot layers. It won't take much for them to put that orbit, my request, and those layers together into something, and then we won't be able to control the information at all."

There was silence around the conference table as everyone thought of the implications of that. Finally Maddox nodded. "I see no problem with that. Does anyone else?"

No one said anything.

"Do we need a vote?"

"Perhaps in the rubber-stamped meeting," Killius said.

"Good idea," Maddox said. She glanced at her own watch. "I expect this to take no more than fifteen minutes of our time. Let's hope I'm right."

Cross certainly did. He hadn't had more than four hours of sleep a night in the past two months. He had too much work to do, and that was compounded by meetings like this, meetings that simply confirmed and okayed what everyone already knew.

"Want me to set a timer?" he asked.

"I already have," Maddox said with a bit of a grin. "My goal is to be out of here before Dr. Archer's cappuccino cools enough for her to drink it."

123

"Hey," Britt said. "It doesn't take me that long to drink it."

"Nope," Shane said. "Only to start."

And the entire group chuckled at the look of mock anger on Britt's face as the screens flared into life around them. The international members of the committee all looked a bit perplexed at the levity, but Maddox ignored their confusion and began the meeting with her usual authority.

And the screens went dark fourteen minutes and forty-nine seconds later, objective accomplished. The tenth planet would be announced to the general public as an astronomical curiosity, nothing more, on the next day's news.

Dr. Leo Cross's name would not be mentioned.

March 9, 2018
20:39 Universal Time

35 Days Until Arrival

The First finished his report to Commander of the South Segment, as was his duty.

No energy, no sound flowed around The First as he stood, the dozen tentacles on each side of his slender torso clasped in a large respectful bundle in front of his thickest warming robe. The dozen movement tentacles beneath him formed a single point on the metal floor, making his stance hard to maintain. It was precisely that hardness, that difficulty, which made the stance an honor to the Commander.

The Commander was watching him carefully. The First saw the Commander's caution dimly, through all ten of his eyestalks. The First held them in an uncomfortable position as well. They formed a circle around his long face, and he had to keep them motionless.

The First hated giving this report to the Commander. He had done so many, many times, and each time he had felt a greater fear. One time the Commander would not approve.

They were alone in the Commander's early meeting room. It was located in the sleep bunker beneath the surface of the southern area of Malmur. The sleep bunker's power sources were in a direct line along the surface and had kicked into action on schedule, as they had done countless times before.

Sometimes The First wondered if he should be thankful for that. Survival above all else. But survival, for him, meant these early meetings with the Commander, and these early meetings never had good news.

The Commander opened his upper tentacles, letting them spread out under his black robes as a sign that The First could stand at ease. The First did so, relaxing only two movement tentacles under him for better balance, and two topmost side tentacles for gestures. He kept all ten of his eyestalks pointed directly at the Commander. To do otherwise would mean instant death.

Silence filled the room.

Clearly the Commander of the South was thinking of the report he had just heard. The First was. He had been terrified of this report, more terrified than he had ever been in the past. This report had not been standard—if there was such a thing as a standard Awakening report. Usually there were problems, but not this many. And not with this kind of range.

The First remembered how he felt as he put the information together, the gradual wilting of his tentacles as he realized how much had happened during their latest long sleep. Two of the planet's six thousand power-storage units had been destroyed in an asteroid collision near the outermost point of the orbit. Five thousand of the planet's residents

125

would not be awakened this orbit so that repairs to the power units could be made quickly and power saved, before the peak storage times. The Commander of the South Segment would be forced to talk to the Commanders of the North and Center to divide the loss of so many workers. Any communication between the three Commanders was always a troublesome occurrence.

Two of the North's harvest ships were also damaged in another small collision, and were being repaired quickly.

The West had lost a hundred and six Malmuria in cold sleep failures. The North had lost seventy-two, and the South sixty. The total was only slightly under the projected birth rate for this orbit, so the population would remain balanced. That, as always, was good news.

The most disturbing news was of the third planet. During the time of the last sleep, the two-legged sentient creatures of the third planet had formed another civilization. It was the third time the creatures had spread out over their planet since Malmuria had found this sun as a new home. During the last Sun Pass such expansion had been forecasted for this Pass, but not thought to be a threat. In the time between arrivals in the past, the creatures had changed habits and building patterns before, but never to this extent.

Sometime since the last Pass, the creatures had discovered technology. They were no longer primitives. Their population had expanded, and they had made small excursions into space. They were becoming civilized.

The First knew that was very disturbing news to the Commander of the South. The news would also force him to communicate with his enemies, the Commanders of the North and Center.

"You have done well, First," the Commander said, gesturing his approval with movements of his top two side

126

tentacles. "Do you have a recommendation about the creatures who cover the third planet?"

The First was startled. Only twice in all the orbits had the Commander asked for his opinion. After the first time he had made sure he was always prepared, but the question still surprised him.

"Ignore their presence, Commander," First said. "Prepare the ships to be energy shielded when near them, a vast waste of power, but necessary. Otherwise ignore them."

The Commander did not respond, so The First went on. "It is all we can do. If they do not know we come, they cannot prepare to act against us. We will do our best to ignore their population centers, but we must accept some destruction of their society."

The ten eyes of the Commander seemed to look right through The First, yet he stood his position, looking directly back. After a short time the Commander waved two tentacles. "Sound advice," he said. "It agrees with my opinion."

"I am honored," The First said.

"You have done your job well," the Commander said. "Observe the Pass and prepare for the next sleep."

The First moved his top two tentacles in the sign of respect. He had just been given the job of being The First again next Pass. "I am honored and will do as you command."

Then both turned away from the other quickly so that neither could see the other's back. The report was over for another Pass. The First glided from the room, passing the Commander's three top generals as he went. He made no indication that he saw them, and they ignored him. He did not fall under their power, nor did he report to them. His only boss was the Commander of the South, and for another Pass, he was to remain The First, the most honored of positions.

March 10, 2018
8:50 Universal Time

34 Days Until Arrival

Dr. Bonita "Zip" Juarez leaned forward in the passenger seat of the International Space Station shuttle and squinted at the space beyond. Thousands of unblinking stars littered the pure blackness above the blue, green, and white edge of the Earth's surface. She loosened her lap and shoulder harness just enough so she could float slightly in the zero gravity, and turned to get a better look outside.

The low-orbit shuttle was moving over the Pacific at the moment and she could see the swirling clouds of a tropical storm forming. But it wasn't the incredible beauty of the planet below that she was looking at, but instead at the tiny flecks floating in orbit ahead of them, slowly growing in size as the shuttle caught up to them.

Home.

She grinned. As much home as she would ever have. She didn't dare tell Mission Control on Earth how much she hated being planet-bound. They would pull her off any mission, order the standard psychological batteries, and then say that she was just plain crazy. Of course, none of the psychiatrists had ever been in space, and few at Mission Control had been there as long as she had. They didn't realize she was like a sailor of old, more at home on the sea than on land. The stars were her playground, and zero g felt more natural to her than gravity itself.

On this last visit planet-side, she actually had to work to hide her discomfort. They'd called her down four months ago to help with the redesign of the Luna shuttles, and to train in flying them. Once she had said that the redesign could have been accomplished on the International Space Station; her comment had been received with such silence that she hadn't made the suggestion again. It wasn't until someone later briefed her on the secrecy of the mission that she had understood: Nothing remained secret on ISS for long.

She wished it did. It would have been better than spending the last four months in full gravity, listening to people call her Bonita or, even worse, Bonnie—rather than the nickname she'd gotten in Top Gun School. She'd been called Zip for the last ten years, and she answered to that, Juarez, or Doctor. And that was it.

Although even she had to give up trying to reeducate every new bozo who came down to check on the shuttle's progress. For a top secret mission, this one had a lot of rotating bozos.

The flecks grew bigger. The largest of them was ISS, her favorite place in the solar system. She had been assigned to ISS twice, once as an assistant in docking and once as management. She preferred piloting. She liked the rush.

The International Space Station had been a dream when she was born. When she was a little girl, she remembered watching her father download information on the joint mission sponsored by sixteen nations to send up the first piece of the station—what was now the outdated, and somewhat dangerous, area they called Zarya. She'd been in Zarya several times, when it was still functioning, and she had felt as if she were on holy ground—even if that ground was a badly assembled station passageway whose docking port and fuel tanks had been shut down because they were no longer safe.

She had watched the ISS go up, piece by piece. They thought the station would be completed in 2004—in those days it only held three scientists and a lot of research. But just after the turn of the century, someone decided to make the ISS an interplanetary way station, home to space travelers everywhere. More modules were added, and ISS began to look like a free-floating jigsaw puzzle put together by a dyslexic child. Now it housed fifty permanent residents and seventy-five nonpermanent ones.

She was going to be one of the nonpermanent ones, she and her crew of eighteen. In less than twenty-three hours, her crew, split between the two modified Luna shuttles, would head toward the tenth planet, what some of the team were now calling Slingshot because no one had bothered to name the poor thing. They were supposed to chase and explore the tenth planet, meeting it almost a full third of the way to Mars.

The Luna shuttles had been towed up here before her. She could see them in the functioning docking area of ISS near the old Service Module. This wasn't the main docking area; the shuttles were there in an attempt to maintain some secrecy.

Secrecy. It was going to be hard to keep those babies secret. Earth loved hearing about Luna shuttle missions. That was why, in part, the scientists in charge of the Tenth Planet Project announced yesterday that they'd discovered a tenth planet. It was the first stage of cover for her mission. If someone blew the whistle, they would say that she was going to explore the planet. No one would mention the four-month prep time, and all that practice.

Fortunately, the shuttles looked no different on the outside. She was always struck by how similar they were to the old Lunar landers, LEMs, from the Apollo missions flown ten years before she was born. God, she loved watching that old footage. It had a patriotic, ancient feel to it, something that she thought the country could never capture again. And she had an echo of that feeling when she looked at the shuttles. They were built like spiders, with legs on five sides and a pointed top. These were a lot more stable than the LEMs, and they were designed to hold a dozen crew comfortably. These particular shuttles had flown repeated missions to the moon over the past six years, doing research and setting up a mining base there.

But now they were to be used for a completely different purpose. She pulled on the strap of her shoulder harness and eased back into the seat, buckling herself in. The secrecy of this damned mission bugged her. She had asked a lot of questions in the four months she'd spent on Earth and didn't get any answers until yesterday.

Now she wished she hadn't gotten most of them.

Yesterday she had had a face-to-face briefing with Drs. Leo Cross, Britt Archer, and Edwin Bradshaw, none of whom she had met before. She didn't pay much attention to them, not with Yolanda Hayes present from the White House, as well as Jesse Killius from NASA. It wasn't until they made her sit through Cross's archaeology presentation that she understood why this mission was being kept under wraps.

She didn't know how the hell she would determine what was causing this planet to chew up the Earth. She had a great grounding in the sciences, but she had a hunch what they were looking for wasn't going to be obvious. And it wasn't going to be something they'd encountered before.

Zip felt an unusual queasiness in her stomach—a rare sign of nerves. Usually she loved it when everything rested on her. But in this case, the price of failure was too high. She was good at what she did, but she would have been happier if they had years to find out what was going on. Cross insisted that they had almost no time at all. Not more than a month.

And by the end of his damn presentation, she believed him.
She only hoped she could find something.
She hoped there was something to find.

7

March 14, 2018
9:15 A.M. Eastern Standard Time

30 Days Until Arrival

It was Cross's mention of his previous work that got Bradshaw into this position. Otherwise, he'd still be in Oregon teaching, instead of being in D.C. on indefinite sabattical. Bradshaw's hands were shaking. He sat alone in the map room at Cross's house, staring at various images on all the different computer screens. One image was, of course, the soot layers, multicolored and marked for their different years. Another was of the orbital path of the tenth planet, and a third was a map of Bradshaw's discovery, his humiliation, the end of his productive life.

Until now.

Damn Cross. The man should have been a psychologist instead of an archaeologist. He had known how to mess with Bradshaw's mind and he had done it so subtly.

First the early comments, the mention that he had read Bradshaw's research. And then the reassurance just as Bradshaw was being hired: *I read it again last night. You were quite clear about the preliminary nature of your research and, contrary to media reports, you never drew a single conclu-sion. You only marked possibilities based on cultural contexts, and you outlined the need for further research. I think you've been in exile long enough, Edwin.*

In exile long enough. So subtle. So nice. So unconnected. And then, when Bradshaw hadn't picked up on the hint, Cross had dropped another—six months ago, when Brad-shaw had gone to Canada to check that soot layer:

On your trip, Edwin, why don't you pick up your research? Bring it back here in case we need it.

Of course Bradshaw brought it back, but Cross never said another word about it. And Bradshaw wasn't going to bring it up. He had promised himself he would never think of it again. But touching it, moving it, digging his fingers through those hard copies in Oregon had brought it to the surface of his mind.

Not thinking of it had become impossible.

He punched up the image on the fourth screen. The rock was shown in microscopic detail. Yet he wasn't looking at the rock itself, but at what he called the fossil.

It was too round to occur naturally. That was what had at-tracted him in the first place: its precision, and that of its seeming exoskeleton, which had tiny circles, perfect circles, like the fossil itself.

His first thought, all those years ago, had been that the fossil was man-made. But that wasn't possible, not in the area he had found it, not as old as it was. In those days he had seen the resemblance to computer chips, but these days his more educated eye saw something else.

He bowed his head and ran his fingers through his thinning hair. This research would be his ruin. It had always been his ruin. And no matter how many times he went over this mate-rial, his reaction was still the same.

134

Cross had to see this.

Bradshaw didn't want Cross to see it. He didn't want anyone to see it until his findings were firm. They never would be, though, because he always stopped in the same place, the place he was now.

For the past three months, after Cross had fallen asleep, Bradshaw had come into the map room and reviewed his research. At first he had scanned most of it in, and then, using the room's upgraded computer systems, he had cleaned up the pictures. And he now saw things he had never seen before.

Since February, he had been checking and rechecking everything. If he was going to show this to Cross, if he was going to open himself to ridicule again, he would do so with the facts firmly behind him.

Maybe that meant a trip to South America. He could tell Cross he was checking more soot layers, because, in truth, he was. Many of these round fossils, and he had found thousands of them, were in soot layers.

He bowed his head. Maybe he would sleep for a few days, get a clear mind, and then talk to Cross. But Bradshaw knew he was stalling, just as he had done since he reopened the research. He hadn't found anything new since Valentine's Day. That was when he realized that these fossils did not operate on a dual system the way most sophisticated tools created by bipeds did. They operated on a system that was based in ten: ten circles, ten branches off the exoskeleton. Even the round shape with its ten bisections showed the influence of a base-ten system. The perfection of the circles, the base-ten system, the soot layers—he hated what he was thinking.

He must have dozed, because he didn't hear the door opening, nor did he know Cross was in the room until the man put a warm hand on his back.

"Edwin?"

For a moment Bradshaw didn't move. He felt like a high school boy again, being caught coming home after curfew by his father. His head still buried in his arms, he smiled at the image and suddenly understood his own psychology: He had been working down here, night after night, hoping to get caught.

"Edwin?"

Bradshaw sat up slowly and rubbed his eyes. "Sorry," he said. But Cross wasn't listening to him. He was staring at the screens before him.

"This is your old research."

"Yes," Bradshaw said wearily.

"I'd forgotten about it. I had wanted to review it before Christmas, but so much had happened—"

"No need to apologize, Leo."

Cross sank into the chair beside Bradshaw. Cross had lost weight in the last six months and his eyes had permanent shadows beneath them. Everyone on this project was showing different signs of stress. Cross's were all physical—and somehow easy for him to ignore.

"I'd forgotten about it," Cross said slowly, "but obviously you haven't."

"No," Bradshaw said. He'd been down here night after night, sometimes only twenty minutes, sometimes hours. "But I was wrong, Leo."

"Wrong?" Cross turned to him, a frown marring his face. "How could you be wrong?"

"They aren't computer chips, or that sort of technology. My ignorance *was* showing, just not in the way everyone thought. And I did do it right. I wanted someone to double-check me."

"We already agreed on that when you joined this team, Edwin. How are you wrong?"

"Those look like some form of nanotechnology. I'm not up on all the current stuff, but I don't remember anything that has that configuration. And besides, it's not a natural human configuration."

"Natural human . . ." Cross turned back toward the screen. He didn't say anything as he studied it.

For the first time since they'd been working together, Bradshaw felt that he finally understood something Cross didn't.

"Even computer code is in binary, Leo," he said softly. "When humans make tools they usually have a dual function. A tomahawk has an edge and a handle."

"Advanced societies make tools whose usage isn't obvious," Cross said slowly. "These are clearly advanced."

"And their purpose isn't obvious," Bradshaw said. "But their configuration is just not something any human society has ever come up with."

"What are you saying?" Cross asked.

Bradshaw listened closely. In Cross's tone there was none of that skepticism Bradshaw had heard from his colleagues fifteen years ago. Nor was there any condescension. Only simple curiosity tempered with something else. Fear?

"Before I answer that," Bradshaw said, "let me show you a few other things."

He tapped a key on the computer and replaced the single fossil image with two of his best images of the nanomachines fossilized in the rock. The images showed a very intricate and alien-looking machine, cut through along an axis to get the two-dimensional image. If Bradshaw had had these two images years ago, his career wouldn't have been destroyed. But he'd only managed to get such good images using some of Cross's equipment.

Cross whistled. "You found confirmation that these are technology."

Bradshaw nodded. "I've gone back over my work and checked everything. The dating of the stone they were found in puts them at a million years old."

Cross nodded as he looked at the images on the screen. "Impressive photos. Could you make out what they were used for? Or where they came from?"

"I have no idea as to their purpose, or their origin," Bradshaw said, careful not to let his voice shake. He didn't want to force out the conclusions. He didn't want to make Cross hostile to them. Instead, he wanted Cross to come to the same conclusions he had. "But I found a number of fascinating details about what the fossils are made of and about the stone I found them in. First, the fossilization bleached their color somewhat. Initially, I believe they were black."

Cross's head snapped around and he stared at Bradshaw. It was clear that Cross suddenly saw exactly where Bradshaw was heading. "And the strata around them?"

Bradshaw swallowed hard. "The strata around them has the same basic composition as we're finding in our 'soot' layers. Only this one was deposited a long time ago. The tenth planet has passed Earth five hundred times since then."

"My god," Cross said.

Bradshaw waited. He knew what Cross was reviewing in his mind. Over the last six months they had found more and more evidence that the regular passes of the tenth planet had been going on for a long, long time. The farthest soot layer back they had found was dated just over three hundred thousand years ago. But both of them knew that finding a layer over a million years old was very possible. As far as they knew, the tenth planet had been passing the Earth and leaving destruction since the formation of the entire solar system.

"How many of these would it take to form a black cloud?"

"Billions," Bradshaw said. "No, trillions. You could get

more then twenty of them on the head of a pin. But I want to be clear that there is no evidence they have anything to do with the layers. They may have been simply trapped in a layer."

He had to be cautious. He had to be very cautious. He didn't want to believe that his discredited research was tied to this project.

Cross gave him a penetrating look. "Do you believe that?"

Bradshaw couldn't look away. He couldn't lie to Cross. Cross had given him this chance, and somehow, back in August, Cross had had one of his famous hunches about Bradshaw's research. Only it hadn't been a big hunch, like the one about the orbit. It had been a small one, and Cross had forgotten it.

Until now.

"No," Bradshaw said, "I don't believe they are something that just happened to get trapped in the soot layer. I believe they caused it."

March 21, 2018
23:18 Universal Time

23 Days Until Arrival

General Garai stood in front of the Commander of the South, his movement tentacles all bunched in a tight point under him, his ten eyestalks focused forward. Having all ten eyestalks out hurt at this late date. The energy filtering through the stalks was almost unbearable in the cold.

He could hardly see the Commander of the South's headquarters. He knew, rather than noted, that the room was designed for larger meetings than this one. Warming robes hung on the walls and balancing spheres were spaced at even intervals all over the floor. The Commander of the South stood on a raised sphere, his ten movement tentacles at rest in the sphere's relaxation depressions, staying warm. Even so, he still stood higher than General Garai, as was custom.

The Commander made a motion with two of his upper tentacles for Garai to stand at ease. Garai did not relax his movement tentacles—to do so without specific order was tantamount to treason—but he did let six of his eyestalks recede into their pockets. He closed the pockets so they would not offend the Commander. All of this Garai did without moving the remaining four eyestalks, keeping them in a makeshift circle around his long face.

"Is all in readiness?" the Commander asked.

"The South will fly thirty-six ships," Garai said, proudly. "As it has always done, since the time of the Great Arrival and First Pass."

For one thousand and eight Passes, since the planet had awoken from its long sleep in interstellar space, caught in a long orbit of this yellow star, the South had flown the same number of ships in the Great Harvest.

The Commander motioned that he was pleased. He knew that the Center General could only fly thirty-five ships, and North had been flying thirty since the time of the great accident twenty-six Passes before. It was the reason why General Garai would be the supreme commander of the mission, as he had been for the last twelve passes.

"Do you foresee any problems?"

"I do not," Garai said. And he did not. Even the population of creatures on the surface posed no great threat. There had been vast numbers of the creatures before and they had made no difference. He would just avoid their areas where possible, as he had done last pass.

"Are the Sulas ready?"

"They are," Garai said.

"Then it is time," the Commander said.

Garai snapped back to one-point attention, bringing his hidden eyestalks out so quickly that he almost made himself dizzy. They made two movements—exiting the pocket and encircling his face—and after that remained rigid. It was difficult to keep them still when he had moved so quickly.

The two Malmuria held the position for a moment, neither speaking to the other, as was custom.

Then, as one, the two turned away from each other, breaking contact simultaneously. Garai felt the surge of pride flowing through him as he glided out of the great room of the South and headed for his ship. Within a very short time he would again be leading the most important mission his people faced every Pass. As in all the Passes before, he would not fail.

March 22, 2018
3:15 P.M. Eastern Standard Time

22 Days Until Arrival

Britt sat at her desk and wished for coffee. Any kind of coffee. As long as it was good coffee, of course.

She ran a hand through her long dark hair and sighed. Might as well send her new assistant to the Union for some Starbucks. Starbucks was so generic, though. In the early teens it had been taken over by profit-minded corporate types who thought it was the successor to McDonald's, not the purveyor of excellent coffee that it had been. Not that she had always thought Starbucks the best. JavaJivin was the best she had tasted in this area.

But JavaJivin was closed as of an hour ago. Health code violations.

The thought made her shudder. How did a coffee shop, which did no cooking on site, get closed for health code violations? She wasn't sure she wanted to know. And what worried her the most about her reaction wasn't that she was concerned for the *baristas* who were out of a job, or the manager who had become her friend. She was worried about where she would get coffee, how she would sustain her ritual.

Maybe Leo was right. Maybe she was an addict. But he didn't seem to be worried about it. And he was slowly making his likes and dislikes known. Their friendship was growing, but she wasn't sure if it would become something more than a friendship.

She hoped it would.

She thought Leo did too.

She grabbed her purse, took a prepaid twenty-dollar smart card out of her wallet, and called in her assistant. He came to the door. He was a junior assistant, a grad student assigned to STScI for just these sorts of things. She'd been using him mostly for data compression and file updating—dull computer work that should have been done a long time ago. She always felt like a bad boss when she had someone do a personal task for her.

But this time she really couldn't leave the office. She had so much work to do. Ever since the tenth planet had been discovered, she found herself doing her regular job and the extra work that Leo and the Tenth Planet Project had required of her. She hadn't been getting much sleep and she'd been living on JavaJivin's espresso. Maybe that was the reason for her upset stomach—the health code violations, not the ulcer she'd been worrying about.

She handed the plastic to her assistant and asked him to bring her a double cappuccino with sprinkles. A treat, just because she was taking the whole JavaJivin thing personally. The manager had warned her that this might happen. He had said that the coffee bar might have to close down, but she had assumed it was because of the economic statistics she had seen on the little MSNBC monitor she kept running constantly on her desktop: the coffee culture was something only diehards like her now participated in. The kids were eschewing all caffeine, claiming health risks, cancer in rats, bad behavior on a caffeine high.

Her personal phone rang and she jumped. Then she grabbed the edge of the desk and took a deep breath to calm herself. Her reaction had nothing to do with caffeine. It was the stress. Only the stress.

"Archer here," she said, punching the hands-free button.

"Britt?" It was Keith Ursa-Michel, the chief astronomer and engineer in charge of Goddard's Space Telescope Operations Control Center. "You on a secured line?"

"No," she said.

"Transfer me."

With two flicks of a button, she did. She picked up the handset. Her heart was pounding and she knew it wasn't from a caffeine high. It was because Keith only called when he had problems.

"I just spoke to White Sands," she said. "Everything is functioning smoothly there. They've reported no more problems with TDRS."

The Tracking Data Relay Satellite system had been giving

them fits for the last week, and it was the worst week it could have happened. Since the announcement of the tenth planet, at least one of the scopes was turned in its direction at all times. That information was downloaded, after a suitable delay, onto the Internet so that people around the world could track its progress.

Fortunately, the engineers had found ways to deal with the TDRS problems this week, but Archer had been living in constant fear that things would get worse.

"It's not the TDRS," Keith said. "I'm going to upload the latest from Brahe."

Brahe was the scope currently trained on the tenth planet. Archer swiveled her chair toward the nearest computer screen, and punched in her access code. She had the capability of looking at the downloads from all the scopes anytime she wanted to. She used to lose a lot of time just staring into space—literally. Now she didn't have the time to lose. She didn't know the last time she had done this.

"Okay," she said.

"Just watch," he said.

The seemingly empty place in space grew in size as the tenth planet approached Mars's orbit. At this distance they should have been able to learn just about everything concerning the small planet, yet they hadn't learned a thing. The surface of the planet was clearly made of a substance that just didn't let any light escape, in any band. So, to the orbiting scopes, the tenth planet looked like a hole in space, blocking the stars behind it as it moved inward toward the sun.

She stared at the image for a moment. It was an infrared image of the planet; the empty place on the image was where the heat from the planet should have shown up.

"Watch first the lower quadrant," Keith's voice said over the picture. "Then central and upper."

She did as she was instructed, growing slightly impatient until suddenly there was a tiny flicker, then another flicker, and another. Finally, there were so many that the hair on the back of her head seemed to stand on end. Three swarms of tiny flickers moved slowly toward each other and away from the planet.

"What are they?" Archer asked.

The image vanished, then started to replay. "Those are," he said slowly, "one hundred or more distinct heat sources. We have someone here analyzing it now, but this is too big for us, Britt."

She wasn't ready to discuss what to do next. Not until he answered a few more questions. "How long did this last?"

"It lasted for exactly sixty-four seconds and then stopped. We're following the area where it happened."

"What would cause that?" Archer asked.

"I don't know," Keith said, and she could hear the exasperation in his voice. "Hell, we can't even see the stupid planet. I have no idea what that was. Something natural from the surface, most likely, as it heats up from getting closer to the sun. I don't know. Your guess is as good as mine."

She squinted as she watched the heat sources flicker in the replay on her screen. "This didn't get out over the Net, did it?"

"Nope," Keith said. "Delay gave us time to block it."

"Thanks," Britt said. "See what you can learn about this, and keep me posted. And I don't have to tell you to keep this quiet."

"Indeed you don't," Keith said. "Hey, Britt."

"Yeah?" she asked.

"Do you find this beautiful?"

She understood the question. She and Keith used to have long discussions about the beautiful images that came through the scopes.

145

"Not anymore," she said.

"Me, neither." He sounded disappointed. "I'll let you know when we've got something."

"Thanks," she said, and disconnected. She replayed the image several times, her stomach twisting. This was it. She knew it. But she didn't know what to do. Or what it was.

Her assistant was at the door, holding her double cappuccino. "Where do you want it?" he asked.

She dimmed the screen. "The edge of my desk," she said, without looking up. "Then you can go for the day."

He brightened, as if he'd been given a reprieve from prison. He set her double down, and walked out. She brightened the screen in time to see the swarms disappear again.

All she could think about was Leo and those "soot" lines he had been studying. It had led them to find the tenth planet in the first place, and she believed that something from the planet caused them and the destruction that had historically gone with them. Maybe what they had just seen were the items that caused the soot lines.

She reached over and punched a button on her computer. A moment later Leo's smiling face filled the screen. But the minute he saw her expression his smile vanished.

"You need to get here," she said. "I think we just found the link between your research and the skies."

"Can you download it to me here?"

She shook her head. "We need a secure line. Better to look at it here."

"Be there shortly," he said and signed off.

What she didn't tell him was that she wanted him here because she didn't want to be alone with this knowledge. She didn't want to be the one to tell the Tenth Planet Project, and she didn't want to be the one to decide the next step.

Not alone.

Because the threat they'd been talking about had gone from theory to something real in the space of five minutes.

She picked up her cappuccino, took off the lid, and stared at the sprinkles floating on top like soot. Her stomach turned, and she replaced the lid, setting the cup aside.

This whole thing was a nightmare, one she hadn't wanted to acknowledge until now. But she knew, the moment she saw those heat signatures, that nothing would ever be the same again.

8

April 3, 2018
13:00 Universal Time

10 Days Until Arrival

Zip Juarez checked her lap and shoulder harness for a fifth time. Then she glanced at Mariko Katae. Mariko was the pilot on this mission—and she was a damn good one, even if she was the size of a delicate ten-year-old. She wore her jet black hair cropped short, and it looked as if she had done it herself, and her flight suit was slightly looser than regulation, but she didn't seem to mind. No one did. When Mariko was at the helm, magic things happened.

Right now, though, Zip envied her and the copilot Serge Rechenko. They had things to do. They were going through the flight check with Mission Control while she waited. She was the one in charge of the mission itself, but at this stage, she could only watch.

It was the one point—the only point—in an important mission where she regretted not piloting. But she had learned, the hard way, that she was a good pilot and, in some circumstances, a great one, but those circumstances had to fit her nickname. In cases when she flew into an area and out quickly, it was always better that she be at the helm. On longer missions, like this one, missions that required some finesse, Mariko was the absolute best in the world, bar none. Serge, who was also good, didn't even compare.

He was muttering his way through the checklist, repeating after Mariko in his thick Russian accent. On the last Luna shuttle mission in which they had served, Serge had tried to convince Zip that his accent was more Balkan than Prussian, but since he had tried to convince her that his accent was closer to pure Russian on the mission before that one, she didn't believe him. She was beginning to think he faked the thick accent because Americans expected it. He had that sort of mischievous sense of humor.

He was a small man, although it was hard to tell when he sat beside Mariko. His hands were delicate for a man, and one of the other commanders had once said that Serge had a technician's fingers. Zip appreciated that. His fingers had gotten them out of a few scrapes she'd never bothered to report to Mission Control.

Behind her the rest of the team waited, strapped into their seats with nothing to do until they arrived at the tenth planet.

The preflight check was finished, and the pilots had started the launch sequence. Zip almost checked her lap and shoulder harness again, and then made herself stop. It was a nervous habit, one she had gotten into when she couldn't do the hands-on work herself. But she wasn't on this mission for hands-on work. She was on it for her brains, and her ability to command. One nice thing about her ability to think and act quickly was that she could process a lot of information that most people didn't even see in half the time it took anyone else. She could make a snap decision and it would be the correct decision, having weighed all the factors and risks while her crew—smart people all—were still examining those factors.

The only difference was, on this mission, she was being asked to command both Luna shuttles. Usually she only commanded the shuttle she was in. But this mission was different, and had been from the start.

She watched the pilots finish the last of the launch sequence. The countdown started from Mission Control, the one inside ISS, but she was the one who issued the launch order—or the abort order, if need be.

She felt tension in her back and shoulders, always an odd experience at zero g when she was usually so relaxed. She did a quick check of the shuttle's interior and saw nothing amiss, no lights, no alarms. Through the windows behind her, she saw the edge of the old Service Module's solar panels. Before her, the unblinking lights of countless stars.

Everything was ready. They were all waiting for her. She took a deep breath. "Launch."

Her word went out to this shuttle and their companion, Luna Two. The secondary commander inside Luna Two would give the final launch order, just in case there were problems with that shuttle.

But there were none. She heard her command echoed in her second's voice.

The computers fired the main engines. The force took away the zero gravity and thrust her back into her chair. A wrinkle in her flight suit dug into her spine under the sudden weight. A three-g burn was standard for the Luna shuttles as they were shoved faster in their orbit around the Earth.

This part of the mission was standard. They would drop even slightly closer to the surface, picking up speed as they went until less than a full orbit later the two shuttles would be flung away from the Earth. The release point usually aimed the shuttle at the Moon, but this time the Moon was nowhere to be seen. This time the Moon was tucked on the far side of the Earth from the direction they would release. This time they were headed for a point in space, empty now, but where the tenth planet would be in two weeks.

"Luna One," Zip said, aware that her every word was being broadcast to millions watching and listening to the launch of the mission to the tenth planet. "Report status."

Beside her, Mariko smiled. "All green, Commander," Mariko said, following mission protocol.

"Luna Two, report," Zip said.

"Status green, Commander." The deep voice of Ennis Latimer, the pilot of Luna Two, was as clear as if he sat beside her. "The engine burn is solid."

"Good," Zip said, glancing at the instruments in front of her. "Shut down in five. Four. Three. Two. One. Mark."

Suddenly the pressure point under her disappeared as the engines shut down. They had done their first job, getting the shuttles started in a fast orbit around Earth.

"Ten minutes until flight path insertion burn," she said. That burn would take place when the shuttles were in the right position in Earth's orbit. The engines' power would break the shuttles out of the Earth's strong gravity well and launch the shuttles toward their rendezvous point with the tenth planet.

At this point in the mission, she felt silly speaking. But for the first time in nearly ten years, this launch was being broadcast live. It was partly a p.r. display, and she had to perform like a trained monkey. She didn't mind, though. It put her in the same league as the first astronauts, the ones whose tapes she had listened to over and over again when she was a child.

Her crew knew what was going on, and they went through

151

the motions as well. On a normal launch, they would be sitting back and joking at this stage, because the computers were now running the flight.

Zip glanced to her right at the speeding surface of Earth below, then to her left at the Moon, now coming into view. She was glad they weren't going to the Moon. She'd been there, countless times. This time she was going somewhere new, taking one of those "small steps for man, giant leaps for mankind" sort of things. Zip had been trying to think of something profound to say.

She glanced at the instruments in front of her, then at Mariko. She was relaxed but watching, letting the computers do the work. Slinging a speeding craft around a planet and out of an orbit toward a distant point in space took more math than she cared to think about. More than even the best pilots could handle without dozens of course corrections. If they were all going to get back in one piece, fuel needed to be saved, which meant the fewer course corrections they had to make, the better they would be. That meant these first two burns had to be right on the money.

From the readings before her, it looked as if they would be. But she had to go through the motions.

Zip grinned at Serge, who grinned back, his blue eyes twinkling. As soon as the broadcast ended, he would say something terrible and witty, and they would laugh themselves sick. She could already see him gearing up for it.

Then she turned to Mariko, who was still watching the instruments.

"Luna One," she said loudly as if Mariko were in the other shuttle instead of right beside her, "report."

"We are dead square in the cash," Mariko said, mangling, as she often did, any American idiom she tried. A muffled laugh behind Zip told her that one of the team had caught the mistake. "All systems are green."

Zip had to swallow once to clear the laughter from her own voice. "Luna Two?"

"We're in the cash too," Ennis said, sounding very serious. Bless him. That would make Mariko's mistake sound like intentional pilot talk to the folks at home. Zip could imagine the commentators on the nets and TV broadcasts pretending they'd heard the expression before. "All systems are green."

"Good," Zip said. "Standby for insertion burn."

She shifted in her seat against her belts, moving to take out the wrinkle in the flight suit before the next engine burn. Six humans in this craft and six in Luna Two, heading for the first time to visit another planet. Her heart was pounding even though she hadn't really exerted herself yet. It was just that few people ever got the opportunity to make first contact with a new planet. In fact, her crews were going to be the first ever to make this kind of contact with a never-before-heard-of planet.

It was a first. And Zip had always liked being first.

April 3, 2018
8:12 A.M. Eastern Time

10 Days Until Arrival

Britt leaned against the couch cushions, her stockinged feet tucked under her. She was leaning toward Cross, near, but not too near. In her right hand she cupped her morning coffee, which she took straight, much to his surprise.

Cross held his own coffee and sat much more rigidly in the

sofa. The remains of the lavish breakfast that Constance had prepared was on the glass-topped coffee table before them.

They were in a room in Cross's house that he rarely used. His mother had called it the movie room with a bit of pride; his father always corrected her and called it the TV room with a bit of disdain. It was, actually, a bit of both, a media room that his mother had kept updating until the day she died. The only change that Cross had made was to remove the Internet-only computer.

Cross had brought down all three large flat screens, deciding not to use the smaller ones. He'd also made sure the sound system was working. He had decided not to dim the lights. He hadn't watched a launch since *Challenger* blew up, back when he was thirteen years old.

It felt odd to do so now. It felt even odder to have Britt beside him.

She came over at 7:30 that morning. She had asked him to watch the launch with her at STScI, but when he found out that they'd be using STScI's TV room, with a single screen, he had invited her here.

He wished he had enough courage to invite her the night before.

The launch itself had gone smoothly, and so had the first burn. The announcers were currently reshowing earlier footage as they waited for the second burn.

". . . And it's going to take two weeks for the shuttles to reach the tenth planet," said a new female voice from the screen. The images were the same. The station must have replaced its anchors. "Then the shuttles will match the tenth planet's speed and stay with it for a ride down toward the sun."

"It should be a fascinating ride, Carol," said an equally invisible male announcer.

154

"That it should," Carol said a bit too brightly.

"And here's where we mute you!" Britt said, grabbing the remote and stabbing the mute so hard that Cross wondered if Carol didn't feel it in her studio somewhere. "I don't think I can listen to that chirpy voice again."

He laughed and stretched. "More coffee?"

"I'm floating already," Britt said. "If it weren't for the second burn, I'd say let's shut this thing off."

"I want to see it."

"Me too."

There was a long silence between them. Cross felt as if he should do something, that Britt expected him to do something, but he wasn't sure what.

"Where's Edwin?" Britt asked. "I thought he'd be here."

Her words startled him. He hadn't told her about the fossils yet, the ones that Bradshaw thought were tiny nanomachines. Bradshaw had made him promise not to say a word until their suspicions were confirmed. Cross wanted to tell Britt, but Bradshaw begged him not to tell anyone.

"Edwin had an appointment," Cross said.

She turned. Her face was only a few inches from his. "On *this* morning?"

He knew what she meant. This was an important morning. It was their planet the Luna shuttles were going to, their discovery. Bradshaw should have been sharing it with them, just as Mickelson should have. But Mickelson was in Afghanistan, and Bradshaw was at his meeting.

So it was just Cross and Britt, alone.

"He has some questions he needs answered as soon as possible," Cross said.

"Feels like something I should know about," she said.

"It is," he said, startled at his own honesty, "but Edwin swore me to secrecy until after his meeting."

155

She raised her eyebrows. "I may have to force it out of you then."

Over her shoulder he saw the engines discharge. The second burn. She must have seen the same thing over his because they turned, in unison, toward the main screen. Britt fumbled for the remote and turned the sound back on.

". . . out of orbit and heading toward the rendezvous point. First they will discharge robotic probes that will photograph the tenth planet from space as well as . . ."

Britt muted the sound again. "I wish they'd say something new."

"They don't know what else to say." Cross sipped his now-cold coffee and set the mug down. "They don't have all the information we do."

"Even *we* don't have enough information," Britt said. She set the remote on the glass table beside his cup. On the screen above them, the shuttles grew small as they headed away from the Earth. "You've had time to think about those flashes."

"So have you," Cross said, not wanting to discuss them. That brought him too close to Bradshaw's research. "What do you think they are?"

"Honestly?" she asked, not looking at him.

"Honestly," he said.

"Spaceships." She whispered the word and bent her head as she did so, almost as if she didn't want to acknowledge it.

"Spaceships?" he asked.

She nodded. Then she closed her eyes. "Engine burns. Obviously you don't think that's what they are."

He swallowed. He had a hunch he knew, but he couldn't tell her. Not yet. "They're awfully small," he said, and wished he could kick himself.

"I know." She sighed and opened her eyes, then she leaned

156

back on the couch, very close to his right arm. "But it's possible that other civilizations are out there. You know that if you run the statistics, it's not only probable, it's certain that there's other life out there."

"But not necessarily on the tenth planet," Cross said.

"Then explain how that thing would know to send flares of light when it was this close to our orbit, and wouldn't do so before this?"

"We don't know it didn't do this before," Cross said. "We haven't been watching it long enough."

"Don't play that game with me," Britt said. "We both know that something happens between that planet and this one, and that something probably launched the other day."

"I hope it's not spaceships," Cross said. "There's a hell of a lot of them."

"I know," she said. She was quiet for a moment. He thought about reaching out and touching her, gently, just to see if her skin was as soft as it looked. "But tell me what kind of natural phenomenon produces that effect."

"It's an alien world," he said. "And you're the astronomer."

Her smile was small. "You have no theories?"

"I have a lot of theories," he said.

"About my spaceships?"

"I comfort myself by thinking that no civilization can survive that two-thousand-year orbit. How would they live? They go too far from the sun to grow anything on that planet."

"Anything we recognize," she said.

"Anything we understand," he said.

"But those were infrared heat signatures," she said.

"I know." He let his hand fall, like a teenager, his fingers brushing her arm.

She looked up at him and smiled. "You can put your arm around me," she said.

157

He felt himself flush. "That obvious?"

"It's taken that long." Her smile widened. "That's not a criticism. We've been very involved with this tenth planet and we're scientists and—"

"What does being a scientist have to do with it?" he asked, putting his arm around her and pulling her close. She was smaller than he expected and warmer, a little radiant sun.

"We're notoriously socially inept," she said.

"Are we?" he asked, bringing his face toward hers.

She tilted her mouth toward his. "Yes," she whispered.

"Prove it," he said.

"All right," she said, and kissed him. The kiss lasted longer than he expected. She tasted of coffee and strawberry jam and something else, something *her*. He brought his other arm around her and pulled her against him.

"Inept?" he whispered as their lips separated.

"Hmm," she said. "I think this'll take further experimentation."

And they kissed again.

April 3, 2018
9:03 A.M. Eastern Time

10 Days Until Arrival

Bradshaw still did not like driving on his own outside of the Beltway. The roads were old and poorly designed; they weren't wide enough for the amount of traffic on them now. The start and stop driving, combined with his natural tendency to run late, and the peculiar character of D.C. drivers, had left his nerves shattered by the time he found the office he was looking for.

The building before him was a late-twentieth-century monstrosity made of glass and steel, designed at the time to look like something modern but which rapidly looked dated. The corporate name—NanTech was emblazoned across the front in red glittery letters. Bradshaw smiled when he saw it. He remembered the trademark infringement lawsuit that had extended through the courts during the last decade; it had made every paper, broadcast, and Net news daily. He had thought the whole thing mildly amusing then—who cared if the company was called NanTech or NanoTech or Nantech? Obviously some corporate wiggy-wigs did, but Bradshaw had simply wished the news story would go away.

Who would have thought that, a few years later, he'd be walking through NanTech's front door. Certainly not him.

But he was going there because the best nanotechnology expert in the entire country, maybe the entire world, worked for NanTech. Portia Groopman didn't own the company; she didn't even start it. She had simply been hired for it straight out of high school, by which time she had applied for two hundred patents on her own. She was a hell of a kid. Homeless for the first ten years of her life, moving from place to place with her family. Taught by her parents—former teachers who had had no insurance, and who had lost their home—she spent most of those ten years in libraries, using library computers to access the Internet. Somehow her interest had gone to nanotechnology.

She had read the works of Drexler by the time she was eight, had developed theories of her own by the time she was ten, and had caught the attention of some important nanotech types by the time she was eleven. They got her a home, got her into the right schools, and got her to apply for patents.

Apparently she chose the NanTech job herself, afraid to survive on her own merits, given her parents' experience. She wanted, she had said in one *Scientific American* interview, to make sure she had a roof over her head and over her parents' heads, and if that meant trusting a corporation to do it, well then, she would.

Bradshaw had read that and his heart bled a little. It was trusting others that had gotten her parents into their predicament in the first place, but he couldn't tell her that. She was only twenty, still too young to understand some things about life.

He felt odd going to see an expert who was younger than most of his students, but he had been assured by everyone in the nanotech community that she was the one to see. *She has an instinctual grasp of the unusual,* a friend of his who had specialized in nanotechnology said. *She's precisely the person you want.*

So here he was, pulling into one of the visitor's slots, and feeling older than he cared to admit. He remembered the days when drivers on the road had a certain courtesy to each other—days so long gone that someone like Portia Groopman probably thought of them as ancient history.

He went into the building, past the electronic security, punching in the code Groopman had given him via secured e-mail. The double doors opened for him, and suddenly he was in a pristine world of chrome and steel. A giant sculpture stood before him, and it took him a moment to realize it was supposed to be a human form covered with or created by tiny machines. He shivered once, walked across the marble tile and got into an elevator.

"Good morning, Dr. Bradshaw," it said in an androgynous digital voice. "Ms. Groopman is expecting you."

And then it zoomed to the thirty-fifth floor so rapidly that

160

he was still recovering from hearing an elevator address him by name as the doors eased open.

He stepped out and glanced back at the thing as if he had been burned. He didn't know how it did that, wasn't sure he wanted to know either, but suspected it had something to do with the keypad he had punched and the name on Groopman's schedule sheet. For the first time in his life, he worried about the little bits of DNA he dropped everywhere—-from the surface of his skin onto that keypad, for example. He wiped his fingers nervously against his pants and turned toward the directory in the center of the gray and chrome hallway.

Everything reflected here. The flowers in the vase reflected, and up close he realized they weren't flowers at all, but nanomachines in the form of flowers. God, he would hate working here. As he looked at the directory, its contents flowed, shifted, and re-formed.

Dr. Bradshaw: Ms. Groopman's office is down the main hallway to your right. Her door will be open for you.

He almost said thank you, but didn't. He was really shaken now. He followed the directions, careful not to brush anything, and entered the door that was open.

Inside was an office twice the size of the president's office at Oregon State. Unlike the hallway, this place was lived in. Stuffed animals covered every surface, and the couch, pushed up against the nearest wall, had a crumpled blanket on it, covered with Reese's candy bar wrappers and a half-eaten Snickers bar. Five cans of Mr. Pibb stood on a glass coffee table, and an ancient computer, decorated with string made to look like a spider web, sat in one corner.

A girl sat behind the main desk. She wore rimless glasses tinted rose and had her hair cut in an eighties angle wedge.

She wore no makeup, but she wore a dress, which surprised him. When she saw him, she smiled.

"Dr. Bradshaw," she said, and held out her hand.

He took it, hoping his wasn't too clammy.

"I was really looking forward to this." She sounded young and eager and excited. "These things are incredible."

"That's what I thought," Bradshaw said, looking behind him for a chair.

"Oh, take Mopsy off that one," she said. Mopsy had to be the larger-than-life-size blue bunny that dominated the stuffed leather chair beside the desk. He picked the bunny up carefully and took it toward the couch.

"Not there," Groopman said. "She might get chocolate on her. I haven't had time to clean up."

He wondered if she sometimes slept here, then realized that she probably did. He slept in his own office sometimes, when his research was going well. "Umm—" he said, turning, looking for an empty surface for the bunny.

"Put her on the other chair with Itchums," she said. "They get along."

He set the bunny next to a small stuffed gorilla who had to be Itchums because of the placement of its hands. Besides, Groopman didn't correct him. She watched, an adult look on her face. She was using the stuffed animals to test him, to see if he would judge her a child because of them. He knew better. People who had no real childhood, like Portia Groopman, often created a childlike atmosphere in their adult lives.

Bradshaw sat in the empty chair, and started to say something, but Groopman interrupted him.

"I suppose you're still not going to tell me where you found this sample," she said.

"I can't," Bradshaw said.

She shook her head. "I'd love to see more of them. Maybe even see the sample they came from."

"I might be able to arrange that," Bradshaw said.

"Good." She no longer sounded like a young girl, but like a scientist, a strong and brilliant one. "I've never seen anything like this machine."

"Neither had I," Bradshaw said. "That's why I brought it to you."

She nodded. "I'm following your information on its composition, since I have no friggin' idea how to read fossilized stuff. I think it's weird that it's made of a material you can't identify."

"So do I," he said.

"And the configuration of the machine itself isn't logical. If we were building a machine like this, we'd go about it completely differently." Then she looked at him and grinned. "You saw the prototypes in the hallway. What'd you think of them?"

"The directory was nanomachines?"

"Yeah," she said. "That's mine. I like it. Every day when I come up, it gives me a phrase for the day."

"And it knows that you're you because . . ."

"The security system feeds information throughout the building. When you leave today, don't be surprised if the door says good-bye to you."

"Nothing could surprise me after this morning."

She laughed. The sound was warm and robust, a child's delighted laugh. "I like working in a place that's fun, don't you?"

"Yes," Bradshaw said, wondering how to turn the conversation back the way he wanted it to go.

"I'd like to keep working on these machines," she said as if she knew what he was thinking. "I feel like I've only scratched the surface."

"What have you discovered?" Bradshaw asked.

"Well." She leaned forward and templed her fingers, like he did when he was giving sage advice and making fun of himself at the same time. "I'm guessing a lot because I'm working off your computer information, not a real machine that I can plug into our system. Even if I could plug it into our system, I'm not sure I'd get more. So what I'm doing is analyzing this by making some assumptions that aren't necessarily true."

"Like what?"

"Like this has a function we understand." She splayed her hands on the table. "This looks alien to me. I mean, really from-Mars alien. So I have to assume the culture that made these things has some things in common with us. You know, like a knife now—with push-button blades and stuff—still has an edge and a point, just like a spear tip did. That's the difference between what you showed me, which is the equivalent of a push-button knife, and what we can do, which is the equivalent of a hand-carved spear tip."

"Got it," Bradshaw said, impressed that she could talk his language.

"So with that in mind, comparing this alien nanomachine with ours, I looked for similar templates. And what I think is this: Your little machine here is designed to break down organic material and store its components."

"What?" Bradshaw felt cold. He didn't like the sound of this, but it made sense with the soot layers.

She hit a button on her desk and a computer screen rose, knocking aside some stuffed kittens the size of his thumb. "Isn't that cool?" she asked. "I had them design it for me, like those old movies."

164

Old movies, apparently, meant anything made around the turn of the century.

The screen blinked on and an image appeared. It was one of the nanomachines. "Remember," she said, moving back to that adult tone. "We're looking at something so small here that it works on a molecular level."

Bradshaw nodded.

A tiny orange circle appeared on the front end of the machine. "This area looks to me like an intake area." The circle moved to a larger section. "Breakdown area." Several circles formed around smaller sections. "Storage areas."

Then a white line formed from the breakdown area to an untouched area. "Waste disposal."

"But how could something like this break apart organic material?" Bradshaw asked.

She shrugged, making a strange I-don't-know face as she did so. "That's where my analogy breaks down," she said. "A primitive guy can pick up our knife and hit it enough to find the button that releases the blade. You got something encased in stone, something so small I can't touch it anyway. I know how it could work in theory, but not on this level, and not this small."

"Then what do you base your guess on?" Bradshaw asked, hoping, just hoping, she could be wrong.

The computer screen disappeared into her desk and she replaced the tiny kittens on top of it. "When I first came to Nan-Tech, I worked on something very similar to this. We made nanites to clean up oil spills."

"You're kidding," Bradshaw said. "We can do that?"

"Not yet," Groopman said. "But we'll be able to by next year. We hope to be able to dump nanites onto a spill, have them eat it, then separate the goo into harmless components, and go dormant. I think this is just a highly advanced form of the same thing."

"Wow," Bradshaw said. The longer he worked on this project, the more he learned about the other branches of science, and the more impressed he was growing. "Is there anything else?"

"Good news, of sorts," Groopman said. "They aren't self-replicating, so there's no chance that any of these could ever get away. These were produced one at a time and most likely they shut down when the storage areas are full."

"Do they move on their own?"

"No," she said. "I'm sure of that."

"What makes you so certain?" Bradshaw asked.

"These nanomachines are basically very simple," she said. "A nanomachine that performs several functions is very complex. Large or small, its interior would be vastly different if it performed more than one function."

"Even if we're talking a more highly developed technology?"

"Even if," she said. "I can guarantee that these machines only do one thing."

"Eat," Bradshaw said.

"To put it simply," she said. "These machines eat something organic, keep most of it, and spit out the rest of it. If there are a lot of machines, you'd find a lot of waste."

"A 'soot' layer," Bradshaw whispered.

"What?" she asked.

"Nothing," he said. Nothing except nightmares. A nightmare that was getting closer with each passing minute.

9

April 4, 2018
8:29 Universal Time

7 Days Until Arrival

On the tenth level of the first ship, the command crew gathered. General Garai stood in the first balance circle, his torso tentacles at rest by his side. He wore a thin warming robe because the atmosphere in the first ship was kept at a comfortable temperature. The other ships of the Southern Fleet had to follow protocol and not use much energy, but in his he could maintain a luxurious level of comfort, although he often chose not to. The levels from the Ancient Days felt unusually hot to him now. The ship was kept at one one-hundredth the Ancient Days' recommended level, and still Garai felt as if he were using too much energy.

He was too young to remember the Ancient Days, the Days when his planet actually orbited its own sun and had its own oceans, its own life. Only the wisdom of his first ascendants had saved his people. They foresaw the disaster, and developed a way to survive it. He had lived much longer than those who brought him into the world with his nine siblings in the egg-brood, but he had been awake only part of that time. The years pass, and he did not live them. He slept. His life would span countless years, but only a few generations. Such was the paradox of his people.

Nine of his eyestalks were in their pockets. The tenth level had light reflectors that made the ambient light seem stronger. It felt almost sinful to look through a single eye, to see as much as he would see if all ten of his eyes were in use.

The nine members of his senior staff stood in their positions around the tenth level. Some had sensors floating around them. Others were rooted into their balance circles, monitoring the space around them. The exterior of the ship was shielded, and those who wanted to see space with their naked eyestalks had to press them against the eyestalk holders built into the hull. It was a dangerous maneuver, particularly during deceleration, and not allowed on any but the most routine trips.

Sensor Watch Three brought all of his eyestalks out of their pockets and had them encircle his face. Then he rose on his movement tentacles.

General Garai turned to face him, acknowledging Sensor Watch Three's desire for communication. They were using standard protocol, often done when the ship was in no danger. Should the ship be in danger, and instant communication was needed, Sensor Watch Three would have slapped his two upper tentacles together and hidden his face as he spoke.

"Proceed," Garai said.

"The creatures from the planet have launched two vessels toward us," Sensor Watch Three said. His fifth eyestalk vibrated as if Three were struggling mightily to hold it still. The news disturbed him then.

"Bring forth images," Garai said. The command had to be on the record. Even though the First ship was allowed to use Ancient Days power levels, it could only do so on routine items. Non-routine items such as using a visual needed to be in the record.

A visual encircled him, replacing the brown light of the tenth level with the brightness of space. Two vessels with a conical shape cut in the center and five spindly tentacles with individual balance circles attached drifted against the blue-and-white backdrop of the destination planet.

Strange, ugly, and useless was the first thought that came to his mind. But he had always thought that of the creatures' constructions. These were no different.

"What is the course?"

"The ships will intercept our great home." Sensor Watch Three's sixth eyestalk started to vibrate.

"You have verified this information."

"Ten times," Sensor Watch Three said, "and then ten more."

"With checks from me and Sensor Watch Eight," said Garai's Command Second. "The information is accurate."

General Garai stared at the images of the two five-legged ships. They were repulsive in their very look. He could not believe that the creatures that had groveled in the dirt at last Pass had come so far.

"Navigation One," Garai said.

The Malmuria in charge of navigation rose on his movement tentacles, but turned only nine of his eyestalks toward Garai. The remaining stalk continued to monitor the ship's path, as he should.

"What sort of energy shall we use should we decide to intercept these two ships?"

Navigation One slid a single tentacle toward his floating control panel. With the touch of the tip, he worked the information, then checked it as he needed to. His tenth eyestalk swiveled and joined the others before he spoke. "There will be

169

minimal energy usage. We will tap less than one-hundredth of a percent of our reserves, if we act now."

Garai turned his back on Navigation One, allowing Navigation One to return to his original position. "Sensor Watch One," Garai said, and watched as One rose on his movement tentacles. "Will we receive an energy gain from these ships?"

Apparently Sensor Watch One was prepared for this question because he did not break protocol position. "We will receive a small, but valuable gain, if these ships are similar to the other ship encountered near the seventh planet. They are bigger, the gain may also be bigger."

A valuable gain. Any energy would help. Survival at all costs needed energy.

"Command Second, use the broadcast light."

Three of the Command Second's eyestalks spun toward him in surprise, then slipped into their pockets as the Command Second realized his horrible breach of protocol. Garai pretended not to notice. He had more important things to do.

The broadcast light—a horrible waste of energy—technology that had existed from the Ancient Days formed around Garai's balance circle. The light would send his image to the bridge of every ship in the fleet for the change in course. In all the Passes that he had been in charge of the fleet, he had never had to resort to such a thing. Never before had he changed plans midflight. And now, because of the creatures on the surface, he must alter the entire fleet's path.

This mission was routine no longer. His hopes for a simple Pass had already been destroyed.

8 Days Until Arrival

"Everyone will come to order." General Clarissa Maddox pounded her coffee mug on the Formica table. Leo Cross had to catch his half-empty mocha cup as it bounced dangerously close to the edge.

They were in the same secret meeting room they had been in for the last session, and the entire U.S. contingent of the team had arrived. Cross had brought Bradshaw, who was going to present his findings to the Tenth Planet Project. Bradshaw had tried to talk Cross into doing it. Then, that morning, he had pleaded illness, like a kid who didn't want to go to school.

Cross empathized, but Bradshaw had to present the work. His findings were important, and if he didn't do the presentation, he wouldn't feel the vindication that was sure to come.

Robert Shane turned from making himself a cup of tea at the beverage table. "You're fifteen minutes early, Clarissa."

"We're starting early," Maddox said, "and when we're official, I'm General Maddox to you."

"Aye, aye, sir," Shane said with a grin.

Maddox glared at him. Cross wasn't sure he ever wanted that look leveled at him, but he had to risk it. He had to buy some time for Bradshaw who was so nervous that he had just disappeared to the men's room for the second time.

"Forgive me, General," Cross said, "but won't it take some time to get our satellite uplinks ready?"

"We're not doing this on satellite, at least not yet. I've delayed the uplinks an hour."

Cross's mouth went dry. So she had heard of Bradshaw's

reputation and was trying to protect the group? That was a silly assumption. Of course she knew of it. Cross had informed them early on and explained the circumstances. Perhaps she was being cautious. But he had to know so he could brief Bradshaw.

"Is there a particular reason?" he asked.

"Hell, yes," Maddox said. "I don't know about the rest of you, but let's simply say that the people I've been answering to are a bit uncomfortable with making decisions the international way."

"The president doesn't want us talking to the other countries?" Yolanda Hayes asked.

"Now, I didn't say that," Maddox said.

"No, you implied it," Shane said, carrying his tea to the table.

At that moment, Britt came in. Cross smiled at her. He couldn't help himself. They hadn't found any time alone since the morning of the launch, but that morning had been worth the long wait. He simply didn't want to have another wait like that.

"Is there a problem?" she asked.

"Sit," Maddox said. "We've started."

"Should I get Edwin?"

"I'll get him in a moment," Cross said, and patted the seat next to him. Britt took it and frowned.

"Let's just say that we need international cooperation," Maddox said as if she hadn't been interrupted, "but it's time we, as the world's biggest superpower, exert some leadership. My orders are to make sure that we have made decisions before we bring them to the international parts of this organization."

"But that's not how this was designed," Britt said. "The

172

Europeans won't like it at all, not to mention the Japanese re-action and the Russians—"

"They won't know," Maddox said. "We've already shown that we can manipulate this discussion and we will continue to do so. We simply cannot suborn U.S. interests to the inter-ests of other nations"

"I thought we were putting the world's interests first," Cross said.

"We are," Maddox said. "But we make sure that the world follows our lead."

"I don't like this, Clarissa," Shane said.

"You haven't liked much about this organization, Robert," she said. "Should I have you relieved?"

"And that's why," he said. "We need to be able to have dialogue."

"Should I come back?" A voice from the doorway made them turn. Bradshaw was standing there. He was slightly green and Cross wondered if he had really been sick. Extreme stress did that to people sometimes.

"No," Cross said. "Join us, Edwin."

Bradshaw came in and stood beside Cross. He smelled vaguely of nervous sweat and toothpaste.

"I understand, Dr. Bradshaw, that you have findings that are very important to this group," Maddox said.

"Yes, ma'am." Bradshaw glanced at the screens. "Aren't we supposed to be on an uplink?"

"When you do the actual presentation," she said. "At the moment, I want you to summarize for us."

Cross put his hand on Bradshaw's arm, to prevent him from saying anything.

"Wait," Cross said. "Clarissa—General Maddox—you can't take control of this group by fiat. We've let you run the meet-ings because you're good at it. But if you're speaking for the

173

president, then you need to say that. Otherwise, we vote on your proposal like anything else."

"I am the highest-ranking official here," Maddox said.

"Technically, yes," Shane said, "but we're an unofficial organization."

"And we could argue," said Jesse Killius, "that I am the highest-ranking civilian official here. And then we run into more trouble, General."

"I'll leave," Bradshaw said and turned to go.

Cross kept his hand on Bradshaw's arm, holding him in place. "Should we vote?" Cross asked.

Everyone stared at him. Maddox gave him The Glare. And he was right; it was as bad as he thought it would be. But he didn't back down.

"All right," he said. "Everyone in favor of having national secret meetings before the international secret meeting raise your right hand."

Maddox raised hers.

"Those opposed."

Everyone else raised their hands, except Bradshaw, who merely looked confused.

"Looks like you were voted down, Clarissa," Shane said.

"This isn't a democracy," she said. "My orders come from the top."

"This is a democracy," Killius said, "no matter how you cut it. And if we're to follow the president's orders, then he has to be courageous enough to go on the record with them. Right now he wants deniability. If something goes wrong with the Tenth Planet Project, he wants to claim that he had no direct knowledge or authority, am I right, Clarissa?"

"Nothing will go wrong if you do this as I ask," Maddox said.

"Don't speak so soon," Cross said. His words made every-

174

one look at him. "I think we have a much more serious problem than you realize." He glanced at Bradshaw. "I guess you will have to summarize a little."

Bradshaw cleared his throat. "We think we know what those hundred-plus heat flares were."

"You do?" Killius asked.

"We can't prove it, not yet. But I found fossils in some of the soot layers, nanomachines over a million years old. I had experts look at these machines. It seems that they come down here in huge quantities, eat just about everything they come in contact with, store the useful parts, and spit out the rest—as dark matter."

"Soot layers," Britt said softly.

Bradshaw nodded.

"And you think those have been sent already?"

"Yes," Bradshaw said.

"Can we intercept them?" Hayes asked.

"I don't know," Bradshaw said. "That's not my area of expertise."

Maddox sighed. "What about our ships up there?"

"Good question." Cross answered that. "They could be in trouble."

"So we abort the mission," Maddox said, as if that were elementary.

"No, General," Shane said. His expression had some compassion in it. "These kinds of missions can't be easily aborted. Space isn't like flying an airplane or driving a car. You can't just turn around."

"Why not?" Maddox asked.

"Fuel for one," Killius said. "Fuel weighs a lot so we provide what's needed for the mission. During this mission we gave those ships enough to get to the tenth planet, use that planet as a help in braking, then come back with that planet. Nothing more. We can't stop a ship dead in space like you see in the movies, and we can't just turn them around. They don't have the fuel for that, nor are they set up on the correct trajectory."

"So what do you suggest?" Maddox asked.

"I suggest we hold the meeting as planned," Hayes said. "Those ships are on an international mission. I think we should keep it that way, and let the international community decide how to play this."

"Do you think those human lives are at risk?" Maddox turned to Bradshaw as she asked that question.

He turned white, then he blushed. "I-I'm only here to report on the nanomachines, General. I don't know anything about space."

"I do," Shane said. "But then, I always have. You know better than to send humans on a risky mission. We should have been satisfied with the probes."

"I think there is a place for people in space, Dr. Shane," Maddox said.

"So do I," Shane said. "But not on missions like this. We all know we did it this way for the p.r. value, so that we could say our people went, like Christopher Columbus, to an unknown land. We all know it would have been better to send probes ahead, and then graduate to something a bit more sophisticated, and then maybe, just maybe, send people."

"There wouldn't have been time to analyze the data," Killius said.

"My point exactly," Shane said. "And now we're worried about human lives when if we had done it my way in the first place, we would only have to think about a few million dollars worth of equipment."

"Recriminations don't help," Cross said, but Britt glared at him and he stopped. What had he said that got such a reaction from her?

"Before we even start reviewing past decisions," Britt said with a bit of an emphasis toward Cross. He took his hand off Bradshaw's arm and leaned back so that the focus wouldn't be on him. "We have to realize that we're jumping ahead here and making all sorts of assumptions that aren't based in fact. We can't do that It's not fair. We need to let Edwin make his presentation."

"And we will," Maddox said. "But tell me one thing, Dr. Bradshaw. If these things eat, what do you expect them to go after?"

Bradshaw cleared his throat. "I'd rather wait, General, for the full meeting."

"I'd rather you didn't," she said.

"I think we need to wait," Hayes said. "If any of this speculation is right, the president will need his deniability. We need the whole world to work together on this, and we really *don't* want to be in the forefront."

Maddox stared at Hayes for a moment. Then she looked at the others and sighed. As she exhaled, the stiffness left her back. She suddenly seemed years older. "I think you're right," she said, "and off the record, I did argue against this strategy myself. When I get back upstairs, I'll tell the powers that be that we need deniability. So, to use Dr. Cross's words, the national meeting before the international meeting won't ever happen again."

"Good," Cross said under his breath to Britt. She bowed her head to hide her smile.

"But," Maddox said, "just to satisfy a scientifically illiterate general's curiosity, Dr. Bradshaw, a general who really hates to delay gratification, what are those little machines coming here for?"

"Food," Bradshaw said.

"I understand that," Maddox said, "but what kind of food?"

"The last times the tenth planet passed us," Bradshaw said, "just about everything within those marked radiuses from those early charts, including *all* organic life, disappeared."

"Leaving the soot layer," the general said.

"Yes," Bradshaw said.

"So even people will go?"

"If they're there, yes," Bradshaw said.

"And if they aren't?"

"We'll still lose everything in the area," he said. "Imagine all those lush New England hills stripped bare and covered with a thin layer of black stuff."

"Oh, my god," Maddox said. Her skin had turned as gray as Bradshaw's was. Cross wondered why she hadn't realized this possibility existed before. "What can we do about this?"

"Let me present my material to the full group," Bradshaw said, "and let's hope like hell someone can prove me wrong."

April 9, 2018
14:17 Universal Time

4 Days Until Arrival

Downtime in zero g. Sometimes Zip wished these crafts had more room in their working compartments. She would love to organize a ballet. She'd had a mental picture of it ever since her first long mission: a crew, floating together, performing moves rather like those of Olympic synchronized swim teams. It would be fun and it would cut down on all the complaining the crew did when the mission got long.

She used hand rungs built into the wall to pull herself toward a portal. The tenth planet still wasn't visible—not that it would be anyway, the way that thing absorbed light—but she couldn't even see the blackness which blotted out the stars.

The ships were still two weeks away from the rendezvous. She could hardly wait. Sometimes it felt as if she were counting the minutes. She didn't say anything to her crew though. They needed to behave professionally, to feel as if this mission were business as usual, which it very definitely was not.

Man, oh, man she wanted to do that zero g ballet, though. Something unusual, something out of the ordinary. She was supposed to be resting; it was her downtime. But every time she closed her eyes, she felt that new planet looming in the distance. *Hurry up,* she wanted to tell it. *Hurry up.*

"Commander?" Rene's voice echoed through the shipwide intercom. "Sorry to bother you, but I am getting something weird here."

She pulled herself to the intercom and pushed the response button. "On my way," she said. Then she hand-climbed the ladder out of the deeper section of the shuttle and into the pilot area.

Rene was monitoring the readings. Serge was at the helm. Mariko was resting in her quarters deep within the ship. Vladi, the Russian member of her team, was running a check on the scientific equipment below. Zip wasn't sure where Percival, the Englishman, was.

Zip drifted in beside Rene, studying the image on the screen. It was the star field behind the location of the tenth planet. Rene had outlined in white for her the small, dime-sized image of the planet none of them could yet see.

"So tell me what's happening," Zip said.

With a quick motion, Rene outlined an area of the star field just to the right of the planet. "I am going to flash ten hours of

179

photos. One photo was taken every hour. Watch what happens to the stars inside my drawing."

The image flickered and she kept her attention focused on the circle Rene had drawn. Inside it the stars seemed to flicker on, then off, then on, then off.

Something was clearly getting between Luna One and those stars.

"Could that be the probe?" Zip asked. The unmanned probe was still out there, but the moment she asked the question, she knew that wasn't possible. It was far, far too small and too far ahead of them to cause such an effect.

Rene shook his head. "I do not think so. It is in the wrong position. I checked."

Zip stared at the circle. "Take some time-elapsed photos of that area. One every three minutes for the next half hour, and see what we get."

"They are going to blur slightly, those photographs, with the movement of the ship." Rene sounded concerned.

Zip smiled. "I know. We need the light more than the clarity at this point. Open up the field and increase the magnification too."

Rene nodded and went to work. Zip watched for a moment, then Rene glanced at her over his shoulder. The message was clear: *Leave me alone.*

She didn't want to, though. She let herself drift to the back of the command area. She grabbed the handrail beside one of the computers and hooked her foot in the catch so she wouldn't float away.

"Load the images over as you get them," she said to Rene, "and I'll work them."

Rene nodded.

Zip filled her screen with the almost white image of the stars behind the tenth planet. It was always startling to her how many stars were out there and how really big the universe was.

She studied the pictures. Rene had opened the field as she had asked and increased the magnification, so that now the tenth planet was a very black circle clearly outlined against the white of the time-elapsed star field. He had even managed to keep things fairly clear, considering what he was using for the time-lapse.

She cleaned up the image as best she could, then brought up the second and did the same. After four images she couldn't wait any longer. She overlaid the four pictures, creating an almost white background with a clear, black circle of the tenth planet.

"Oh, my god," she said. Clearly over the star field were small shadows, seemingly dozens of them, like small black dots in the white.

Rene moved over and glanced at her screen.

"What can cause those?" she asked, pointing to the small dark dots in the screen of white.

Rene gripped the handrail beside her. He looked very serious. In fact, he had looked serious from the moment he called her up to the command area. That wasn't normal for him. He should have found something to laugh about by now.

"I do not know what can cause those," he said. "Perhaps if you add in more pictures, they may vanish."

Zip did as Rene suggested. She cleaned up five more images and overlaid them on the others. Now the black dots were even clearer. And they were clearly moving. There was no doubt in her mind that something was ahead of them. Many somethings.

"Send these images to Mission Control," she said to Rene. "Wake up Mariko, and make sure the others are up here. I want everyone working on this. And keep doing what you're doing."

"All at once?" Rene said, in a feeble attempt at humor.

"All at once," Zip said.

He nodded, and returned to his own console. Zip floated forward and buckled herself into her command chair. Serge looked over at her.

"A problem?" he asked.

"We have some work to do," she said.

"All right." He continued to monitor the ship's passage, waiting for her instructions. She was focused on the computer screen in front of her. She was taking the image from the shuttle's main scope and magnifying it, focusing it down and down until finally she had the image of one of the dark dots filling her screen, only an outline of it against the backdrop of the stars.

"What is that?" Serge asked.

"Damned if I know," Zip said. "But there are a bunch of them between us and that planet."

Serge swore to himself in what sounded like Russian.

Zip punched a communications link. "Luna Two."

"Go ahead, Luna One," Ennis said.

"There're some *things* in front of us. I'm downloading the location to you now. Track them and let's see if we can get a fix on how far away they are."

"Understood."

For the next fifteen minutes every crew member aboard both ships worked to discover what was ahead of them, downloading the information to Mission Control. Zip didn't like the feeling she had in her stomach. It was a familiar one, one that suggested things weren't going as smoothly as she had hoped. Every time she asked Mission Control for an on-

182

the-ground update, they gave her an excuse. When she asked what the orbital scopes were reading, they said they didn't have anything yet.

That much she believed. In order to get the data from an orbiting scope, Mission Control had to triangulate with the data from the two ships. It would take time. And time was what she was afraid they didn't have.

Seemingly slow, but actually fairly fast, they learned more. They confirmed there were many objects in front of them, on a direct intercept course with the two shuttles. How many they didn't yet know. The objects were clearly moving at them at a high speed, faster than the shuttles were moving. At the speeds the objects were traveling, and the speed the two Luna shuttles were traveling, the objects and the two shuttles would pass each other in less than thirty minutes.

Those in the shuttle would not see the objects coming, or be able to see them after they passed, since the speeds were so great and the objects seemed to be black, reflecting no energy or light. The objects would actually be visible to the naked eye for less than a tenth of a second.

"Are they ships?" Percival asked.

"Possibly," Mariko said, her voice almost a whisper.

"Considering that they are flying a direct intercept orbit for Earth," Rene said, "it is more than likely. But what kind of ships? And what or who is flying them?"

Zip shuddered, remembering the last briefing with Dr. Cross. He had hoped they would find what the connection was between those soot layers on Earth and the tenth planet.

She had a hunch she knew.

But she didn't *really* know. She couldn't say exactly what the objects were, or why they were going to Earth. She just felt that the objects were ships, headed to Earth to cause mass destruction for some unknown reason. But belief was different from fact. She needed fact, and she doubted she had time to get it.

If only she had the ability to maneuver this ship, like the spaceships she'd seen in countless movies and on television. To fly a ship like an airplane, dodging in and out, going under or over, those objects coming at her. That would be wonderful.

But she couldn't. Space technology was still primitive, even by Earth standards, and she had only so much fuel. If she made a mistake, or a miscalculation at this point, she'd kill them all in a long, cold death in deep space, far beyond the solar system. She didn't have the time to have the shipboard computer do all the math it would take to reconfigure burn ratios and changes, and get that approved by Mission Control. There was no moving these Luna shuttles, at least not quickly.

Besides, this meeting was going to happen almost instantly, with no chance that either side could slow down to even try to talk.

The only hope she had was that those things would miss her ships. The computers said that none of the objects were on direct collision courses with the two shuttles. But that meant nothing as far as Zip was concerned. She didn't know if the objects had more maneuverability than she did, and could change to strike them.

Maybe they were just going to pass, like cars on a highway, never knowing the thoughts of the other.

Frantically, Zip and her crew worked to get all cameras ready and focused, working on orders from the computers as to direction and focus. Whatever these objects were, it was clear now that they were heading for Earth faster than the two Luna shuttles were heading for the tenth planet. Far, far faster.

Her crew worked as hard as it could, getting ready, trying to find out more about what was headed their way. But as the time passed she didn't learn much more than she had when the objects were discovered. They were simply black spots against the star fields.

She had always wanted a First Contact situation. She had dreamed what it might be like, being the first to meet another race. If those black shapes were actually ships, this kind of First Contact hadn't been in her dream.

Five minutes before the shuttles reached the objects, she made her crews strap in. That limited their work, and some complained, but she didn't answer them. She wanted her crew safe first. They had to get through this, and then go on to the planet itself.

If these were ships approaching, that mission to the tenth planet had just gotten a lot more dangerous. But they had no choice. There was no turning around.

"Commander," Mariko said in her delicate voice. "We approach them in twenty seconds."

"Stand by," Zip said, for Mission Control's benefit more than anything else.

The magnified images on the computer screen before her were of a dark, almost flat shape that reflected no light. They were also huge, with a span that would easily cover any football field. She double-checked. The images were being sent to Mission Control.

"They're like the black shadows of space," she said softly to Rene.

He nodded.

"Ten seconds," Mariko said.

"Systems functioning normally," Percival said.

Given the rather strange conditions, Zip thought.

"Five seconds."

185

Zip felt her fingers grip the edge of her chair. She just hoped those back on the surface were enjoying the show. She wasn't sure if she was. She'd analyze how she felt later.

"Three seconds," Mariko said.

Vladi sighed behind Zip, and in that sound, Zip thought she heard fear.

"Two."

Serge straightened his back, as if his posture would help him in the next few moments.

"One."

The lights seemed to dim.

"Now!"

Zip didn't know what she expected to happen. Perhaps she had expected to die instantly. Or perhaps she thought she was going to be hailed, like commanders were in all those late-twentieth-century movies.

But she wasn't expecting the loss of light.

And the immense and sudden tiredness.

The lights went out, and the computer screen faded to a tiny dot, then went black. The normal humming and clicking sounds, the faint reminders of electronics, disappeared.

It felt as if every ounce of energy had been sucked from every part of the ship.

And Zip had never, in all her life, felt so totally exhausted, as if massive amounts of her own energy had also been somehow drained.

"Merde," Rene whispered beside her. He sounded weak.

Zip took a deep breath and forced down the instant panic of being plunged into total darkness, the only light coming through the portholes from the stars, since the sun was behind and below them.

"I want a verbal roll call," she said. "Name and condition."

"Mariko. Fine but tired."

"Rene. Tired too."

"Serge. Yeah, tired."

"Percival. Bloody fucking exhausted."

"Vladi. Very tired."

There was no response from Luna Two, and Zip really didn't expect one. The radio was dead as well.

Zip was exhausted too, but she wouldn't tell them that. Let them think she was strong. It helped to have something to believe in.

First things first. She had to take care of them, then the ship, then the mission.

"Can we get environment controls up?" she asked.

"Nothing doing, Commander," Percival said. "Even the torch batteries are drained."

"The flashlights are dead?"

"Yes, ma'am." Percival sounded a bit more energetic than the rest, but he had also been the farthest away. Or was he displaying classic British reserve?

"Are you getting that too, Mariko?"

"Yes," Mariko said, even more softly than before. "So sorry."

Zip's eyes were beginning to adjust slightly in the faint light. She fought down the overwhelming desire to fall asleep and made herself think. They were totally cut off from Earth, drifting through deep space toward an unknown planet. Something in the passing ships had drained all their power almost instantly. There had to be a way to get some of it back.

"Does anyone have any piece of equipment, no matter how small, working in their area?"

Together her crew murmured nos.

"Can anyone see Luna Two?"

"They are dead too," Serge said, looking out the porthole at the ship floating a distance beside them.

The word *dead* echoed through the shuttle. She could already sense the intense cold around them. The warmth of the sun was behind them, shielded, with no way for them to turn the shuttle. Her breath would soon begin forming mist in the air. With all the electronics on board, the shuttles had passive systems that bled off the normal heat from the electronics into space.

That heat-bleeding system took no power to work.

Now, slowly, the heat of their shuttle would bleed away, like a bad wound on a body. They would freeze to death long before the air in the cabin became bad. She couldn't remember the exact timetable, but she knew their lives were measured in hours if they didn't get the power going.

"Okay, people," she said, putting as much energy in her voice as she could. "We need to figure out a way to get some heat going. Any power at all. Report if you have any luck."

She forced herself not to think about the coming cold, the complete exhaustion, but to focus on the task. But the more she thought, the more she realized there was nothing she or anyone could do. Nothing.

Everyone worked in silence for what she guessed was a long ten, maybe fifteen minutes. Finally she called roll, asking for details of what they had tried.

Nothing had worked, from any of them. The craft was completely dead of all power. Impossible, but true.

And the cold was becoming a real thing around her, the air chilled noticeably.

"Keep working, people. There's got to be a way."

Two hours later, more tired than she had ever remembered being, she finally forced herself to stop. Ice was forming on much of the surfaces around her, and no one had managed to even come up with an idea that might work. The idea of trying to go outside and turn the capsule, or rig up some solar panels, was exciting for a short moment, then rejected when it was discovered that even the independent systems of the space suits were drained of power.

"Maybe we should huddle together, for heat," she said.

"I cannot free my shoulder harness," Percival said.

"Mine is frozen shut," Vladi said.

"Mine too." Rene sounded as if he were speaking through mud.

They couldn't even touch each other for warmth. Not that it would matter soon. No matter how determined she was, she couldn't fight the cold.

There was nothing as cold as emptiness.

Outside the Luna shuttle wasn't actually cold, simply the absence of heat, with the heat inside the shuttle draining away.

In front of her in the faint light was a panel of dead instruments, as useless without power as a cement wall. The shuttles hadn't been set up for solar power, but ran almost completely on batteries, with dozens of backups. But every battery had been drained as the objects passed, leaving every instrument dead.

She had no idea how those objects that passed them could have done that, but they did. And for just a moment she wondered what would happen on Earth when those objects arrived there. But she knew she would never know the answer to that question. She forced that thought away.

Not important.

She blew on her hands, but her breath formed ice crystals on her fingers.

The air hurt as it went into her lungs. What had she been taught? That the cilia in her lungs, moist with her breath, would freeze and she would be unable to breathe properly. Not that it mattered. By then she would be unconscious.

Death by freezing was the kindest death there was: sinking, slowly, into a deep, endless, uncontrollable sleep.

But she didn't want to die.

She didn't want to sleep.

She had to find a way out of this. She'd found ways out of tight spots before.

She couldn't hear the others. No one else seemed to be moving, speaking, *trying*.

But she had to try.

She would get them started again.

This would be a temporary thing.

She tried to unbuckle her lap belt, to get out of the chair, to move around, but her fingers had stopped working it seemed.

Her breathing had become shallow, the air thick. Did air freeze? She couldn't remember.

Slowly, she turned her face toward the half-frosted porthole. She could see stars.

Without a crew and power to make corrective burns, the two shuttles would miss the tenth planet and head on out into deep space. More than likely, they even had enough forward momentum to escape the pull of the sun. If that was so, they would drift forever among the stars.

There was nothing she could do to change that now.

She felt the lethargy in her body grow. But she wouldn't sleep. She had vowed she would never die in her sleep.

She forced her eyes to stay open until the end, staring out at the distant stars.

She so loved the stars.

DEFENSE

10

April 12, 2018
8:56 A.M. Eastern Standard Time

1 Day Until Arrival

Cross looked at the plate of scrambled eggs, bacon, and hash browns that Constance set before him. The eggs were steaming, the bacon was crisp, and the hash browns looked lightly grilled, just as he liked them. The coffee was hot and smelled heavenly, and the orange juice was freshly squeezed.

He wondered how he could get through the breakfast.

He had to eat something. Before Constance had left the day before, she had asked him how she could help him get through this rough period in his life.

"Make sure I eat," he had said to her.

And this morning, true to his wishes, she had given him a good, old-fashioned breakfast.

He didn't have the heart to tell her that it turned his stomach.

Everything did. And the single daylong heartburn pill he took—the strongest you could get without a prescription, according to the ads—wasn't strong enough. His stress levels had risen so high he was jittery.

He picked up the *Washington Post*, reluctant to see what its headlines would be this morning. He had stopped listening to the radio and he couldn't watch television. The repeated footage of the Luna shuttles, their cameras going dark, would haunt him for the rest of his life. He even shut down the instant news feed on his main computer, and he stopped having his wrist computer beep him whenever there was a major news story.

Maybe he was hiding, like Bradshaw had suggested, rather tentatively the night before, or maybe he was protecting himself.

Or maybe he was learning what life was really like for people like Mickelson, who made life and death decisions every day. Cross had never done that before. Zip Juarez and her team were in space at his instigation. He hadn't sent them, but he had started the wheels in motion to get them there.

Maybe he should have argued harder when the Tenth Planet Project started pushing for a manned space flight. Maybe he should have listened to Robert Shane, and then pushed for the robotic probes.

Maybe.

Maybe.

Maybe.

"Your eggs are getting cold," Constance said gently. "Do you want something else?"

She knew how upset he was, and still she was trying to help him. She was a good woman and he was a bad boss, never really giving her the time of day, forgetting, sometimes, to say hello in the mornings, or to ask after her family.

God, the guilt he was feeling over the shuttle mission was spilling into everything.

"No," he said. "The eggs are fine."

And as if to prove it, he took a forkful and ate them. They were delicious. He hadn't tasted anything that good in a long time. Maybe his stomach was upset because he hadn't eaten. How strange.

He took another bite, and then another, and then drank some orange juice, which tasted heavenly. He kept the *Post* turned down, so he wouldn't have to see it until he was done eating, so that he could continue enjoying the meal.

He knew what it would say anyway. It would regurgitate yesterday's headlines and then it would analyze them. Newspapers had become the home of the analysis story, the in-depth story that the headlines the day before couldn't cover properly.

Yesterday's headlines had been about the last images Luna One had sent before its cameras went dark. The tabloid broadcasts were talking about aliens. They showed the strange little craft, and then enlarged it so that it was little more than a dark-shaped blur.

Aliens was the buzzword all day. Even the staid network newscasts had used it.

Cross had spent the day before in an angry huff. Someone had leaked the image. He had people searching for the source of the leak. He was afraid it had come from the Tenth Planet Project staff themselves, but that was finally discounted. Britt said that most likely the leak had come from NASA, where the images had been processed. She was double-checking that now.

Whoever had leaked the information had done them no favors. The entire world was in an uproar. They were frightened that little green men would come out of tiny ships and zap the entire planet. The Sci-Fi Channel had announced a change in its programming: It was running all the alien invasion movies from the decades-old *Them!* to last year's extravaganza *Rendezvous with Rama*.

Cross was very glad he had not attached his name to the tenth planet announcement. If he had, the archaeologists that he had contacted all over the world would have put together the tenth planet, the death of the Luna shuttles, and the soot lines. And then the hysteria would have been even worse.

Cross was amazed no one had leaked that information. Amazed and grateful.

Bradshaw was a bit worried about the girl he had contacted at NanTech. He was afraid that she might put the pieces together and contact the press. So he was talking to her at this moment.

He had planned to talk to her a bit later in the project, to get a bit more information, but now he was going to bring her into the secret meetings, if she wanted to join. If she didn't, he would have her sign some paper that the science advisers had drawn up, ensuring that she keep all the information confidential. She was supposed to have called half an hour ago to report on her response. She hadn't called yet, and that too made Cross nervous.

Everything was making him nervous. He hadn't slept well since the shuttles lost power. He hadn't realized how people died in those sorts of circumstances. At the meeting of the Tenth Planet Project, Shane told them all what the crew would have experienced. Deep intense cold at temperatures unfathomable for normal humans. Cold that killed over a number of hours, long before the oxygen would run out. He did say that freezing was an easy death. They had simply gone to sleep. But Cross couldn't imagine those last few hours, knowing they were doomed, trapped in the dark in space.

196

The vibrant woman Cross had met, the woman who had held out a callused hand and winked at him as she said "I'm Zip," was now dead, a body frozen in a coffin that would drift until the end of time.

He would see her face for the rest of his life. He saw it now, whenever he closed his eyes. He saw it, and he would wake, apologizing to a woman who would never ever be able to hear him.

"Are you all right?" Constance asked.

Cross nodded. He pushed his plate away—he had eaten most of the food, except the toast—and he felt somewhat better. Mickelson had called last night to see how he was holding up, and Cross had explained his guilt over the deaths.

"It's something you don't get over," Mickelson had said. "So just keep going forward. If you don't, there'll be a lot more deaths. That's what you have to think about."

Good words. Words that Cross had to put into practice. He had to learn, quickly, how to be a man who constantly moved forward. He did no one any good in the condition he was in.

With that in mind, he snapped open the morning's *Post*, expecting to see the same damn pictures he'd been seeing for the last two days. Instead, the headline read WORLD LEADERS ADVISE ALL: REMAIN CALM.

The body of the article talked about how all the problems were suppositions, how the shuttles weren't designed for the kind of use they had gone through, and could have experienced an identical malfunction, and how the images could have been spots on the cameras.

It was all bullshit; Cross had been at the meeting where some of the words he read had been invented. But it was necessary bullshit, and he hoped it would have the desired effect.

Of course, not all people were remaining calm. The inside

197

pages had story after story of riots in some city streets, of people who were calling psychic hotlines, of groups getting together to meet the aliens. The business section had several articles about the effect of the images on the world's financial markets.

Cross hoped the world leaders could keep some sort of order. The last thing they needed right now was worldwide panic.

He set the paper down just as his personal phone rang. He hit a button on his watch so that the call transferred to the larger phone in the corner of the kitchen. Then he picked it up.

"Yes?" he said.

Constance moved beside him, taking his plate, but leaving his coffee.

"Portia will join the meeting at eleven," Bradshaw said. "I'm going to stay here and help her put together a quick presentation to make all this clear."

"Good work," Cross said. "Thanks."

"You're welcome," Bradshaw said and cut the connection.

Cross leaned his head against the cool kitchen wall. Bradshaw got the girl to help. The more minds working on whatever was coming at them the better. The Tenth Planet Project's daily meetings hadn't accomplished much. All this work, all these years, and now, suddenly, he had a deadline that he didn't understand, and he had to find a way to prevent something he wasn't even sure was going to happen.

Move forward.

He would.

He had to.

April 12, 2018
20:49 Universal Time

1 Day Until Arrival

General Garai stood on the balance circle in his private area on the sixth level of the first ship of the Southern Fleet. He had ordered the doors closed. His private area was dark and cool as most areas on the ship were. Only the tenth level, the command level, was allowed more comforts.

He wore two warming robes, one over the other, and had all but five of his tentacles hidden between them for warmth. His race's bodies were not evolved to live in such cold. His planet had circled close to its own sun. But that was a long time ago. He must not think of it now.

All ten of his eyes were out of their pockets. He had to see the colors on his screens clearly and that was difficult in this dim light. The sphere represented the third planet, and black areas were the areas with populations of the intelligent bipeds that had started giving the Malmuria trouble soon after they had first came to the third planet.

The creatures had a short-term memory. The Malmuria discovered that early on—if they stayed too long, the creatures cleared what they could from a feeding area to stop the harvest. But the creatures had no long-term memory. The Malmuria had expected a fight on their second visit after first encountering the creatures, and the creatures had acted as if they had never seen Malmuria before. Apparently the length of the orbit was longer than the historical record the creatures kept.

Not that that solved his current problem. The second sphere contained the projection his harvesters had given him. During the approach to the planet the harvesters had studied, as they always did, the areas of highest yields on each land mass. Some of the areas, due to the time of the planet's rotation around the sun, were covered in ice, or had little growth. But it was still a very rich planet and each fleet would harvest one area of the surface. He was in charge of picking the areas, and it wasn't as easy as it had been in the past.

The projection in front of him now showed the highest yield areas. He had seven to choose from, not as many as last Pass. A few of the areas were the same ones harvested last time. Usually he did not like to harvest the same area of the planet two Passes in a row, but this time he would have no choice. The creatures who had spread out over the surface of the planet had destroyed many fertile areas.

At first he had thought that to be a fatal problem. Then he had calmed himself and looked again.

Using two tentacles, he combined a blue, white, green, and black sphere with the yield sphere. They created a single sphere, showing the richest yield areas and the high habitation areas. He studied it for a moment, and realized that the situation was not as dire as he had thought. There was still plenty of space with low population densities or no real population at all. The deaths of the sentient bipeds would be minimal.

He picked three areas, all the same size, all equally as rich in growth, and all with minimal populations. Then he put the Southern mark on one, the Central mark on another, and the Northern mark on a third.

Then he opened the doors, and left the single sphere floating. His chief harvester came in, balanced on his tentacles, but Garai did not look at him. That was not protocol. The harvester knew what to do. He would take the sphere and send the information to the other two fleets.

They would not acknowledge the receipt of the information, but their ships would immediately turn slightly to show that they now had a destination.

Garai went into the pod and wrapped two tentacles around the center pole, a signal that he needed to be taken to the tenth level. Only certain Malmuria were allowed on that level, and the pole would not let him rise if his tentacles did not fit properly into the designed slots.

Slowly he rose and as he did, he felt the chill area around him grow slightly warmer. Sometimes he wondered what it was like to have a contained life on a single place, a place where food grew and where water was plentiful, where warmth was something that was taken for granted.

His people had that once, long before he was born. They did no longer. It was too bad the third planet's atmosphere was poison to them, or they could have returned to the warmth. But that was not to be. Ever.

Sometimes he wondered how he could miss something he had never had. And would never get.

April 13, 2018
12:23 P.M. Brazilian Andes Standard Time

Arrival

When viewed from above the trees of the rain forest, the cruise ship *Aventuras del Brasil (Brazilian Adventures)* looked like a branch that was floating on top of the water. The ship's sleek design was a marvel of modern engineering and of modern economics: more passengers could fit, less space was wasted on equipment, and there were a large number of viewing decks all over the ship.

Aventuras del Brasil was full, stem to stern, on this trip, but only a handful of people stood on her decks. The heat, even in April, was intense, and passengers usually sat in the air-conditioned cabins, watching the scenery through the windows.

But not Archibald Spencer. Archie had spent a small fortune for this trip, as he spent for every trip his wife scheduled, and he was determined to squeeze every farthing from the experience.

He rubbed the sweat off his neck and leaned against the metal railing. Bugs swarmed around him, and he wondered if he shouldn't apply more bug repellent. The guidebooks said that the shots he had received should take care of any exotic diseases, but he didn't quite believe it. He had never been in a place where there had been so many bugs.

He stared at the smooth brown waters of the Amazon. The cruise ship was going relatively slow—he'd missed the announced reason why, probably some rare plant the size of a pencil that the bevy of old spinsters on the top deck could see with their computerized binoculars. They would shout gleefully when they found it, and he would squint, pretending he could see. He hadn't brought any binocs, computerized or otherwise, and they cost over £50 in the ship's supply store. He wasn't going to spend double on something that he could get at home, no matter what Penelope said.

And she had a lot to say. She thought this the trip of a lifetime. She spent much of her day indoors, in the air-conditioning, playing bridge with an American threesome who were a bit too loud for Archie's taste. When the ship docked, as it did way too often, she lathered him up with more repellent and dragged him into the wilds. The last time it was to see fire damage. The time before, he was in some sort of swamp. He didn't understand why they couldn't take a cruise somewhere cool—he'd heard that the Norway trips were gorgeous, and he'd always wanted to see Canada and Alaska—but the wife planned the vacations, and she did so with her interests in mind. His counted for nothing. When he complained, she said that he needed to broaden his horizons and open his mind.

Privately, he thought that he wasn't the one who was closed. But a man didn't say that, especially to a woman like Penny.

He turned slightly and froze. Dark shadows had swept down the river from the north, suddenly making the bright day almost seem as if it were night. Archie had never seen anything like that, and he didn't remember reading about it in the brochures. Surely they would say if the Amazon had dark patches, or sudden storms.

But this didn't look like a storm. This looked like holes in the sky, dark holes, like something he would see in a movie. The blackness came toward the ship, and he looked up, unable to comprehend what he was seeing.

The sky seemed to be filled with huge, black shapes, all hovering above the river and the jungles beyond. He could see blue sky between the shapes, but the shapes themselves seemed to have no distinct characteristics besides their blackness.

His heart was pounding hard. He heard the old ladies up top exclaim in awe and shock. A woman's voice rose as she called for a cruise ship official.

As if they could do anything about it.

Maybe they were used to this. Maybe they knew what to do. Surely they would move the ship out of the way or move it against the river's edge or find a spot to anchor until these shapes had passed.

Surely.

The day became blacker and blacker.

Archie stood, shocked, watching upward until finally he realized what he was seeing. The shapes had dropped a mist-like, black cloud that was descending on everything.

"Bloody hell," he shouted as he ran for the first-class entrance. He could see Penny inside, looking up at the sound of his voice, looking startled, setting her cards down. But he couldn't get to her.

The cloud covered him, black particles choking him, filling his eyes and mouth and lungs, covering his skin. Around him the black mist swirled with his every motion.

He staggered toward the door. Penny had gotten up but that bloody American was holding her back, looking frightened. Archie reached toward the door, feeling the black dust on his skin. He couldn't think about it. He needed to get help.

And then the pain started, like needles at first, and then growing and growing. He lost the power to move, although he tried. He tried to ignore the whole thing, to keep going, but he couldn't. Surely someone would come out and help him.

Surely . . .

The pain intensified and he lost all rational thought. He swiped at the black dust to get it off, and then he screamed as his skin seemed to vanish off his body.

Every nerve in his body felt like it was on fire.

Blood poured out of his skin onto the deck, only to be covered with the black dust.

The black cloud continued to float down, covering everything as Archie wriggled in agony on the deck, then slowly stopped moving.

The old ladies on the upper deck were dead too, and the crowd inside wasn't enjoying the air-conditioning anymore. It had shut off as the creatures had gone through it. More creatures covered the windows, and the wood, working their way inside.

People screamed. Some ran. But no one escaped. They were quickly all covered in black dust.

And they all died the way Archie had.

Soon the bodies were gone, eaten completely by the black dust. The wood on the ship was eaten through a short time later, and the ship sank. All that remained was the steel skeleton in the mud on the bottom of the river.

And for a hundred miles to the north and south of the wreck of the *Aventuras del Brasil,* every living thing in the Amazon rain forest was leveled, reduced to black dust on the ground and floating in the river and streams.

11

April 13, 2018
11:36 A.M. Eastern Standard Time

Arrival

General Clarissa Maddox stood, hands clasped behind her back, as she stared at the screens around her. Somehow she had known this moment would come. She just didn't know what to tell the others.

They were in the military briefing room in one of the tunnels below the White House. On the screens to her left, the news stations from all over the world chattered in various languages about the darkness. The Net broadcasts were on the next set of screens, and below those, several junior military officers monitored written Web news reports.

In front of her, several large screens showed continuous live shots from the secret military satellites in orbit around Earth. Live images from spy planes and, in some cases, outdated radar showed on various other screens.

None of the images looked good.

Thirteen minutes earlier, the 101 objects that had left the tenth planet, and that her secret Tenth Planet Project had been monitoring, had arrived in Earth orbit. They had then split into three groups and descended over different areas of the planet, circling at a height of four thousand feet.

That simple maneuver alone made it clear that the tenth planet had released ships. Spaceships with intelligent life behind them. And now that intelligent life had dropped a large, black cloud of god knows what from every ship. The black cloud destroyed everything it covered, and while the clouds were doing their awful work, the ships retreated into space. Now they simply hovered in low orbit over the areas they had attacked.

Maddox had been finishing a debriefing when the attack started. She had hurried to this room, as had the other four members of the Joint Chiefs of Staff. Several of the science advisers were here as well.

The room was completely silent.

Everything they had been taught was wrong.

Maddox supposed she was in a better position than most. She had been working on this project for months now. But she had been reporting directly to the president, not to the other members of the Joint Chiefs. Not even Jamal Harrington, the chairman, knew what she had been doing, only that it was something ordered by the president.

And now it was too late to brief him.

General Harrington was standing beside her, his position identical to hers, hands behind his back, feet spread slightly, his mouth open just enough to register his shock. Beside him, Admiral Kilyra and General Tucker had similar reactions.

The Joint Chiefs often ran war scenarios, but they had never run a scenario like this one: not one with an enemy from space, and not one that involved a technology no one understood.

Maddox should have spoken up sooner. She should have said that this was a possibility so that some scenarios could be run, so that someone could have seen if anything could be modified for alien attack from space.

But she hadn't said a word.

She had been too afraid of getting laughed at. Aliens from outer space. If she hadn't seen it herself, she wouldn't have believed it.

She would never have believed it.

"If these attacks weren't so orchestrated," Harrington said, his voice slightly shaky, "I would think they were random. What could these things possibly want in those regions? Don't they understand that our weapons are in populated areas? If they wanted to take out our power structure, this isn't the way to do it."

Maddox had been thinking the same thing. The aliens had dropped the clouds over a section of the upper Amazon, a section of Central Africa, and the large rain forests of Central America. The areas were all untamed and had no military value that she knew about.

"Are there secret installations in any of those places? Things perhaps put there by the countries under attack?" Admiral Kilyra asked, but there was no real force behind the question. If there were such installations, these five people should know about them. The Joint Chiefs were the heads of all the branches of the U.S. military. Military intelligence reported to them.

No one answered him.

"General Harrington," said one of the officers assigned to the room. "We have a secured line with the president."

"Clear the room," Harrington snapped.

The officials and monitors, all junior military staff from the various branches, quickly filed out. They knew better than to remain at a moment like this.

Harrington touched a button on the computer before him,

and all the network anchors winked out. Fifteen copies of the president's face filled the screens. Each screen showed the same thing: a tired, puffy-eyed man who had aged ten years in the two he had been in office. Maddox would have bet that the president looked younger as recently as two days before.

The Joint Chiefs had been waiting for this moment. The president had been in a conference with world leaders as to what to do about the aliens and the panic that was sweeping some areas. The president wanted a concerted worldwide effort, with all countries agreeing on the same thing. He had been worried that some countries would want a peaceful solution.

But he needn't have worried. The meeting had only taken ten minutes—the shortest worldwide summit in history. Maddox knew what the president was going to say before he said it.

They were going to fight back.

Still, she stood at attention and listened as Harrington and the president spoke.

"We have decided on a worldwide effort to get rid of those things," the president said. "You are authorized to use all means necessary, except nuclear, to stop those ships from coming into the atmosphere again."

"Yes, sir," Harrington said. "But, sir, some of our most effective equipment—"

"The agreement was no nuclear weapons. They'll do too much damage to us as well as those ships. We're not going there." The president's dark eyes narrowed. "At least not yet."

"Yes, sir."

"Coordinate your efforts with Europe and Asia when possible. The Central American countries are already launching what weapons they have. We've got teams trying to contact the aliens, and another team that is studying possible alien visits to this planet before. But for now, do what you can."

"Yes, sir," Harrington said.

"Good luck." And with that the president broke the connection. The network anchors reappeared and their speech, in all the various languages, sounded like babble. Harrington muted them.

Maddox's heart was pounding. No nuclear. That would make things more difficult, although she understood the rationale for it. There hadn't been any authorized nuclear weapons tests in the atmosphere in twenty years, not since India—or was it Pakistan?—performed some tests to show their military might. No one knew what a concentrated force of those things would do to Earth anymore. And no one really wanted to find out.

Harrington pushed another area on the computer before him. Maddox looked over his shoulder. He was looking at their capability of striking at a fleet of ships in low orbit without using the old land- and submarine-based nuclear-tipped intercontinental rockets. Maddox knew what he would find: damn little.

Fighting an alien fleet in orbit around the planet had just never been a scenario the Pentagon had taken seriously, let alone alien ships parked in orbit over Africa, South, and Central Americas.

Maddox looked up at the still photos of the alien ships that had been sent less than fifteen minutes ago, when the things were hovering close to land. They were black shapes, barely discernible against the light of the sun. No openings, no windows, nothing sticking out of their dull blackness.

She shuddered. She had been taught by the best in the art of war. Yet in all her years, the world had been small enough and the U.S. military powerful enough, that she had never had the problem of being able to see the enemy and not reach them. She had never even envisioned it.

Until this moment.

210

April 13, 2018
3:10 P.M. Eastern Standard Time

Arrival

Britt Archer came up behind Cross and put a reassuring hand on his shoulder. They hadn't had any time to talk since the events of that morning, and they certainly couldn't talk here, at the meeting room for the Tenth Planet Project. But he appreciated the simple touch, and the warmth it conveyed. He wished he had met her under other circumstances, wished too that he had time now to build a life with her.

He wasn't sure any of them would have a life to build. He had a hunch that their problems were only beginning.

He let himself into the meeting room and saw Robert Shane talking with Bradshaw and Portia Groopman. Groopman was a tiny thing with a cap of dark hair that made her look dainty. When she met Cross her mood had been a mixture of who-cares-about-the-adults and curiosity. He could see the intelligence in her eyes, and also a frustration in them. Everyone saw her as a nanotechnology genius who had risen above her past. No one saw her as a twenty-year-old who couldn't drink legally and who shouldn't even be out of college yet.

And she certainly shouldn't be here, explaining to scientists one of the ways the world might end.

Everyone was here except Clarissa Maddox. Cross wasn't sure she'd show at all. He'd heard, through the Project grapevine, that the world powers were trying to make some sort of concentrated response to the attack.

He just wasn't sure what kind of response they'd make.

The lights blinked on the satellite uplinks, which, he had learned, meant that they were ready to be flashed on as soon

211

as this meeting convened. But who would convene the meeting if Maddox didn't show?

Britt took her place beside Cross. She covered his hand with her own, seemingly uncaring about what the others thought. He put his free hand on top of hers.

She had an idea of what he'd been going through the last few days. He suspected she'd been going through the same thing. But ever since those clouds had landed on Central America, all the doubt he'd been feeling was gone.

He remembered Mickelson's words: *If you don't move forward, you'll lose a lot more lives.*

Mickelson was right.

The images coming through the televisions were horrendous. Most showed the destruction at a merciful distance, film taken from video cameras that didn't have the capacity to see details. But one shot, taken with a long-distance wide-angle lens, was being replayed all over the world. Cross had seen it dozens of times already. It was of a woman in Africa caught at the edge of the black cloud, her skin dissolving, disappearing, blood flowing everywhere.

He squeezed Britt's hand and then let go. She smiled at him, but her smile was distant, sad, as if she too were thinking about the imagery, thinking about the death.

He was about to start the meeting himself when Clarissa Maddox came in. She wore full uniform and her hair was pulled back so tightly it looked as if it tugged her skin.

"Sorry to be late," she said. "I am supposed to be conducting a secondary briefing of my troops, but I thought this more important. I only have a few moments before I need to be back at the White House. So let's get this meeting under way and over with. Are the satellite links still operating?"

"Yes," Yolanda Hayes said. She had seemed subdued since she came into the building.

212

"Excellent," Maddox said. "I understand that there's been concern that these ships would take out our satellites and the space station. This has not happened so far."

"Their interest seems to be Earth," Killius said. She was shuffling a few papers before her. The calls to NASA, Cross had overheard her say, had been incredible since those ships appeared. People seemed to believe NASA would have all the answers. Killius looked exhausted and rather frightened. No one had any answers.

"One of our missions will have to be to protect our equipment," Maddox said, more to herself than to anyone else. "We lose that, we lose our ability to communicate on a worldwide level, and we really will be in chaos."

Cross shuddered. Britt looked at him as if she had felt that shudder too.

"It's her job," Britt whispered. "She needs to worry about defense."

He nodded as the satellite links came on. The familiar faces of the international members of the Tenth Planet Project appeared on the split screen.

Maddox explained again her short time limit. Then she turned to Bradshaw. "I understand you think these things are the machines you found in the soot layers."

"I don't think so," Bradshaw said. "I know it." He glanced at Groopman. She swallowed nervously.

Cross could see the movement in her neck from across the table. Poor kid. She was in farther over her head than he was.

"This is Portia Groopman," Bradshaw said. "She is probably the worldwide expert on nanotechnology. She currently works with NanTech, but on this project she's all ours. She's been studying the fossils we found of these things. Portia?"

She stood, like a child about to give a presentation in class. She kept two fingers from each hand braced on the tabletop and looked at Maddox, then at the screens, as if she wasn't sure whom to talk to. Cross wanted to tell her to speak to the group, but he was afraid he would destroy her already shaky confidence.

"The 'things' as Dr. Bradshaw calls them are nanomachines." Groopman's voice sounded tiny and wavery, not at all the voice of an expert. She cleared her throat as if that were the problem. "They're doing exactly what I thought they'd do, only they're much more efficient. They seem to eat almost all matter, and the soot, as Dr. Bradshaw calls it, is a by-product of the materials they can't use."

"We understand that," Maddox said. "I want to know how much damage they've done."

Groopman flushed and looked at Bradshaw. Neither of them were prepared for this.

"I'll take care of that question in a minute, General," Cross said. "Let's let Ms. Groopman finish, and then I'll address the upcoming problems."

"Don't tell me there are more problems, Dr. Cross," Maddox said. "We have plenty as it is."

"I know that, General, but—"

She held up her hand so that he would stop speaking and turned to Groopman. "What else can you tell us about these machines?"

Groopman glanced at Bradshaw. He nodded to her. "I could show you schematics," she said, "but you said you wanted to know quick. So—" She took a deep breath and went on. "I've been making a study of these things. They have only one purpose. They eat. They combine the raw parts down into a substance—probably a form of molecular paste—that they can store. And then they shut off."

"That's it?" Maddox asked.

"Yes."

"How do they get back to the ships?" Britt asked.

"They don't," Groopman said. "They're a simple design."

"Then what's the point of them?" Killius asked. "Why gather materials if you can't use them."

"The ships will have to come back for them," Groopman said. "It's the only explanation."

Maddox let out a small grunt. Some of the international scientists asked Groopman a few questions, but Cross didn't pay any attention. He was watching Maddox. Her brain was working hard. Did she think they could attack those ships inside the atmosphere?

Cross waited for a pause in the conversation before he said, "I too think those ships'll come back."

"And what do you base this on, Dr. Cross?" Maddox asked.

"I think Ms. Groopman's analysis is excellent," Cross said. "I also think there's a step she's leaving out."

Groopman frowned at him like he was another student stepping on her presentation.

"I think," he said, "that the ships pick up those machines, take the paste or whatever the nutrients become, from the storage, and then send the machines down again."

"I hope this is idle speculation, Doctor," Maddox said.

Cross shook his head. He stood. Groopman remained on her feet for a moment, then Bradshaw tugged at her arm. She sat.

Cross went to the computer where he pulled up a screen. It showed the devastation that had occurred so far. Part of the upper Amazon was covered in black, as was a large area of the Central American rain forest, and a big section of Central Africa. Cross stared at Central Africa. He had been wrong when he had said that there weren't a lot of people in these areas. Millions must have died already in Africa alone.

"That's what's going on now," he said.

"We know." Maddox's voice sounded gruff, almost brusque. Cross was finally beginning to understand the military mind. They weren't brusque because they were unfeeling; they were brusque because they didn't want to lose their intellectual focus when faced with overwhelming emotional facts.

Cross hit a button on the keyboard, and a large gray area covered various places on the map. "This," he said, "is the devastation from the last time the tenth planet came near us."

There were gasps all over the room. He didn't need to say more. Everyone could see it. The tenth planet's destruction the last time was four times greater than it currently was.

"You think this means they'll come back?" Maddox asked.

"When you put this map together with Ms. Groopman's discoveries about the nanomachines, yes, I do."

"Four times," Shane whispered. "If they were to hit a population center—"

"It's already bad," said one of the international members. Cross didn't look to see which one.

"And it's going to get a lot worse," Britt said.

"What else do we have?" Maddox asked.

Her request for information was met with silence.

"Do we know what propels those ships? What kind of creatures we're dealing with?"

Silence.

"Why the hell can't we see what these things look like?" On this last, her voice rose slightly.

Silence.

"Damnation," she said. "Get working on this, people. I need answers. We all need answers and solutions and we're out of time. I don't want more meetings. I want information, and ways to keep these things from ripping up our planet more times." She stood. "Dismissed."

216

She turned and left the room almost at a run. The information was probably enough for her to continue the military planning.

Cross was still standing. "I don't think we have time for good science," he said to the entire group. "We can't postulate, experiment, and then double-check. We need theories, we need creativity, and we need solutions."

"And General Maddox is right," Britt said. "We need it all now."

No one spoke for another moment, and then, as a unit, they started dividing up tasks.

It didn't reassure Cross, but at least he was moving forward. And right now, that was the best he could do.

His best had better be pretty damn good. He glanced at the difference in the black area and the huge gray areas attacked last pass. Millions and millions of people were going to die very quickly if they didn't stop this. And stop it soon.

April 14, 2018
4:51 Universal Time

Arrival: Day Two

Supreme General Garai settled into his balance circle on the tenth level of the first ship of the Southern Fleet. He had watched, over the last few hours, as all the fleets, Southern, Central, and Northern, released their Sulas and then retreated to low orbit. Both the Central and Northern commanders had broken protocol to request permission to use the energy fields on the strange metal objects floating in orbit with them.

Garai had denied the requests. His orders were firm: get

supplies, and get supplies only. The objects seemed to have no function that his staff could discern. They were not weapons. They were little more than reflectors and toys sent into space. The creatures below were so primitive that they did not understand, apparently, that things sent aloft should have a purpose.

Not that he should worry about them. He had done what he could in attempting to avoid them. In fact, he had tried harder on this Pass than on any other, simply because there were so many of them now.

But as his Command Second had pointed out, the fact that there were so many of them meant that the lost ones wouldn't be missed. Garai hadn't even thought of them being missed until the Second had mentioned that. Garai's worry was an old one; a memory of carelessness by the Fifth Commander of the North who had forgotten that the creatures had the ability to recall things that happened on short notice. His Sulas had been attacked with flame and burning sticks and it had created a short, messy diversion that had destroyed much of the organic material that the Northern Commander had come for.

That Northern Commander had been relieved of his position.

Garai did not want to make that sort of mistake himself. He did not want to provoke those primitive creatures into making an attack that would destroy the very things he had come to this planet to harvest. The less the creatures noticed, the better off the Malmuria would be.

He had been tempted, though, to let the Central Commander turn on his energy field for that large station the creatures had built in orbit. That, he knew, had been the staging area for those pathetic ships. But, he felt, that would give the creatures on the ground too much warning. He would attack the staging area if he had to, but only then.

The First Harvester had come up the pole and was standing on his movement tentacles, his eyestalks in position around his face. "We are ready to retrieve."

Garai turned away from the Harvester in acknowledgment. "Proceed," Garai said to his Command Second. "Put all energy fields at full range."

Garai knew that the energy fields would not be functioning during the actual pickup of the Sulas, but he had no thought the creatures would cause a problem at that moment.

He watched as his fleet broke orbit and dropped into the thick, poisoned atmosphere of the planet. How a race like the creatures could even develop in such a mixture was a puzzle to him, but the organic compounds grown in the air could be eaten by his people, with processing, and that was all that was important. Without such a possibility, his people would have been dead long ago.

"General," said Sensor Watch Six. "The creatures are sending objects toward us."

"Objects?" Garai said.

"They appear to be weapons of some sort," said Sensor Watch Six.

"How much energy do they carry?"

Two of Sensor Watch Six's eyestalks rose straight up in surprise. "A great deal."

"Use the energy field to retrieve the energy from them. Do so with all objects the creatures send."

"Yes, sir."

Weapons. Garai let himself feel pleasure. The creatures had learned how to make less primitive forms of energy than the fires of their past. How wonderful for his people.

Perhaps this Pass would be more beneficial than any other.

219

Perhaps they would gain more than the Sulas' harvest. Perhaps they would get ahead in energy for the first time in his lifetime, thanks to the "weapons" of the creatures.

What a victory for him.

What a victory for them all.

12

April 14, 2018
8:55 A.M. Eastern Standard Time

Arrival: Day Two

Clarissa Maddox stood in the center of the war room, her hands clasped behind her back. She hadn't slept in fifteen hours and she felt wider awake than she had in months. She was angry, but she didn't show it. She was angry at herself.

They were losing this battle, and it was her battle. She was one of the first women to graduate from the Air Force Academy, the best scorer in her class in Top Gun School, and the first female chief of staff of the air force. And then, based on her performance in those Middle Eastern border skirmishes ten years ago, she became the first female general of the air force, and finally the first woman ever on the Joint Chiefs of Staff.

She had more medals than anyone else on the damn Joint Chiefs of Staff, and most of them were combat medals. She had been known as creative and demanding.

And until today, she had never lost a fight.

She had never faced an enemy like this one, though. Not ever.

She stared at the satellite screens showing the alien ships.

She hated their blackness, the way they looked like a heat shimmer on a highway on a hot summer day. A black mirage, something that would vanish if she touched it.

The military satellites sent the visuals and even when she switched to infrared they didn't say much.

Her staff was looking tired. Fifteen people in this room, monitoring equipment, her own chief of staff, Paul Ward, behind her, offering suggestions of his own, which she was ignoring. Maddox was the commander in charge of NATO forces—the acting commander. The United States led the military, through the president who gave his orders to Jamal Harrington. Harrington coordinated everything, but he put Maddox in charge of the actual day-to-day, moment-to-moment fighting.

In the last day, Maddox had managed to get dozens of fighter craft into the area of the Brazilian and Central American locations. NATO and South African forces had taken on the African site. They were at a disadvantage: There were very few NATO bases in these areas. Fortunately, the local governments were requesting help, but still, deploying forces at this late date was so different from having them there. All she could manage, at the moment, were two hundred fighter planes from fourteen nations in patterns around the alien planes, keeping their distances.

Their armed forces covered the ground well and the air adequately. But they didn't begin to understand space. And they should have. Now that she was standing here, wishing her tired mind would come up with an alternative plan, she remembered all the warnings she'd heard from scientists, all the science fiction novels she'd read, the movies she'd seen, that had used statistics to show that there would be, based only on the number of planets and the number of stars, additional life in the universe. Intelligent life. Knowing that, and knowing that the United States had had spacefaring capabilities for more than fifty years, you'd think someone would have thought up an outer space defense.

But no.

So she had to stand here and watch their ancient systems fail against these black objects. Missiles rose, just like they did when she was a cadet, watching the Gulf War on CNN, only when they got close to their dark targets, the missiles suddenly lost all power, and fell to the ground. They didn't even explode there. The missiles were suddenly and completely useless.

How to fight an enemy that neutralized your weapons? It was as if they were attacking tanks with bow and arrows, which, she was pretty sure, they were. The only way an arrow worked against a tank was if the tank's top were open and the arrow went down inside.

Open.

She felt the first bit of hope she had felt in days.

"Get me General Harrington," she said to her chief of staff.

Ward nodded, and within a moment Harrington actually came into the war room. "Problems, Maddox?"

"Obvious problems, sir," she said. "But I have an idea and I am requesting permission to use nuclear weapons."

Harrington put his arm around her shoulder and pulled her toward the corridor so the others couldn't hear the discussion. "The president has forbidden their use."

"I know that, sir, but I propose to use them on those ships when they pick up those nanomachines. The ships have to be vulnerable at that point. There have to be open somewhere to get the machines inside, even if they're small openings. If we hit them with all we've got, then we might have a chance."

Harrington shook his head.

"Sir, I'm proposing limited nuclear use over an area that's already been destroyed."

"I know," he said. "I made a similar argument earlier." He smiled at her, and the smile was tired. "Although my argument wasn't nearly as creative. I didn't think about those ships opening up to retrieve the machines. I simply figured we'd hit them in the destroyed regions and no one would care. But the president does. And he says much of the international support comes from the fact that we aren't using those weapons."

"I don't see why we can't use our most destructive equipment," she said. "The conventional weapons aren't doing anything. And if we don't stop them now, these ships will do the same thing more times. Imagine if they hit New York, sir, or Washington?"

"I have," Harrington said. "And so has the president. But for now the order remains."

Maddox shook her head. "Is anyone trying to talk to these ships? Speakee English and all that?"

"We're broadcasting in all known languages, including the dead ones. We're not getting any response at all."

"Excuse me, sirs," Ward said loudly as he approached. "The ships are reentering the atmosphere. They look to be returning to their original positions."

Where they had dropped the cloud. Maddox excused herself and went back to her command position. "Tell everyone to hold their fire," she said. "These space ships seem to be going lower this time. We wait until they start sucking up those nanomachines, and then we'll hit them with everything we have, right in their bellies."

Harrington was behind her. "I'm going to notify the president about what's happening."

"Let's hope this works," Maddox said.

Harrington nodded and disappeared through the door. He seemed almost relieved that he wasn't commanding the actual fight, the bastard. Well, she'd show him. And that weak-ass president. No nukes. If she had nukes this would work, she was convinced of it The trick now was to make it work without the nukes.

"Everything in position?" she snapped.

"As much as we can be," Ward said. "Some of the alien ships are already hovering, much lower than before."

"Picking up their little machines," she said. "Well, let's see if they can pick up their equipment and defend themselves at the same time. Start the attack. Tell the pilots to target the openings where the nanomachines are being picked up."

Then she stood, hands behind her back, watching the dozens of large screens on the wall show her the most important battle she, and the planet Earth, had ever fought.

April 14, 2018
9:59 A.M. Brazilian Andes Standard Time

Arrival: Day Two

"Go for the belly, gentlemen," Captain Thomas Ezzel's commander relayed the attack orders clearly and loudly in Ezzel's headset.

"Understood," Ezzel said, and banked his Blackwing Stealth Six fighter into a low turn, the four g forces shoving him solidly in his seat, a feeling he was used to, felt at home with.

Around him four other jets moved with him in practiced

ease, all staying in formation. In the three years since the academy, he hadn't actually been in a real combat situation. Lots of scrambles, lots of drills. But never real, until this moment.

He could feel tiny beads of sweat forming on his forehead, and he focused on the job ahead, just as he had always done, letting the routine comfort his nerves. He would do just fine. He always had, and today would be no exception. His mom and Julia, his wife, back in Arizona, would be proud of him. He would not let them down.

Those big, black ships were like nothing he'd ever seen before, but he knew he could do some damage. And the brass were finally giving him a chance to try.

That thought sent a little shiver through him. He was shivering anyway, not with cold, but with excitement.

He flipped his eyepiece over his eyes, and said, "Going to VR mode."

"Understood." Command's voice came back strong.

The landscape suddenly was outlined, all contours shown in graphic detail, covered in grid lines, like an old computer game he used to play in his bedroom when he was a kid. Only VR had been invented for fighter pilots, since they were moving too fast to react to ordinary sight. VR allowed a pilot to see, through the computer, for miles ahead, every bump in the ground.

In essence, he was flying with his eyes covered, only seeing the images the computer sent him. But these days he was more used to flying with it on than without it. It took him only an instant to adjust, then he relaxed slightly. This was home to him, flying at Mach Three a hundred feet over the ground, virtual images flashing past. The advanced Blackwing Stealth Six felt like a comfortable leather glove around him.

A virtual reality control panel hovered in the air in front of him to his right.

"Going to visual targeting."

He touched a place in the air where a virtual switch hovered. An orange target site appeared in front of his dominant left eye, aimed where he looked, relaying distance data constantly. Every missile he fired would hit where he looked, laser locked.

"Coming up on targets," the voice in his ear said.

"Missiles armed and ready," he said. Now, when that target in front of his eye went to a point, the missiles would fire automatically.

He didn't expect to feel this relaxed in his first real combat mission. But this wasn't exactly the mission he had expected to be his first.

Julia, his wife, would be worried, and she would be yelling at him for taking this so lightly, but he wasn't really taking it lightly. This is what he'd been training to do since high school, fighting missions like this to keep the world safe.

To keep his kids safe.

Right now they'd be getting ready for school if this were a normal day. But it wasn't. He had no idea what Julia was doing with them in their small home in Arizona. Playing with them? Letting them watch television? Getting them ready for school as if the world were going to continue unchanged?

Thoughts of his family calmed him further, reminded him why he was doing this. He hoped to hell they'd never see what he was seeing, not in Arizona. Not at home.

And they wouldn't, if he was successful.

On his screen were the images of the huge alien ships over the Amazon, thirty miles dead ahead. Or what was left of the Amazon. Now the area below those ships was only a huge blackness, devoid of life. Nothing was left standing. It was the most incredible thing he had ever seen. The VR showed it all in clear detail, covered in faint grid lines showing elevation and distance.

What kind of alien monsters would do this?

"Pilots." Command's voice filled his world. "Break and engage enemy at will."

Ezzel was the third from the left of a wing of five. He went ten degrees left and up slightly, as he was trained on break maneuver.

The other four planes were instantly shown in his VR imaging as small, blue dots, moving into their break positions from formation. The computer would watch them for him, warning him if any got too close.

His worry was dead ahead.

The computer showed the alien ships as huge, football stadium–sized ovals. No bumps, no obvious power source. The area under them looked like a canyon to the computer, formed between the ship and the ground. Lots of room.

He visually targeted the underside of the one closest to his position and moved down, right onto the deck, skimming the ground no more than fifty feet above the surface at twice the speed of sound.

He continued to focus on the underside of the alien ship as the distance closed, the square target in front of his eye becoming smaller, more defined, as the VR took him in.

The alien ship was hovering at six hundred feet. Ezzel was coming in under it.

The target he held on the underside of the alien ship narrowed down to a point, then flashed red.

"Missile launch," the computer said.

Two missiles suddenly appeared in his virtual image, streaking at the underside of the ship.

"Go babies," he said as he veered to the right.

The computer VR display showed the missiles striking the ship. Direct hit.

Ezzel desperately wanted to flip off his VR controls and see the damage, but he didn't. Instead, he banked even harder right, the g forces smashing him back into the seat as he immediately targeted the next alien ship twenty miles downrange.

He barely had time to set target, arm missiles, and fire, but he managed it, sending two more arrows of supersonic destruction into the underside of an alien craft.

His speed took him completely through the forty-mile area of destruction and back over the green jungle. Taking as much g force as he could, he swung around in a tight turn and headed back in. He had six more missiles to deliver.

In front of him the alien ships were starting to climb. He targeted the closest, setting missiles.

"Break off attack!" Command ordered.

He flicked off missiles targeting and shoved the jet into a hard right turn, slamming his body into the seat once again.

But he was just a fraction of a second too late.

His speed took him directly under one alien ship.

Suddenly the power to his entire jet shut down.

Blackness covered his eyes.

Before he could even get his hand to his face to flip up his VR visor to go visual, his jet flipped like a playing card in a high wind, end over end.

Shit, he thought, fighting to right it with a dead stick. How would he explain this to Julia?

How . . .

The jet smashed into the black, soot-covered hill with a yellow ball of flame.

He died instantly, not even knowing what had happened. And not knowing the extent of damage he had done to his unknown enemy.

April 14, 2018
5:12 P.M. Universal Time

Arrival: Day Two

General Garai pocketed all ten eyestalks for a moment so he could think without interruption. Never before had a harvesting been so unusual. The creatures from the planet had attacked before, in previous Passes, but they hadn't been developed. And there had never been anything in the air around his ships.

It was annoying.

It was distracting.

It was inconvenient.

He had to concentrate on retrieving the harvesters and making certain he gave the correct commands. In the darkness, being unable to see for just a moment gave him clarity. He wished he had time to go through the rest of the clearness ritual, with all torso tentacles raised and movement tentacles lowered.

But he did not have time, and things were not as easy as he wished. Of course, things never were. On the last Pass, before the last sleep, the area they had chosen had received an early freeze shortly before they broke into the poisonous atmosphere. They had to pick new sites quicker than they ever had before.

Those sites had been richer, and he had been praised, but it had been a near error that had caused the success.

As it would be now.

The thought calmed him, and he raised all ten eyestalks out of their pockets, only to focus all of his vision on Sensor Watch Three, who was standing in the nearest balance circle on all of his movement tentacles. Garai wondered how long Sensor Watch Three had been there, watching him, and decided not to reprimand him.

"You have news?" Garai asked, leaving his eyestalks to float freely as a sign of displeasure.

Sensor Watch Three's eyestalks were all facing forward. "The creatures are mounting a massive attack."

"And this, you felt, was not worth disturbing me over?"

"They have only just begun. I thought to give you a moment more. It is better to have a clear commander."

Garai waved two torso tentacles in a dismissal. He grabbed the nearest sensor sphere and looked for himself. Sensor Watch Three dropped his eyestalks and turned away, knowing that he had just been reprimanded for not following the proper procedure.

Flying machines hovered. The sensors showed massive power buildups in areas close to the destruction. Garai stared at those power buildups, wondering if he could raid them as the ships came down.

He dropped four tentacles in an unconscious no. If he took additional risks, he might harm the ships. And the ships were the key to their survival.

"How long until retrieval is complete?"

"Ten decaunits," Harvester One said.

Almost no time at all. Garai hadn't realized they were so close. His concentration had indeed been broken.

"Will the creatures' weapons arrive before we are finished?"

"Yes, Commander." Sensor Watch Four was the one who answered this time. His voice was soft, and although he did not turn around, he faced all his eyestalks toward Garai in deference.

Garai stared at the sphere before him. The power levels on the flying machines and the weapons were marvelously high. If he could think of a way of stealing the energy while doing the retrieval, he would.

But while it was theoretically possible to do energy retrieval and harvester retrieval simultaneously, it had never been done. And getting the Sulas now was more important than stealing energy from the creatures' machines. He would try to do that as his own ships returned to orbit.

"Continue retrieval," he ordered.

The words were barely out of his mouth when the first creature weapon, a long narrow thing that looked like a Malmurian face, struck the second ship of the Southern Fleet and exploded. The light and energy were absorbed by the ship's skin at contact and there was no damage.

Five of Garai's tentacles rose with pleasure. He hadn't thought the creatures would send their weapons to *impact* the ships. He hadn't thought they would come to him, give him energy without him having to use fields to retrieve it.

The Southern Fleet continued to retrieve. Another creature weapon hit the second ship.

"They have striking capability," Sensor Watch One said.

"That is not possible," Garai said. "It would take more expertise than these creatures are capable of. They do not have the minds for the calculations. This is simple luck."

"Forgive me, Commander," said Command Second. "They have the minds to create flying machines in the first place."

"Targeting and flying are different acts," Garai said. He watched as his ships were now in position. "Continue harvest."

The entire ship shuddered as the weight of the full Sulas became apparent. This was the difficult part each Pass. Each Sula weighed only a bit more, but that bit, combined, made retrieval a tricky business. Done wrong, it could damage the ship.

Another weapon struck the second ship, then another, and yet another. They were hitting the same place.

"The sixth and tenth ships are reporting hits as well," Sensor Watch Four said.

"What?" Garai hit his own sensor unit with a tentacle so that he could see the ships of his fleet. And what he saw displeased him. Their absorbent skin was not absorbing the energy. The weapons were destroying the fine webbing near the impact sites. Some Sulas were actually being dropped. "Tell the fleet to speed up the harvest."

"Message sent," said Command Second.

The weapons were hitting ships with increasing intensity. Some even broke through the outer ring of ships and hit the first ship. It shuddered with the impact and the power flickered momentarily.

"How soon until retrieval is complete?" Garai asked, clutching the information sphere.

"Two decaunits," said Sensor Watch Four, voice shaking.

"We have ten ships damaged, Commander," said Sensor Watch One without bothering to turn his eyestalks.

"Continue retrieval," Garai said. He stared at his own information sphere. The creatures' weapons were pelting the ships. Several more were getting through to his own, and he couldn't evade. The ship rocked and he almost lost his balance, the first time in his entire life that six of his movement

233

tentacles at once had ever touched the floor outside of the balance circle.

It was a bad omen.

"Retrieval finished," said Sensor Watch One.

Garai regained his balance. His left top torso tentacle was wrapped around the information sphere, squeezing it. He made himself loosen his grip. "Turn on our energy absorption fields," he snapped, wishing he didn't have to order everything to get his staff to do it. "Move to low orbit for processing."

The ship shuddered for a moment as the energy retrieval fields went on. Then it started to rise, sluggishly. The Sulas, in their holds, were not balanced.

"Even out the Sulas, and remove the nutrients," he said. "We must be prepared for our second harvest."

"Yes, Commander," said Harvester One.

Garai released the information sphere and watched as the creatures' weapons were again falling uselessly to the ground, their energy absorbed by their intended victims.

"Commander."

Garai turned. His Command Second had his movement tentacles splayed on the floor, his torso tentacles flattened against his sides, and his eyestalks turned so that the eyes looked downward.

Bad news.

Hideous news.

The kind of news that could cause Garai to order that Command Second be removed and his body sent to the energy centers for recycling.

"Report," Garai said.

"We have lost two ships, Commander." Command Second's fifth torso tentacle rose slightly and then fell, in apology.

234

"Lost?" Garai wasn't sure he'd heard the word correctly.

"Destroyed." Command Second sank lower onto the deck. His eyestalks touched his torso tentacles, something done only in moments of great shame. Garai wasn't sure he had ever seen anyone make that movement before.

"All life is lost," Command Second said. "Central also lost two. Northern lost three."

Garai almost allowed more of his tentacles to touch the deck again as he reeled under the news. Seven ships gone forever. How could this be? He would be forever known in the history as the commander who lost seven ships in a single harvest. No commander had ever lost a ship in a harvest. Ships were damaged during the long sleep and had to be repaired. They were not lost.

Garai did not show his own shame. He would do that when he returned to Malmur. He had a mission to finish. The lives of his people were at stake.

"Rise," he said, and then turned so that he would not have to look on Command Second again. "You have your orders. We have very little time. Inform me when the Sulas are ready for the second seeding."

He heard the slap of tentacles as Command Second stood. "Yes, Commander," Command Second said. Garai still did not look at him.

Instead, Garai grabbed a second information sphere, the one on which he kept the map of the planet below.

The creatures had struck in defense of their planet. He understood that.

He had underestimated their ability.

He would not do that again. But his time as commander of the fleet was almost finished. When they returned, he would be removed in disgrace, and his body recycled into energy.

He had done what he could. If only those creatures had a long-term memory, then they would know that the Malmuria meant them no harm. In all the Passes, the Malmuria had worked to minimize damage to the creatures.

And now that the creatures had the capability of hurting the Malmuria, they had done so, in a way so devastating that the Malmuria would not be the same. Ever.

Seven ships. Seven ships lost meant food would not be gathered, which meant that thousands and thousands of Malmuria would not survive the next sleep.

All because Garai had been careless, because he had not realized that the creatures had grown into tacticians. They were still primitive. Their weapons would have been ineffective if Garai had ordered the energy retrieval fields on while harvesting. But he had not.

And he had given the creatures the idea that they could destroy Malmurian ships.

He had to show them that they could not do so. He would not allow the creatures' short-term memories to function, to come up with another plan to defeat the Malmuria.

Garai had to retrieve more than energy. He needed to take honor from this defeat. He needed to devastate the creatures as they had devastated him. Perhaps then they would not presume to attack another Malmurian ship.

He studied the map. There were many very fertile areas for harvesting food near high-population centers. He would find the best harvesting area, get the richest food, and show no mercy to the creatures.

He would not regain his seven ships. But he would stop the creatures from touching any others.

He would die in shame when he returned home, but he would do what he could now to save his world and his people by taking as much energy from the creatures as he could at the same time. They owed his people that much now.

And he would make them pay.

13

Arrival: Day Three

Tax day. It was tax day, but Americans were not talking about taxes. Cross doubted any of them had thought of it, except for him.

The only reason he had was because he was in the media room with Britt. She was in her position on the couch, only this time she was in his robe and a pair of his slippers, and she looked more tired than any human being had a right to.

Twelve days before, they had been here together and it had been a glorious occasion: The Luna shuttles had been launched to the tenth planet.

Only twelve days before.

He hadn't expected so much to change in twelve days. Let alone last night.

He and Britt had come to the media room to watch the battle on the three flat screens. Bradshaw wasn't there. He had gone, with Portia Groopman and a few others, to the edge of the Central American destruction to see if they could find some nanomachines to study. Cross was worried for them,

238

but Bradshaw had reminded him that they were all adults. They all had their parts to play.

Cross had tried not to think about it as he channel-surfed until he found the best coverage—CNN, a Brazilian channel that broadcast in Portuguese, but it didn't matter since all Cross needed was the imagery, and the new British all-news station that threatened to dwarf every other channel on the planet. Each station was running different views of the battle: CNN had crews in Africa, Brazil was running views from the Amazon, and the Brits covered all three.

It had made for frightening, rousing television. He and Britt had watched in horror as the ships had come down, their blackness covering the destroyed areas, the nanomachines floating back into the holds in clouds of blackness, sucked from the ground by some unseen force.

And then the attack had begun, and he found himself cheering as their planes—American planes—destroyed one of the ships. Other weapons worked as well, but he finally felt patriotic for the first time in his life.

It felt so strange. He had no image of the kind of lives that were being lost on the alien vessels, and he actually found that he didn't care. They had destroyed parts of Earth and he wanted them to pay. The intensity of his emotion had startled him.

But the joy he had felt in that defeat disappeared quickly. The human life lost became clearer as the evening wore on, and unlike the alien life, he had a vision of this. He knew about grieving families and dead children, and losses that could never be replaced.

The numbers that were being reported were horrendous: An estimated quarter million dead under the aliens' first black clouds. Sixty-five fighter jets lost in the attack that downed the seven alien ships. Seven down, ninety-four left.

Sixty-five pilots who gave their lives in defense of their planet.

Now the remaining alien ships were simply parked in low orbit, in three groups. And Cross knew exactly what they were doing. History had told him. They were preparing to drop the clouds again, to harvest more of the planet. Their first drop had only been one-quarter of their harvest area from the previous Pass of the tenth planet. So, if Cross's facts were correct, the planet had three more destruction cycles to go through.

At 3:00 A.M. an exhausted Britt had fallen asleep, cradled in Cross's arms. He had looked down on her once, saw the flickering of the television screens on her skin, had even, once, seen the numbers of the devastation flit backward across her face. It was like an omen, a bad omen, and he wanted to turn off the televisions, but he couldn't.

He was mesmerized by all of this.

He was out of the loop at the moment. Right now, he had to trust everything to people like Doug Mickelson and Clarissa Maddox. Normally that wouldn't have bothered him. He had done it his whole life. National, international events had no meaning for him. He felt they were things out of his control, things he could do nothing about, so he ignored them.

But his research had brought them to this. He was tied in, and it felt strange to be out of the loop on the battle. It felt very, very strange.

He found himself asking what would have happened if he hadn't discovered the soot lines. Where would Earth be now?

Startled beyond belief, even more startled than it was now. The dark ships would have appeared, sunk into the atmosphere and leveled the three areas with no warning at all. By the time the world even thought of retaliating, the ships would have been gone.

240

Seven alien ships were destroyed because he had found this early. Seven ships and sixty-five dead human pilots.

Sixty-five lives that could be attributed to him.

Were sixty-five lives worth seven ships? He didn't know. He would be inclined to say yes, because he didn't know the people who had died. But then he thought of Zip Juarez and the excitement he had seen on her face the one time he met her, and he knew that he would have felt the loss.

He was shell-shocked now. These aliens were more powerful than he had ever imagined. And he was afraid things would get worse before they got better.

This was only the first quarter of their harvest. He knew there had to be three more.

Around 6:00 A.M., CNN rounded up some MIT professor who was an acclaimed orbital mathematics specialist. The professor had argued, quite clearly, that the aliens only had two more days in orbit over the Earth before their window for catching the tenth planet as it moved sunward closed, and they were stuck here for over six months, until the planet came around the sun and started on its trip outward.

But that didn't make sense to Cross and his knowledge of how much area they harvested the last Pass. Their first cloud drop and pickup took just over twenty-four hours. If the next took as long, they would be finished, as far as the mathematician was concerned, but only half done as far as Cross could tell. Either he was wrong, or the mathematician was. Cross hoped he was. It would mean a lot fewer people would be killed.

Cross had awakened Britt then, and had asked her what she thought. She had blinked sleepily at him, then frowned, got up and asked to use the map room. He said that was fine.

She disappeared for an hour.

He used the time to shower and fix them breakfast. It had

been a long time since he had cooked in his own kitchen. Constance would hate the mess when she arrived, but she would probably appreciate not doing the cooking. He made eggs and bacon and cappuccino for Britt. Then he had brought it all to the map room on a tray.

Britt was sitting at his main computer, her hair sticking up in spikes because she had run her fingers through it a dozen times.

"I'm not an orbital mathematician," she said. "But I've been looking at this. I think he's right."

Cross set the food tray down, took a piece of toast off it, and started to butter it. "But it doesn't make sense. They've only harvested a fourth of what they've done before."

"Maybe this was the preliminary run," she said. "Maybe they take more on the second one."

He shuddered. It was an involuntary motion. If this was the beginning, the next few days would be hell.

He didn't know how right he was. And he didn't know how soon things would change. He and Britt ate breakfast, then he shut off the computers, closed the map room door, and spent some time with her, both of them seeking more than an hour's pleasure, seeking some kind of comfort, some kind of reassurance that life would continue.

Then she had toddled off to the shower, and he had gathered the breakfast dishes, taken them to the kitchen, and come back to the media room.

Where he stopped as the CNN announcer said the alien ships were coming back. He listened to the report, and then went to his bedroom. Britt was just getting out of the shower. He handed her a robe.

"They're coming back," he said.

"We thought they would." She sounded calm, but she didn't look it. Her hands shook as she put on his robe.

242

"They're not going to the same places. It looks like they're going elsewhere."

She looked up at him, her face freshly scrubbed and vulnerable. "You . . . you said that wouldn't happen."

"It didn't happen in the past," he said. And it hadn't. All the evidence showed that the ships had harvested areas close by the first harvest areas.

"Where are they going?" she asked, her voice breathy.

"I don't know," he said. "I came to get you."

Because he couldn't watch it alone. He didn't want to watch it alone.

She stuck her small feet into a pair of his slippers and let him lead her back to the media room. There, on all three stations, were maps of the world.

The ships had picked their targets.

One group of ships flew toward the west coast of North America. Another moved into the fertile areas of central France, and the third toward South Vietnam.

Britt had led Cross to the couch, and they had been there ever since, Cross thinking inane thoughts about tax day, wishing things would be normal again and knowing they never would, Britt making small wounded noises in the back of her throat.

CNN focused on California, the British channel on France, and Cross found an Asian station that had live images from Vietnam. But he couldn't take his eyes off CNN.

California.

The United States.

Home.

The ships took positions over California's fertile south-central coast, from Monterey to San Luis Obispo. Britt clutched Cross's hand. His mouth was dry, his entire body taut.

The news reports were horrifying. Some people tried to go

243

into the ocean—on ships, on rafts, on anything. Others got in their cars and drove. A few headed north, and several tried to go south, but everywhere, traffic, for miles.

Some put video cameras in the windows, and local reporters fed live reports to the networks. Cross heard the voices of people who thought they might die, and hoped they wouldn't.

People were going underground, into basements, into concrete buildings, hoping, hoping they would survive. And some were shooting guns into the air, as if firing at black nothingness would solve anything.

Cross let the images flow.

Britt's grip had cut off the circulation to his hand.

He didn't want to watch this, but he couldn't stop.

The ships dropped the black clouds.

Britt moaned and buried her face in his shoulder, but Cross did not look away. Not as camera crews filmed live shots of the clouds descending on them. Not as the pictures turned dark, then the cameras were dropped and human screams filled the airwaves before the networks cut it off. Cross didn't look away as cameras inside buildings recorded through windows. People looking up as the cloud descended, then batting at the black clouds, then literally being dissolved into dust.

The cameras didn't stop recording until the buildings around them melted away, and then the casing of the camera itself.

Image after image: a boy cradling his younger sister, trying to protect her with his body; a couple running screaming for a building that was turning to dust.

Image after image: all ending with a black cloud, and then a blank screen.

Disconnect.

A moment of horror, and then nothing.

244

Finally Cross reached up, grabbed a remote, and shut off all three screens.

The media room became mercifully silent.

Britt raised her head. She hadn't been crying, but she looked as if she wanted to. She stared at him.

"What went wrong?" she asked.

"Seven ships," Cross said. He finally had his answer. He knew what would have been different if he hadn't found the tenth planet when he did. The aliens would have harvested according to their normal pattern.

The world had had time to defend itself, to destroy seven ships, and now the aliens were mad.

"You think they did this in retaliation?" she asked.

He nodded.

"Isn't that a human reaction?"

He looked at her, then brushed some hair from her face. "I think," he said slowly, "we've just found out that it isn't."

"They've killed millions of people because we destroyed seven ships."

"Yes," he said. And he wasn't sure he wanted to find out what the aliens would do if the world destroyed even one more ship. What kind of destructive capabilities did they have?

He was afraid they would all find out.

April 16, 2018
10:42 A.M. Eastern Standard Time

Arrival: Day Four

The devastation was horrible.

Clarissa Maddox had once stood at Fisherman's Wharf in

245

Monterey, staring at the majestic blue of the Pacific, thinking she was the luckiest woman in the world. She had been promoted, straight out of the Air Force Academy, and she had been standing there, on leave, with a man whose name she didn't remember, thinking that life was very, very good. It was a memory she used to go back to whenever she needed to feel relaxed, whenever she needed to be in a good mood.

Even the memory held nothing for her now. Fisherman's Wharf was gone. Monterey was gone. It had all vanished in a black cloud.

A cloud she hadn't been able to stop.

She rubbed her eyes with the thumb and forefinger of her left hand, then leaned toward Ward, her chief of staff. On the screens around her the satellite photos showed dark areas of devastation. Her staff in the room had doubled, all thirty extremely busy following her orders. Everything was ready for this last attack. She had even talked with Harrington, and begged for the ability to use limited nukes, but the president had balked.

Pansy-ass politician, still afraid of what might happen to him in a future election if he ordered a nuclear strike and it failed, getting that junk into the atmosphere, destroying yet more of California. Of course he was afraid. He should be. He was going to be thrown out of office no matter what, that was what would happen to him. He'd lost part of California. If the United States survived, if the world survived, what people would remember was that he'd lost California and hadn't let his general fight the battle she wanted.

She wanted to use tacticals to blow those fuckers out of the sky.

Harrington had argued that it wouldn't work, not after the last attack. She had said the last attack didn't mean anything.

246

It had been a gamble, she had told him, and she had been right.

She had thought, incorrectly it turned out, that if the alien craft were vulnerable when they were picking up those damned machines, they'd be vulnerable when they were dropping the machines off.

She had been wrong.

Very wrong.

The weapons and planes she had sent against the aliens when they dropped the clouds of killing black nanomachines had done no damage at all. When she fired missiles and planes, they got within half a klick from the ships and dropped to the ground like stones. She had lost a dozen good pilots before calling off the planes, and she finally decided to stop throwing missiles at the ships as well.

She had to wait.

God, she hated that.

The waiting had been awful too. The news media didn't help, broadcasting those images of destruction all over the world. She hadn't been able to shake the one of the screaming children fleeing an engulfed bus, and neither, it seemed, could the rest of the world. That was the image so many channels were showing over and over, and all the while those hypocritical reporters were telling people to remain calm.

Calm? With images like that? It was no wonder there were riots in London and Seattle, that people were fleeing parts of China for the countryside. In the Midwest, people were disappearing into bomb shelters built in the 1950s. She hadn't even known any of those were left. There were runs on stores, and banks, and a lot of people were heading out to sea, thinking those creatures weren't going to attack over water.

People were never rational in these situations.

At least the military—all of the military, all over the

world—were remaining calm. Otherwise she'd be even more worried. She trusted that the European Union and NATO forces would handle the French landing, and the Chinese would take care of theirs.

She had to.

She was concentrating on California.

The plan was that Earth forces would again hit the aliens when they were hovering low over the ground. The alien ships would be vulnerable again, just as they were the last time they picked up their machines. It had to be a flaw in the works, something the aliens hadn't foreseen when they designed those ships.

And why would they? They clearly hadn't been attacked on Earth before. Earth had never had the capability of attacking them before now. She suspected, although she was no scientist, that the energy drain the planes experienced was a normal by-product of the ships themselves, probably something to do with that darkness. It was less of a defensive reaction than a natural one.

She was counting on that.

Ward had already asked her what she would do if the aliens could modify their ships, if they had been caught by surprise the first time, and would be ready this time.

She had thought of that, and she hadn't answered him. But she did have an answer. She'd berate Harrington and the president. She'd get her nukes and she'd blast those goddamn ships out of the sky. That was what she'd do.

But right now, she didn't have nukes. So she was going to throw everything she had at the group that came down over California, since they were in her own backyard. She was going to hit the aliens with more firepower than many nuclear bombs combined.

"Here they come," said one of the lieutenants down front.

Maddox looked up. The alien crafts were breaking orbit and slanting in, just like she expected them to. Her heart was pounding. She wished she were out there, so that she could go after them herself.

"Get everything into position," she said, "and have everyone stand ready."

" Yes, sir." Ward snapped into attention beside her.

She didn't even notice when he left. She was staring at the screens. The black ships were blotches against the sky. If only she knew what they were. If only she knew their weaknesses.

She only knew one, and she was praying to god that they would get this second chance.

Because she doubted they would get any more.

April 16, 2018
7:59 A.M. Pacific Standard Time

Arrival: Day Four

Brian Hernandez stood on a hill overlooking what remained of San Luis Obispo. It had taken him all night to get there and get set up, but the trek had been worth it. Toni had driven through hell and back—good thing the station had sprung for four-wheel drive on the equipment van. Mose and Krystal were already setting up cameras, and Toni was using the sound equipment from inside the van to see if she could pick up any ambient noise.

Brian's sources were guessing that the black cloud wasn't composed of alien insects like other stations were reporting, but some sort of nanotechnology. He doubted there'd be chewing sounds, but anything would work.

The devastation made his throat hurt. He'd done fires, serious fires, the kind that wiped out communities, but he'd never seen anything like this. The trees, the community, the *buildings* had been leveled. The last-minute feeds from all the cameras folks had left running had been nightmarish, and he knew in that sea of black dust ahead of him were remains of people as well.

What was the creepiest to him was that the air smelled fresh and that the ground was flat. Only a layer of dirt or soot, as the other stations were calling it, covered everything. It had no smell. If anything, he could smell the ocean now, even though it was a few miles away. The salt tang with a hint of fish made him think of better days.

He'd vacationed up here once; a friend of his had a house near California Polytechnic Institute, and Brian had house-sat there for an entire summer. He'd spent time on the Cal Poly campus, he'd driven to the ocean, and he'd generally bummed around. That had been the summer his desires had crystallized. He had spent half the summer writing an investigative magazine piece on spec, and had been bitten by the journalism bug. Only no one read anymore. He'd gone to Northwestern after that, then apprenticed at a few local stations. He'd worked his way up to daytime reporting for KTLA, and he'd hoped someday to get an anchor spot.

That dream was gone now. It seemed petty in the face of what was before him. Sometime over the last few days he remembered that he didn't want to be another pretty face reading the latest government scandals. He wanted to tell stories that would make a difference. And if he got what he wanted here, this one would.

He scrambled over part of the hill. The silence in this place was unnerving. Toni had ventured that there would be a barely audible sound of munching. Krystal had thought there would be a high-pitched buzz like you'd hear when a saw went through wood. Mose hadn't said anything, but then Mose never did. Brian hadn't known what to expect. Although he hadn't expected the silence.

It was unnatural. There should at least be wind through trees. But there weren't any trees. There wasn't anything.

He turned to Mose. His hair was in long cornrows, done, he'd once said, so that he wouldn't have to think about it on assignment. It made his head seem artificial, especially when it was pushed against the digital long-range camera they'd taken from the station. The camera was the latest thing in spy technology, or so the station manager had said—long-distance zooms that picked up things previous cameras had missed.

Toni crossed the hill, her dark hair limp around her face, and handed Brian his ear and mike chips. "I got the station on-line," she said. "I didn't tell them how we got here."

Those last were a warning to him. They'd blown one police barricade so fast that the cops didn't seem to know what hit them. It had been on a section of 101 near Nipomo where they simply didn't feel safe going off the road. They would get in trouble later.

If there was a later.

"All right," Brian said, and put the chips in place. Toni hiked back to the van. He waited for her to get in before signaling Krystal. She turned her head and the older handheld toward him, her blue eyes somber. He'd been interested in her once, until he realized that she was interested in how things looked and nothing more. She was perfect behind a camera. She thought in images and moments, not in any sort of fluid way.

"Brian?" a tiny voice asked in his ear. It was Johnson at the studio.

"Yeah."

"We aren't going to live feed you until the fighting starts. We're afraid they'll pull you out before that."

"Sensible," he said. "You're getting stuff from Krystal and Mose?"

"Yeah," Johnson said. "It looks barren there."

"We're just outside San Luis Obispo."

"I know."

"Brian." Toni's voice cut in. "We're getting something."

Krystal had already pointed her camera skyward and Mose, a few feet down, followed. Brian looked up. The alien ships looked like black holes in the sky, where the blue sky seemed to have been punched open. At just the sight of them Brian shuddered.

Suddenly around them the ground seemed to explode as two stealth fighters no more than two hundred feet off the top of the mountain flashed past. The impact sent Brian sprawling in the grass. He looked over, and saw that Mose and Krystal were down.

Mose got his camera back up and in position first, as Brian scrambled to his feet.

"This is great stuff!" Johnson shouted. "Give me voice-over."

Brian indicated that Krystal should turn her camera toward him. She did.

"This is Brian Hernandez for KTLA. I'm just outside San Luis Obispo where an alien ship hovers overhead. You can see the destruction from that very ship behind me, and in the distance, the roar you hear are two American Blackhawk Stealth jet fighters . . ."

He continued speaking, describing everything in clear detail, as the two jets that had passed over them started a run up toward one alien ship.

252

With a movement of his hand below camera range, he indicated that Krystal should turn her camera skyward.

He spoke almost on automatic, a skill he had developed years ago, and for which he was thankful. It allowed him to distance himself from the scene in front of him.

As he watched, the jets sputtered and then they simply fell out of the sky, like a kid's toy far too heavy to remain aloft. Their speed took them below the alien ships into the side of a far ridge line, where they exploded in huge, orange fireballs against the blackness of the ground and the alien ships.

"Je-zus," Johnson said in his ear. "Keep going, Brian."

Brian hadn't stopped.

Neither had Mose and Krystal.

Both cameras were sending back images that were just part of the massive battle being fought along a hundred-mile stretch in the area. One alien ship was above him, and in the distance he could see three others.

Four fighters flashed past the news team, flying between them and the alien ships, again rocking the cameras with their sonic impact. Mose followed the planes with his camera, while Krystal kept hers trained on the alien ships.

Brian kept talking, describing, shouting sometimes to be heard over the noise of the firefight.

He couldn't believe he was here.

He couldn't believe he was seeing this.

He couldn't believe this was a place where he had once lived and enjoyed himself.

The scene that was playing itself out above him was like something from a nightmare. The planes swung high in a wide arc that took them a few miles downrange. The alien ship turned and moved over the ground, slowly, part of the blackness from below seeming to be sucked up into the ship as if the ship was a giant vacuum cleaner.

253

"Two more fighters coming in from the south," Mose said. "I'm on them."

As he spoke, Brian watched as the four fighters that had swung north went high and started down on top of the alien ship, like they were going to do a strafing run.

The two planes from the south moved to do the same thing.

"They're going in," Brian said to himself.

"What was that?" Johnson asked.

Brian realized that his thought had gone out over the air.

"Those pilots," Brian said. "They're flying into the alien ships. It seems that they have decided if they lose their power, they'll have their planes aimed at the alien ships. They'll be missiles, like the kamikaze Japanese aircraft in the Second World War. If the weapons won't destroy the target, the aircraft will. These pilots are sacrificing their own lives for all of ours."

His voice shook. He could hear distress in it, something he would never normally allow. He prided himself on his control, but even that was breaking now.

Everything seemed to go into slow motion.

The four fighters coming in from the north were slightly ahead of the two from the south. Suddenly, a good quarter mile away, the four fighters seemed to suddenly go limp in the sky, clearly their power gone, their jets nothing more than masses of hurtling metal coffins for their pilots.

Almost at the same moment, the two planes from the south also seemed to die in midair, their speed flashing them forward toward the alien ship.

But seemingly instantly, the alien ship moved upward.

The collision of the six jets in the space where the alien craft had been a moment before flashed to every working monitor in the country.

The explosion rocked the ground under Brian.

The alien craft went back to slowly hovering over the ground, sweeping up its deadly nanomachines as if nothing had happened.

In the distance there were other orange fireballs as other fighters crashed.

Brian said nothing. There were no words for this.

Mose had managed to keep his camera trained on the destruction. So had Krystal, but tears were running down her face, and she was gasping as if she couldn't believe what she was seeing.

He doubted anyone could.

This was not how it was supposed to have been. They were supposed to win this battle.

They were supposed to win.

His voice wasn't working. He felt himself sink to the ground. The earth still felt normal beneath him, the tickle of newborn grass, the dampness of the spring dirt. Only a half mile away was blackness caused by something he didn't understand. Above him, the black thing that was an alien spaceship was disappearing into the blue spring sky.

The battle was over.

The aliens were getting away.

And Earth had lost.

14

Arrival: Day Four

Supreme General Garai stood for the last time in the command balance circle. Information spheres swirled around him, but he did not touch them. He did not touch anything. Soon his touch would become a reminder of the disgrace.

The staff kept to their stations. Most had five of their eyestalks pocketed. There was no point in using all ten for visuals, and even less point in using all ten to honor their commander. Garai was now in disgrace, except they were the only ones who knew it. They understood, though, that once they reached Malmur, the entire world would know. Garai was lucky they let him continue to speak to them. Perhaps they felt they had no choice. He was, after all, the most experienced among them.

They also knew that if they were not careful, they too would be blamed for this awful defeat.

"Harvester One," Garai said. "Have all the Sulas been retrieved?"

Harvester One did not move a single eyestalk in acknowl-

256

edgment. He kept the base of his tentacles flat on his own balance circle. "They have," he said.

Garai studied the information sphere before him, the one that showed the creatures' planet. He took an older information sphere, one that showed the planet during the last Pass, and stared at them. In the last Pass, the planet had been bluer, the swirling clouds in the poisonous atmosphere whiter. The land itself had been greener; there had been more areas to harvest. All of it had been caused by the creatures' expansion.

Garai had noted that in his initial approach to the planet, but he had thought it inconsequential. He thought it inconsequential no longer.

His greatest problem now was communicating what he had learned to his own commanders before they gave him his punishment. He hoped they counted his past seventeen performances in his favor. They needed to listen, or they would lose more to the creatures on the planet below.

Garai had shocked those creatures on his second harvest, but he remembered their resilience. They would respond as angrily as he had. The commander of the next harvest had to be even harsher.

"Command Second," he said, "have any more ships been lost?"

Command Second did not move a tentacle. "No. Two from the Central Fleet have sustained slight damage."

Garai let the information spheres swirl. It was nearly over. All of it. "Return to orbit and prepare for standard departure."

"Acknowledged," Command Second said, as he would to an underling. His response, ungracious and uncompromising, made Garai touch a single information sphere. He turned its image to his own planet, Malmur.

He had served his people well over his time. His only mistake had been in underestimating the creatures. And that mistake had cost seven ships. On the next Pass thousands of his kind would not be able to wake up due to lack of ships to harvest food. Many more this Pass would have reduced rations, making the long, cold sleep much more dangerous. The birth rate would be reduced for many Passes to come, until a balance was again reached with the number of harvester ships and the population.

All because he underestimated the creatures.

He deserved his punishment. His people would pay for his mistake long after he was gone.

He stood at his command position until his ships were safely away from the third planet, then he took the pole to the coldest area on the first level. It was a small narrow punishment area, unused in all his years as commander, beneath the storage sections. He let himself in and waited.

He would remain there, in shame, until they landed. Then he would attempt to inform his superiors of the methods they needed to subdue the creatures. And then he would await his punishment. He would welcome it. In being recycled as energy, he would serve his people one final time.

April 16, 2018
12:17 P.M. Eastern Standard Time

Arrival: Day Four

Clarissa Maddox remained standing, although it was only her training that kept her upright. She had been wrong. The president and Harrington had been right; nukes had not been the way to go. Only their reasons didn't really matter either. The nukes would have hit that energy draining field and fallen to Earth, just as useless as the conventional weapons had been.

She had done her best against the alien ships, and she had lost.

Now they were leaving, and she knew it had nothing to do with her.

Her own analogy kept coming back to her. It was like fighting tanks with bows and arrows. Only this time, the tank's hatch had remained closed. This time, the arrows bounced harmlessly away.

So many lives had been lost.

And California . . . she shook her head. She kept seeing Fisherman's Wharf and the bright blue of the Pacific. The Pacific would still be there, only this time she would have to stand on a flattened gray landscape to see it.

"General," said Ward from the front of the room. "We've received confirmation. Ninety-four alien ships have broken orbit and are headed on an intercept course for the tenth planet."

His words were met with silence. No one cheered. No one could. Everyone knew those ships were leaving for their own reasons.

The images on the fifteen television screens showing various channels, all muted, were of people standing in the streets staring at the sky as if they could see into outer space. The silence seemed to be a worldwide phenomenon. No one could believe the aliens were leaving.

But they were.

Maddox wondered what Cross would say. He had said there would be four attacks. There had only been two. But he had also said the areas would be close together. They hadn't been. She suspected that was because of the success of her first mission. She had destroyed seven of those ships before

259

the aliens put their defenses back on. And they had made the Earth pay.

"They're really gone," one of the junior staffers muttered.

He had probably been talking to himself, but in the room's quiet, his murmur had sounded like a shout.

"You'd better hope they are, Mister," Maddox snapped. His words finally got through her own stupor. She couldn't act as if she had won. She had not. She had sat in all those briefings Cross and his people had done. The one thing that was clear was that these aliens saw Earth as their own personal greenhouse. They didn't care what they leveled, so long as they took whatever it was that they needed.

They were leaving, whether for a short regrouping, or two thousand years. But the key was that they would be back. And when they returned, Maddox would know how to defeat them. If she wasn't around to fire the weapons herself, she would make damned sure her descendants would know what to do.

"Well," she said. "Enough of this moping. We have work to do."

Then she turned and left the room. Her first job was to convince Harrington to shore up the planet's defenses. Her second was to find the aliens' vulnerabilities. They had to have some. And she would do everything she could to find them.

April 16, 2018
12:17 P.M. Eastern Standard Time

Arrival: Day Four

Cross sat alone in the media room. The television screens had been rebroadcasting images from the horrific battles that had taken place in France, China, and California. The images that came out of San Luis Obispo were the worst. They showed again and again the jets tumbling out of the sky like toys, and then exploding behind a rise.

Britt had left the room in the middle of the repetition, as if she couldn't take it anymore, but Cross had to stay. He wanted to know what would happen next, and he felt somehow that the news would tell him that.

He was completely stunned, then, when the announcer broke in on CNN with news from the International Space Station. Cross had watched the ships leave Earth and enter orbit. He had expected that. What he hadn't expected was the footage from the ISS:

The blackness that was the alien ships was silhouetted against the unblinking stars and then, suddenly, the ships broke out of orbit and headed back toward the tenth planet. After the tape rolled, several experts commented that the ships were gone for good.

Gone for good.

Cross felt a shudder run through him and then something like joy.

He had been wrong.

The ships were gone.

The mathematician had been right. Perhaps the fact that people had attacked had shown the tenth planet that it wasn't worth harvesting here. Or maybe they always overharvested.

Or maybe, maybe, he had misinterpreted.

He sat for a moment.

After the alien ships had finished their pickup of the nanomachines in the three areas, instead of going back into a low, holding orbit, as Cross and everyone else had expected, the three groups of ships went into an accelerating orbit, finally accelerating away from Earth and slightly sunward.

An orbital specialist from NASA appeared on MSNBC

and said the alien ships would rendezvous with the tenth planet just after it moved inside the orbit of the planet Earth. It was the only window the alien ships had of catching their planet from Earth, without wasting a vast amount of fuel in acceleration and braking.

Cross was too stunned to feel relief. He had expected more of the destruction. Somehow he had thought that it would just continue.

The commentary moved from expert to inane in a matter of moments, the announcers trying to cope with the significant changes that had happened to the world, to the way people thought, in just the past few days. They couldn't.

He couldn't, and he had been prepared.

Then he stood, without turning off the remote, and went in search of Britt.

He found her in the map room. She was bent over his main computer and muttering to herself.

"They're gone," he said, without preamble.

"I know," she said. She pointed to the small television screen in the middle of her larger screen.

"You don't seem happy about it."

She turned in her chair. "You were right, Leo."

He frowned at her. "I wasn't right. They were supposed to harvest twice as much—"

"They will," she said.

He started to shake. She had to be wrong. But he knew she wasn't.

"I've been working on the orbit ever since our conversation yesterday. It bothered me."

She punched an image of the solar system on the screen. It showed an orbit of the tenth planet coming in from deep space and swinging in close to the sun like a comet, then moving back out into deep space. Cross had looked at this a hundred times before in the last few months, and it had always bothered him too.

Britt didn't look at him. Instead, she added dotted lines on the largest screen, showing Earth's orbit, and Venus's orbit. Then she marked the tenth planet's current position on its orbit with a white dot and Earth's current position in its orbit with a green dot.

"This is the position of the planets now," she said. "But watch what happens when I put the screens in motion."

She hit a button, and as she did so, the scene changed.

"This is ten days elapsed time every second."

The dot that was the tenth planet moved in closer and closer to the sun, moving inside Venus's orbit as it went around the sun, then started out.

In the meantime, the green dot that indicated the planet Earth moved along its orbit. At six months elapsed time, Britt stopped the motion on the screen.

Cross sat down. He let out a small sigh.

He had been right.

He had been right and he hadn't known why. That showed the limits of archaeoastronomy. The words *black death from the sky* had occurred at different times near the two-thousand-and-six-year time span, and he had thought it errors in record-keeping. But it hadn't been.

"It's going to be almost as close to us a second time, on the way back out," Cross said. "They harvest coming in and going out. Two harvests."

Britt nodded.

"We have to call in everyone on the Tenth Planet Project," Cross said. "We don't have much time."

On the other screen, MSNBC coverage had moved from the ISS footage to coverage of the world situation. Riots were still going on in major cities. France was barring footage of its destroyed areas.

"God," Britt said. "How are we going to tell them?" She wasn't talking about the project. She was talking about the world.

"I don't know," Cross said. "But they have to know."

The tenth planet was coming back.

And this time, Earth had to be prepared.

181 Days Until Second Harvest

DEAN WESLEY SMITH was a founder of the well-respected small press Pulphouse. He has written a number of novels—both his own and as tie-in projects—including *Laying the Music to Rest* and *X-Men: The Jewels of Cyttorak.*

KRISTINE KATHRYN RUSCH is the Hugo and World Fantasy Award–winning former editor of *The Magazine of Fantasy and Science Fiction.* She turned to writing full-time two years ago. She, too, has written a number of original and tie-in novels, including the *Fey* series and *Star Wars: The New Rebellion.*

Printed in the United States
by Baker & Taylor Publisher Services